Berkley Prime Crime titles by Ali Brandon

TWICE TOLD
TAIL

ALI BRANDON

BERKLEY PRIME CRIME
New York

BERKLEY PRIME CRIME
Published by Berkley
An imprint of Penguin Random House LLC
375 Hudson Street, New York, New York 10014

Copyright © 2016 by Tekno Books
Penguin Random House supports copyright. Copyright fuels creativity, encourages
diverse voices, promotes free speech, and creates a vibrant culture. Thank you for buying
an authorized edition of this book and for complying with copyright laws by not
reproducing, scanning, or distributing any part of it in any form without permission.
You are supporting writers and allowing Penguin Random House to continue to
publish books for every reader.

BERKLEY is a registered trademark and BERKLEY PRIME CRIME and the B colophon
are trademarks of Penguin Random House LLC.

ISBN: 9780425261606

First Edition: November 2016

Printed in the United States of America
1 3 5 7 9 10 8 6 4 2

Cover illustration by Ross Jones

Book design by Kristin del Rosario.

This is not a dedication; rather, it's a humble and heartfelt "thank you" to all the readers, reviewers, booksellers, and bloggers who have taken Hamlet and Darla—and me!—into their hearts. Your kind words and enthusiasm for a certain snarky black feline and his compadres has made this series a joy to write. Sadly, after this outing, it's time to say good-bye, at least when it comes to new adventures featuring Hamlet and his friends.

But the wonderful thing about books is that, once written, their characters live on in the imagination forever. And so, Hamlet and Darla and James and Robert will always be hard at work at Pettistone's Fine Books, with Jake and Mary Ann and Reese popping in for their regular visits. And super-feline sleuth Hamlet will never give up his book-snagging ways. When it comes to murder in Brooklyn, he and Darla will always be on the case.

As for me, you can keep up with my future doings at www.dianestuckart.com. So, again, thank you for your support over the years. Hamlet and Darla and I love you all. Sending warmest purrs to ya! ~ Ali

ACKNOWLEDGMENTS

The Black Cat Bookshop Mysteries wouldn't be what they are without the support of many people. And while numerous folks have my undying gratitude, I owe the greatest thanks to the following:

To Larry Segriff, my editor at Tekno Books for most of the series duration—your patient and low-key approach, along with good commonsense editing, made working with you a pleasure.

To Shannon Jamieson Vazquez, my editor at Berkley Prime Crime for the first five Hamlet novels—your sharp and brilliant editing made me a better writer, and the Black Cat Bookshop Mysteries better books. It was a privilege to partner with you.

To my husband, Gerry, who has always been Hamlet's biggest fan, and even insisted we add a couple of black cats to our already-large menagerie—thanks for all your love and support over the years. I couldn't have done it without you!

To my family and friends who bought my books and constantly spread the word, and the love—you're the best!

And, finally, to Denise Little, my friend and original editor at Tekno Books, whose gentlemanly black cat, Hamlet, was the inspiration for my own snarky feline—thank you from the bottom of my heart for giving me the opportunity to write this series. I hope I did you proud.

ONE

"OH MY GAWD, DARLA, YOU GOTTA HELP ME! MY WEDDING gown I custom-ordered finally showed up. I did a fitting last night and, Darla, it was horrible!"

The nasal Jersey tones emanating from Darla Pettistone's cell phone belonged to Connie Capello, the brash Snooki wannabe who had an irritating tendency to refer to herself as the future Mrs. Fiorello Reese. The self-bestowed title had been moderately amusing the first few times Darla had heard it. But in the four-plus months since Connie's engagement to Darla's ex-almost-boyfriend, NYPD Detective Reese, she had grown a bit weary of the joke.

Suppressing a sigh, Darla stepped away from the counter where her bookstore manager, Professor James T. James, was busy ringing up an order. Conversations with Connie tended to drag on. Since Darla was the eponymous owner of Pettistone's Fine Books—a converted Brooklyn brownstone that featured the bookstore on two levels, and her own apartment on the third—she put particular stock in presenting a professional image in front of her customers. Personal phone calls were to be kept to a minimum during business hours.

"Slow down, Connie," she urged, even as she wondered why the woman was unloading on her, and not on one of her twelve—or was it thirteen?—bridesmaids. She and Connie were really no more than acquaintances, not BFFs who paged through bridal magazines together.

"It's probably just pre-wedding jitters that make you feel like that," she continued. "You showed me the sketch back in September, and it was a truly lovely dress."

"Yeah, well, it ain't lovely on. I swear I looked like a freakin' cow in it!"

Darla highly doubted that last. The woman was almost as tall as Darla's best friend, the six-foot-tall ex-cop-turned-private-investigator, Jacqueline "Jake" Martelli. And, in Darla's opinion, Connie was in perpetual need of a Big Mac or three to fatten her up. Still, she could hear the tears in Connie's voice, meaning that the bovine illusion was definitely real to her.

"It's really awful," the woman raged on. "The stupid dress makes my butt look fat and my boobs look flat, and it was supposed to be ivory, but they made it ecru. So I don't just look like a cow, I look like a freakin' corpse of a cow. And now it's too close to the wedding to get another gown special-made for me-e-e-e."

First-world problems was Darla's first thought, a notion she promptly shoved away as uncharitable.

She knew how stressful weddings could be. Heck, she'd had nightmares before her own (ultimately ill-fated) nuptials that the cake, of all things, wasn't quite right. And with Connie's fashion obsession—the woman wore heels and full makeup just to pop down the block for a latte—the perfect gown would be particularly essential. Besides, when one paid big bucks for a single-occasion dress like a wedding gown, one expected to look fabulous in it.

Managing a consoling tone, she dutifully replied, "I'm sure the gown just needs some alterations, and then it will be gorgeous on you. I know a nice little old lady a couple of blocks down who does sewing out of her daughter's dry-cleaning shop. She altered a tweed jacket I got from my sister last year, and it fits like a dream now. I can give you her address and phone number, and you can—"

"It's too late for that." Connie cut her short with another wail. "I got mad and stuffed the stupid thing in the incinerator last night, and now I gotta buy a new wedding dress off the ra-a-a-ack!"

That last pathetic howl was loud enough that Darla had to hold the cell phone away from her ear, while James and his elderly customer both shot her stunned looks.

Darla gave them an apologetic headshake and headed toward the staircase that led to the coffee bar that Darla had installed upstairs the previous spring. Her teenaged goth-clerk-turned-barista, Robert Gilmore, ran the bar with such efficiency that the add-on to her book business was already beginning to show a bit of profit. But since it was almost 11 a.m., her early-morning regulars had pretty well dispersed, leaving only a couple of stragglers until the next small rush at noon.

And since it was a Thursday, that rush was more likely to be a trickle.

By the time Darla had waved to Robert and settled at one of the wicker bistro tables to continue the call, Connie's wails had dwindled to a few sedate sobs.

"I'm so sorry," she told the woman once she was sure

Connie was listening again. "I can imagine how disappointed you are. But I'm not sure how I can help you."

Then, as a thought occurred to her, she quickly added, "Wait. Maybe you could try Davina's Bridal. It's a little store maybe ten or twelve blocks from here, and they got a nice write-up in one of the city magazines recently. What did the headline call it? 'Couture Looks at Rack Prices,' or something like that. They do custom gowns, but I've looked in their window before, and it seems like they have lots of ready-made dresses in stock, too."

"Really?" The sniffling sounds abruptly ceased. "Oh, Darla, you're brilliant! I told Fi"—Connie pronounced her nickname for Reese's given name as *Fee*—"that you'd have the answer. I'm going to call right now and see if they can fit me in after lunch."

"Darla saves the day again," Darla muttered to herself as the phone went silent, without even a final good-bye from the woman.

Still, she smiled a little as she tucked her phone into the pocket of her khakis. Much as she probably should, she really couldn't dislike Connie Capello. Despite her often dismissive attitude, the woman had an amusingly brash way about her that Darla found—if not exactly endearing—refreshing. Of course, she could do without Connie's constant jokes about Darla's Texas accent.

And her red hair and freckles.

And the fact that she owned a bookstore.

But Connie did have her good points, Darla conceded. For one, she did seem to truly love Reese. For another, Connie had given no indication that she cared that Darla and her fiancé were friends. That alone gave the woman major props in Darla's book. And she was as generous with small gifts as she was with snippy digs. Darla was still using the uber-expensive red lipstick Connie had given her a few months ago.

"Hamlet, no!"

The cry came from Robert, who was busy at the sink cleaning a handful of logoed coffee mugs. Fearing the worst, she half rose from her chair to see what mischief the book-store's official mascot, Hamlet the cat, was getting into now. Forget other people's wedding disasters. *She* had to contend with *cat*-astrophes!

Sure enough, the big-boned black feline was purposefully striding along the coffee bar's polished wood countertop. He was headed, Darla saw, toward a milk pitcher trailing leftover foam as it waited to be washed.

Rule number one, Darla reminded herself. *No cats in the coffee area.*

Rule number two. Cats do whatever they want to do!

Fortunately, Robert was on board with the first rule, even if a particular furry troublemaker embraced the second edict.

"No," he repeated, rushing to stick a sudsy arm between Hamlet and his milky objective. "You know better than that, little goth bro. You're not allowed to drink out of anything except, you know, your own bowls."

Darla smiled as she resumed her seat. The teen was heavily into the goth subculture: black wardrobe, dyed black hair, piercings, vampiric makeup (the latter two of which he'd willingly toned down since taking the job at Pettistone's). He'd worn his hair five or six different ways since Darla had known him. The most recent style had been one of those asymmetrical cuts, with hair buzzed almost all the way up on one side, and a long swoop of locks combed over onto the other side of his head. Fortunately for Darla's somewhat compulsive need for proportion, he'd finally tired of that look and shaved both sides, leaving a broad cockscomb of dyed black hair on top.

His ongoing joke with Hamlet was that the feline subscribed to the same lifestyle, given his inky black coat; hence, the "little goth bro" reference.

"And you're not supposed to be on the counter, either," Robert said, continuing his lecture. "The health department dude, he doesn't like cat paws on food prep areas."

At that last, Darla shot a worried look at the two current customers in the coffee bar with her and Robert. If they were anti-cat (although Hamlet's fuzzy face was all over the coffee bar's mugs, and a sign at the front door warned of a feline mascot), they might be inclined to make a complaint call to the city. Fortunately, both women appeared engrossed in their respective books and unconcerned with any cat antics.

Darla let out a relieved breath. It was physically impossible to ban Hamlet from the loft. The cat had come to the brownstone ten years earlier as a feral kitten adopted by Darla's late great-aunt Dee, who had willed the place— Hamlet included!—to Darla. And with a feline's canny intuition, Hamlet had found every secret passage between the apartment and bookstore in the old building, even finding his way outside and into the adjoining buildings. The best Darla could hope for not to run afoul of health codes was prompt and effective damage control any time the feisty feline flouted the rules.

Hamlet, meanwhile, was shooting Robert a cold green look, while irritation fairly bristled from him. While the youth was one of Hamlet's favorite people, the feline wasn't used to being dictated to. Darla could almost hear him thinking, *You're not the boss of me, human.*

Robert obviously caught the meaning behind the cat's

stare, for he lowered his voice and assumed a conciliatory air. "If it was just me, I wouldn't care. But sometimes there are, like, rules. So hop down, and I'll put a little foam in a saucer for you."

With a grudging *mm-rumph*, Hamlet sprang like a small black panther from bar top to floor. Robert, meanwhile, tipped the pitcher over a small plate, the resulting mound of froth quivering as the youth lowered the crockery to the ground. Hamlet's velvety black nose quivered, too, but he waited patiently until Robert stepped away before plunging his face into the foam and lapping away.

"You know, he really shouldn't be drinking that," Darla told Robert with a tolerant shake of her head. "The dairy isn't good for his tummy, and it's fattening. I think he's put on a pound or two since we opened the coffee bar."

"Don't worry, Ms. P., it's mostly air," he assured her. "And I only give him the foam a couple of times a week."

Hamlet, meanwhile, paused and shot Darla the same look he'd earlier turned on Robert. *You could stand to drop a couple of pounds yourself*, she could almost hear him thinking. Unfortunately for Hamlet's snark-cred, the cute sprinkling of foam on his black whiskers overruled what should have been a peeved emerald green stare.

"Okay, but just go easy on the treats," she conceded. "I don't want him getting in the habit of begging. Thanksgiving is coming up sooner than I'd like, and it's going to be hard to keep his paws out of all the food I'll be cooking that week."

"Yeah, well, too bad I'm going to miss it," Robert replied. "But thanks for letting me have Thanksgiving week off. I talked to my dad again, and he's real excited we're going to spend the holiday together."

Darla gave him a doubtful look. "I'm glad you two are reconciling, but if you change your mind about going to

Connecticut, you know you're welcome to spend Thanksgiving Day with me and Jake and the Plinskis."

"I've already got my train ticket," he reminded her. "Don't worry, it should be, you know, fun. And I'm looking forward to meeting my new stepbrothers. Pop even said I can bring Roma with me," he added, referring to the tiny gray-and-white Italian greyhound he'd adopted earlier that year.

Despite Robert's upbeat attitude, Darla wasn't quite convinced. She knew that the youth's parents had been divorced for several years, ever since Robert's mother had abandoned her husband and son to move to California. And while the elder Gilmore had fulfilled his parental obligation as far as providing food and shelter, he had remained pretty well absent from Robert's life throughout his high school years. The absence had turned to outright estrangement when he'd kicked the teen out of his house the day he had turned eighteen. Robert had been left virtually homeless until Darla hired him and arranged for him to live in the garden apartment belonging to her elderly neighbors, the Plinskis.

But just two weeks ago, Mr. Gilmore had called his son out of the blue to inform him he'd gotten remarried over the summer. He'd invited Robert to a Thanksgiving reunion of sorts so that he could meet his new stepfamily. Though wary at first, Robert had grown increasingly excited over the past few days at the prospect of potentially healing what was more than a yearlong family breach, especially since his father had also confessed that Robert had a new half brother due in the spring.

"Fingers crossed," Darla told him with a smile. "And don't worry, there should be plenty of leftovers to carry over into Black Friday, when you get back. With luck, that's going to be our busiest day this year!"

"Ugh, don't even mention Black Friday," came a woman's voice drifting up the stairway.

Robert and Darla turned to see Jake Martelli headed toward them. Though the temperature was in the forties outside, her only concession to the chilly weather was the bulky black knit sweater she wore with tight jeans and her ubiquitous Doc Martens . . . this pair bright red in anticipation of the upcoming holiday season. Not that a coat was necessary, since Jake was Darla's tenant. The trip from her place was a matter of running up the steps from her garden apartment below the brownstone and into the bookstore's front door.

A dusting of snow left over from the day's brief flurry clung to her curly black hair, so that for a moment her appearance echoed Hamlet's earlier frosty look. Then the loft's warmer temperature abruptly melted the flakes while she flung herself into the bistro chair next to Darla's.

"Hi, Robert," she said, giving the youth a wave. "Any chance you can get me a caramel latte?"

"Sure, Ms. Jake."

While Robert scooted behind the counter to fill her order, the PI turned to Darla.

"Bad news, kid," she said with a moan. "I just got an email from Ma. She decided—and I quote—there's too many old geezers wandering around Fort Lauderdale right now, so she's booked a flight to come stay with me for the Thanksgiving holiday."

"Nattie's coming up for a visit? That's great," Darla replied, genuinely pleased.

She glanced over at Hamlet, who had finished off the foam and was tidying his whiskers, licking one big paw and rhythmically swiping it across his face. She'd met Jake's mother, Natalia Martelli, when she, Jake, and Hamlet had traveled to

Florida as guests of the Feline Association of America's championship cat show. The invitation had come when Hamlet's Karate Kitty video—the one set to music showing him performing martial arts moves—had gone viral.

The trip had served a dual purpose, keeping Hamlet out of the way while the coffee bar was being installed as well as figuratively cashing in on his temporary celebrity. They'd stayed much of the time at Nattie's Fort Lauderdale condo, where the woman had lived the past few years after a lifetime spent in New Jersey. Nattie had served as their tour guide and driver . . . not to mention being the unintended focus of some rather dastardly happenings related to the cat show.

Darla smiled ruefully at the memory. Seventy years old, and with flaming red hair that—unlike Darla's natural auburn—came straight from a bottle, the elderly woman was what Darla's father would have called "a pistol." And while the Amazonian Jake and her five-foot-nothing mother were total opposites in appearance, they were more alike in attitude and manner than either woman would admit.

"And she's already told me that she wants to be out the door at six a.m. the Friday after Thanksgiving to hit all the big sales," Jake said, hand to forehead. "She even sent me a list of the stores already mapped out. Can't I tell her I need to help you out in the bookstore, or something?"

"Sorry, no way am I going to be party to sabotaging a mother/daughter outing," Darla shot back, grinning. "You're just going to have to suck it up and spend time with her."

"Well, next year I'll be smart like you and plan my family vacation for the dead of summer, when nothing's going on and we can just bake on the beach."

Darla nodded. She'd finally managed her long-awaited trip back to Dallas to see her parents and siblings in August. And while she would have preferred a spring get-together—nothing was better than a drive through the Texas countryside during bluebonnet season—the end of summer was a slow time for the store. But that had meant she'd spent a lot of time sweltering in hundred-degree-plus weather, one thing she didn't miss now that she was for all intents and purposes a Brooklynite.

Except when it was forty degrees outside!

"You'll have fun," Darla assured her. "And I hope she'll want to join us for our old-fashioned Thanksgiving."

"She'll love it. But just be forewarned that she'll probably do the little-old-Italian-lady thing and bring a big dish of her traditional Thanksgiving lasagna."

"No problem. Nattie's a fantastic cook. But speaking of traditional . . ."

While Robert brought over Jake's latte and she began sipping her drink, Darla related her earlier phone call with Connie concerning the disastrous dress.

"I just hope she finds something she likes over at Davina's," she finished. "If she doesn't get a new dress, and soon, I have a feeling good old Fi is going to be in for a rough time."

The PI grinned a little at Darla's usurping of Connie's nickname for Reese before she shrugged.

"Actually, she's been less of a bridezilla than I expected," the woman observed. "I mean, that whole twelve-bridesmaids thing is a bit over the top, but you've gotta take into account all the sisters and cousins a good Catholic girl like her has. She could have had twice as many and still have female relatives to spare."

As Darla laughed at that, Jake added, "And my friend—the one who's Connie's cousin's mother-in-law—texted me a picture of the bridesmaids' dress. She let the girls pick it out, and it's really cute. Cocktail length and red with a great wrap waist. And according to Reese, she's even made a list of all the guests' dietary restrictions for the caterers. You know, so none of the vegan–celiac–paleo–lactose intolerant types can complain about the food."

Darla nodded, still puzzling over the cousin's mother-in-law friend of Jake, when her cell phone gave off a little New Age riff that was her current ringtone. She glanced at the caller ID and groaned. "Speaking of the bride, guess who's calling? I guess that means Connie couldn't get into Davina's, after all. So I'm going to have to listen to another round of her dress woes."

"Let it go to voice mail," Jake advised with a grin.

Darla shrugged as the cell kept ringing. "She'll just call back. Better get it over with now." Ignoring Jake's warning shake of her head, she answered the phone with a cautious, "Hi, Connie. Anything wrong?"

"Darla, you gotta help me!"

She winced at the familiar strident, nasal tones. *Connie dress disaster, Part Two.* "Connie, I'm sorry, but I've got a store to run. I really can't—"

"You was right," Connie cut her short, sounding surprisingly upbeat. "The guy at the shop—his name is Daniel—said he had a cancellation at two, so he said to come in. I'm so excited. I just know they'll have the right dress for me."

"That's great," Darla replied, hoping the other woman didn't hear the sigh of relief in her voice. With luck, this would be the one and only Connie pre-wedding disaster to involve her. "Be sure you text me and Jake a picture of the dress you decide on."

"Oh, you'll get to see it in person," Connie cheerfully shot back. "I can't make such an important decision like this alone. Fi will be by at quarter to two and pick you up so you can help me choose."

|| TWO

"SO, KID, WHAT DO YOU THINK?"

Jake stood on a wide wooden platform before a gilt-framed, trifold mirror, preening at her reflection as she held a poufy wedding gown beneath her chin. Turning to Darla, who was perched atop a nearby white wicker settee, she said, "It makes a statement, doesn't it?"

"It makes a statement, all right," Darla conceded, putting down the inch-thick bridal magazine she'd been idly flipping through, "but not one I'd want to hear."

She gave the dress that Jake was displaying a considering look. As far as wedding gowns went, this one fell into the category the bridal magazine termed "ball gown." Its skirt was a flurry of layered white tulle that cascaded from a tight, white lace bodice into a bell-like silhouette. A wide sash of white satin between skirt and bodice was meant to emphasize a tiny waistline, as was the cabbage-sized white satin rose pinned atop that band. The scooped neckline was trimmed with similar but much smaller white satin roses from shoulder to shoulder, ending in a tulle explosion of capped sleeves.

Darla suppressed a smile as she glanced across the room. Another bride's entourage—three giggling, midtwenties blondes who likely were sisters or BFFs, accompanied by a trim, middle-aged woman whose hair was an even brighter shade of platinum and likely was the mom—were staring at Jake's impromptu fashion show. Darla didn't blame them.

Her smile broadened. The style Jake had chosen was better suited to a girl in her early twenties than a fifty-year-old woman. It didn't help that the padded hanger still attached to the gown made it look like Jake was reenacting the iconic *Carol Burnett Show* skit parodying *Gone with the Wind*. The only saving grace lay in the fact that it was cut for a bride a good eight inches shorter than Jake's six-foot height. Her Doc Martens peeped from beneath the gown's ruffled hem to add a refreshing bit of bad-girl vibe to the ensemble.

Too bad Reese hasn't stuck around to see this.

"Yep, a statement," Darla repeated, "but it doesn't say 'you,' know what I mean?"

"Yeah, you're right."

Grinning, Jake strode off the platform and rehung the tulle confection on an intricate wrought iron hook alongside another dozen or so gowns on display at Davina's Bridal Boutique. Darla merely shook her head and settled back in her seat.

It had been years since she had set foot in a bridal salon. Davina's was far more luxurious than the suburban Dallas store where she'd shopped for her own wedding gown.

Thick carpeting in a muted rose shade spread underfoot in the seating area where she and Jake waited, with the remainder of the floors a placid white-washed wood. Oversized framed photographs of blushing brides and luxurious bouquets stood out against walls hung with a soothing, monochromatic floral print: white flowers over a cream background. Three oversized crystal chandeliers added light and sparkle to the place, while faint strains of classical music drifted from a hidden speaker.

More like a spa than retail, Darla told herself, wondering if Pettistone's could do with a chandelier or two. The only real concession the place made to being a retail outlet was the discreet sign near the front that said, "We Offer 6 Months Credit Same as Cash."

Jake, meanwhile, had resumed her seat on the matching wicker settee across from Darla's. Propping her Doc Martens on the footstool in front of her, she observed, "Guess it's a good thing Connie is the one getting married, and not me. And I still don't know how you roped me into dress shopping with you two."

"Roped you?" Darla replied, giving her friend a disbelieving look. "I'm the one Connie shanghaied. You volunteered to come along."

Jake gave a cheerful shrug, lifting the complimentary glass of champagne that had been pressed into her hand as they first entered the bridal shop. "Okay, guilty. I didn't have any clients scheduled, so I thought it might be fun to do something girly for a change."

Gesturing to the plate of pink-iced petits fours on the glass-topped table between them, she added, "I've seen those wedding dress shows, and all the high-class places offer refreshments. You think I'm going to pass up free bubbly and little cake thingies? No way."

Darla suppressed a sigh. Actually, *no way* had been her own first thought when Connie had informed her that the two of them were going wedding dress shopping together.

While Jake had listened in amused interest, Darla had promptly launched into a protest, reminding the woman she worked for a living and couldn't just go gallivanting off to look at dresses. Connie had countered just as quickly, bringing out the big guns in the person of her fiancé.

"Hi, Darla." She'd heard Reese's familiar voice as Connie apparently handed over the phone to him. "Hold on a sec."

She held as she heard him say in a muffled aside, "Hey, Conn, run upstairs and grab my tweed overcoat out of the bedroom closet, would you?"

Then, coming back onto the line, he'd spoken softly and quickly. "Look, Red, I'd consider it a major favor if you'd go shopping with Connie . . . just for a couple of hours, okay? She's driving me crazy with this whole dress thing. All the ones in the magazines I told her I thought were fine, she hated, so she doesn't want me going with her. Not that I want to, anyhow. You know, the whole 'bad luck for the groom to see the dress before the wedding' thing."

"Can't her mom go along?" Darla had countered, suspicious that Reese had lapsed into his old nickname for her—the one he'd quit using once he got engaged.

"Mrs. Capello is, to quote her, f'ing PO'd that her daughter destroyed a dress that cost more than Mrs. C.'s living room furniture."

Darla had winced at that. Praying that the mother of the bride owned IKEA and nothing more high-end, she asked, "What about her bridesmaid posse, then? Why doesn't she take some of them along?"

"Not gonna happen," was his flat reply. "Right now, they're all ticked off at each other because of some stupid argument over the bachelorette party. Connie's afraid they'll talk her into—and, again, I quote—a butt-ugly dress that'll make her look like the Queen of the Cows."

Darla couldn't help a reflexive snicker, though she asked in concern, "But what about the wedding, if everyone is mad? Are they all going to leave her standing at the altar by herself?"

"Hey, I'll be there," Reese had reminded her. "Besides, the girls are all her sisters and her cousins. Take my word for it, they'll be over it in another couple of days. And her ma will come around, too. But in the meantime, it's wedding dress this, and wedding dress that. I can't take much more of it."

He paused, then lowered his voice further, obviously expecting Connie to return with the coat at any moment. "Look, I'll even give her my credit card so she can take you out for an early happy hour afterward. C'mon, Red, for old times' sake?"

Darla had hesitated, weakening as the desperation in his voice made her wonder if she was being a bad sport. Since the announcement back in July, the best she could say was that she had been polite about her friend's upcoming nuptials. Maybe it was time she showed a little more enthusiasm for his and Connie's big day. And it wasn't as if she didn't have both Robert and James to cover the store after lunch.

"Sure, sounds like fun," she'd brightly lied. "See you at one forty-five."

Her agreement had earned her a heartfelt *I owe you one, Red* from Reese and a muffled chuckle from Jake as her friend had correctly interpreted the one-sided conversation she'd heard as capitulation. To Darla's surprise, however, the PI had arrived back at the bookstore just as Connie and Reese pulled up to the curb. After a quick consultation out on the recently shoveled stoop, the consensus had been that Jake should join the official dress hunt. At the time, she couldn't guess why the PI would have raised her hand for this kind of mission, but the free-booze thing did explain it.

Darla looked at the dwindling level of champagne in her own glass and said, "We're on, what, gown number five now, and Connie still hasn't found *the one* yet? Ugh, I'm going to need a refill."

"Here you go, dearie," a man's soothing voice beside her said as an open champagne bottle made a miraculous appearance. "This should take the edge off."

Darla turned to see the portly, middle-aged man who earlier had introduced himself to them. His name was Daniel Lawson, and he was one of the bridal shop's two owners. *The "Da" in Davina*, he'd explained with a chuckle.

A cloud of expensive—meaning it didn't smell like spicy chemicals—body spray clung to him, and he was quite dapper in black tuxedo pants and a pleated white shirt. He wore his bleached blond hair like a short spiky crown in contrast to his exuberant black eyebrows. All he needed was a neatly trimmed mustache and beard, Darla had told herself, and he could be the big brother of that cooking show host who specialized in finding hole-in-the-wall restaurants.

A bubbly stream of sparkling wine rapidly poured into her glass as Daniel added with a confidential air, "Believe me, I understand. Sometimes it's a bit much, putting up with all this bridal hullabaloo when one isn't engaged or married oneself."

"Oh, I like weddings just fine," Darla protested, unsure whether to be offended over his assumption that she wasn't wedding material, or embarrassed that her lack of enthusiasm was that obvious. "And I'm divorced, so I've been through my own bridal hullabaloo. It's just that I had to take time from work to do this, and it's dragging on longer than I thought it would."

"Oh no, dearie, I'm so sorry. I didn't mean you," Daniel gushed in distress as he refilled Jake's glass, too. "I'm speaking about myself. I mean, after sixteen years, you'd think a proposal would be in the offing. But, nooooo. Sometimes, I'm really tempted to—"

"Girls, look!" came Connie's strident tones from the direction of the dressing room. "Here it is. I think I've finally found *the one!*"

Fistfuls of white satin clutched at her hips, Connie came rushing out of the dressing room in yet another gown, followed by the tiny brunette shop assistant who'd been helping her. Connie clambered onto the same platform where Jake had paraded a few moments earlier while the young woman—*Liz? Lori?* Darla tried to recall—stood below her, tucking and rearranging folds of fabric. Finally satisfied, the woman stepped back.

"So, girls, whaddaya think?" Connie demanded with a triumphant smile. "Is it the perfect dress, or what?"

Perfect if you were a Kardashian.

Darla exchanged a shocked glance with Jake. Though the strapless, ankle-length gown with just a hint of a train was sewn from appropriately virginal white satin trimmed with seed pearls, there was nothing demure about its neckline.

How the gown's bodice was staying up, Darla couldn't guess, though she suspected toupee tape might have something to do with it. The décolletage didn't so much plunge as it nose-dived south almost to Connie's navel, leaving exposed a broad expanse of tanned flesh. The last time she'd seen a dress like that, Darla told herself, it had been on a Vegas showgirl at a decidedly R-rated performance.

Finally, she managed, "Uh, Connie, you were planning a church wedding, right?"

"Of course," the other woman replied as she began a leisurely pirouette. "Why?"

"Because you're showing an awful lot of cleavage," Jake

answered for Darla, adding as Connie finished her slow twirl, "and I don't mean just up front."

Connie had been admiring herself in the trifold mirror. At Jake's words, she glanced over her shoulder, and Darla winced.

Had Connie sported a so-called tramp stamp tattoo, said ink would have been visible in this gown, given that it was backless and plunged even lower in the rear than in the front. More problematic was the fact that the mere twisting of her torso exposed even more southern real estate. The resulting view was one that—while doubtless appropriate for an attention-seeking actress on the red carpet—was far too risqué for the altar.

"Well, I think it's sexy," Connie stubbornly proclaimed, giving the gown's train a little twitch in emphasis. "It looks like something Beyoncé would wear. And I'm sure Fi will love it."

Yeah, I bet he will . . . not, Darla told herself. She knew Reese well enough to suspect that while he'd appreciate lingerie cut down to there, he'd be far more prudish about what his future bride wore to church.

"Oh my, that's awful," Daniel murmured beside her, apparently forgetting it was his store and, hence, his stock choices. Setting down the champagne bottle, he gave his plump hands a quick clap.

"No, no, that will never do. Liz"—he addressed the brunette assistant—"go get the Carolina Herrera white lace that just came in. You know the one. It should be Ms. Capello's size."

While Liz hurried off in search of that gown, he added to a pouting Connie, "My dear, you have far too elegant a figure to prance about in—well, there's no other word for it—something so vulgar. Ah, ah," he went on, raising a finger as she opened her mouth to protest, "I know what I'm talking about. Davina's has dressed thousands of brides over the years."

Leaving the champagne with Darla and Jake, he marched over to the platform where Connie stood poised and helped her down. "Let's go try on the Herrera, dearie. And if I'm right, I'll make you a great deal on it."

Connie gave her reflection a final longing glance. "Okay, fine," she conceded with just a bit of a huff.

As Connie and Daniel headed toward the curtained dressing area, Jake turned to Darla and muttered, "Wow. All I can say is that if Connie wore *that* to the wedding, we'd be attending a whole lot of funerals the next week."

Darla snickered. "Can you picture it, Connie walking up the aisle and people fainting right and left every pew she passes? And good old Fi standing up at the front with his groomsmen having no idea why all the friends and relatives are keeling over like dominoes."

"Well, let's just hope Daniel manages to wrestle Connie into a suitable gown. I've about hit my limit on champagne, and I've got a heck of a sugar buzz going from all those petits fours."

Despite the disclaimer, however, she joined Darla in another sip of the sparkling wine as they critiqued the other bride-to-be while she modeled a surprisingly chic white satin bridal tuxedo. When the novelty of that debate faded— Jake had been pro-tux, while Darla had found the style a bit too avant-garde for her tastes—they sat in companionable silence for a few moments before the PI said, "And you might as well get used to all this bridal stuff. I have a feeling we have another wedding on the horizon."

"Another wedding?" Darla shot her a puzzled look, trying to figure out that one. Then, as a possibility occurred to her, she exclaimed, "Wait! You don't mean James and Martha, do you?"

Martha Washington—*no relation to the president's wife*, the woman would laughingly tell new acquaintances—was leader of the book discussion group that met every couple of weeks at Pettistone's. She and James had been dating for almost a year. To Darla's mind, they made a surprisingly compatible couple despite the fact that Martha was a good thirty years younger than James and came from a totally different background. (The dreadlocked, English-accented Martha was an army brat with a father from the Deep South and a mother from a London suburb, while the former university professor was Brooklyn born and raised.)

Both continued to insist the relationship wasn't serious, though Darla had always suspected otherwise. But marriage?

Jake, however, was shaking her head. "No, not those two. I'm talking about Mary Ann."

Darla's previous bafflement morphed into disbelief. The notion of James marrying was incredible enough, but Mary Ann . . .

"Hold your horses. You mean Mary Ann Plinski? As in, the little old lady who lives next door to us? Our Mary Ann?"

"One and the same," Jake replied with a satisfied smile. "Rumor has it that things are getting pretty hot and heavy between her and her new boyfriend."

Darla took a considering sip from her glass as she mentally digested that. "Well, I guess at their ages they don't have a lot of time to waste," she finally conceded. "But it's only been, what, two months?"

She had been surprised but pleased when, a few weeks earlier, the septuagenarian had stopped by the bookstore with her big news. Apparently, the computer-savvy Mary

Ann had been feeling nostalgic one night and impulsively done an Internet search for her long-lost high school boyfriend. Fortunately, in dealing with a name like Hodge Camden, her "hit" list had not proved extensive.

By the next day the old woman had located her particular Hodge sharing pictures of his grown grandchildren on Facebook. She'd followed up that bit of sleuthing with a private message, which Hodge had returned within the hour. He let her know that a) his wife had passed away a year earlier and b) he hadn't forgotten their high school days.

The messages had led to a lunch meeting (he now lived in Queens) which then led to them seeing each other almost daily. Mary Ann had even brought Hodge by the bookstore to introduce him. A jovial, snowy-haired charmer who was surprisingly robust for his age, he had impressed Darla with his solicitous, old-style manner.

"Just one problem," Jake added. "It seems like Mr. Plinski isn't too thrilled with the whole high-school-sweetheart-reunion situation. Mary Ann told me that they had a big argument the other night about her relationship with Hodge."

Darla frowned. Mr. Plinski was Mary Ann's older brother . . . "Brother" also being Mary Ann's nickname for him. Darla assumed that Brother had an actual first name, but she'd never heard it used by either of the elderly siblings. Together, the pair owned the brownstone next to Darla's, which housed their antiques and collectibles shop, Bygone Days, as well as their apartment above and Robert's garden apartment below.

"Why is Mr. Plinski concerned?" she wondered aloud. "I figured he'd be happy that Mary Ann has found someone after all these years. I hate to say it, but with his past health problems, it's not like he's going to be around forever."

Jake shook her head. "Mary Ann wasn't too specific, but

I got the idea that Hodge and Mr. P. were high school rivals, which is why Mary Ann broke it off with Hodge all those years ago. They didn't get along then, and apparently Mr. Plinski still holds a grudge."

Darla frowned a little, doing the math in her head. Based on her age, Mary Ann would have been in high school in the mid-1950s. World War II would have been long since over, and the Korean War as well. Kids who were Mary Ann's age would have been sock-hopping it, watching *Leave It to Beaver*, and liking Ike. So any drama would likely have been of the soda-shop variety.

Jake, however, was continuing, "—bad feelings even after all these years. From what Mary Ann said, the last time Hodge stopped by, things got heated. In fact, Mr. P. even threatened—"

What Mr. Plinski had threatened, Darla didn't learn, because Daniel abruptly burst through the curtains. "Attention, ladies," he told them, smiling broadly. "I think Ms. Capello has found *the one*, and I'm not talking about her fiancé."

With a flourish, he drew aside the curtain. Unlike the previous times when she'd pranced out like a model on a runway, Connie moved uncertainly toward the mirrors, dress hem again clutched high as Liz trailed after. The assistant helped the bride-to-be onto the platform and went through the tuck-and-fluff ritual again while Daniel directed, tsk-ing and tutting.

Darla watched with interest. What she could see of the gown—sleeveless, with white lace overlaying satin— appeared promising. Maybe this really *was* the one.

"Fingers crossed," she muttered to Jake. "I'm about dress-shopped out."

"No peeking," Daniel meanwhile was warning Connie

when she tried to get a glimpse over her shoulder at the mirror behind her. "I want your first look to be a moment of pure perfection."

Then, apparently satisfied that said perfect moment was at hand, he gestured Liz away. "No one move," he commanded as he stepped to one side. "Just look."

The sleeveless lace mermaid wedding dress had a sweetheart neckline that accentuated Connie's ample bustline without going into showgirl territory. The gown itself seemed to have been sewn specifically for her, sliding over her curves without gripping too snugly. The lace overlay lent a simple yet elegant touch, with the fabric's pure white hue complementing Connie's olive skin.

"Perfect!" Darla exclaimed, any niggling jealousy evaporating at the sight of the bride-to-be in full regalia.

Ignoring Daniel's earlier command, she popped up from her chair for a better look. The man had pulled out the big guns this time by also decking out Connie in a stunning veil—elbow-length, Darla pegged it, drawing from her recent bridal mag education. A lacy headband perched tiara-like on Connie's teased tresses, from which two lace-trimmed tiers of tulle gently billowed down halfway to her fingertips.

"Home run, Connie. You should be on the cover of a bridal magazine," Darla told her with an admiring smile.

Jake gave a vigorous nod and stood as well, lifting her glass in a toast. "It's just stunning. No way you're leaving here without buying that dress."

"Are you girls sure?"

Expression hopeful, Connie slowly turned to face the mirror and then gasped herself.

"Oh my Gawd, you're right, it's perfect! And the veil, too."

She preened a moment, then gave a half turn and looked over her shoulder to admire the view from behind. "Bite this, Beyoncé," she exclaimed with a little hip waggle. Then, to Darla, she said, "Can you hand me my phone outta my bag? I need to get a picture of this."

While Connie posed on the platform taking a series of selfies, Daniel was giving the gown a final, critical look.

"We need to do a couple of tucks and adjust the hemline a bit. As I told you on the phone, my seamstress is out this afternoon, but if you'd like to purchase this gown, we can schedule an alteration appointment." He whipped out a small notebook from his trousers pocket and finished, "Shall I pencil you in for, say, next Tuesday?"

"Hmm, let me think. I'm not totally sure," she replied, her expression suddenly bland as she obviously realized her earlier enthusiasm had put her at a disadvantage in bargaining. Handing her phone back to Darla—who was amused but not surprised to see that the final selfie was a Beyoncé-style butt shot—she planted her hands on her hips. "I mean, it's nice and all, but there might be something nicer out there. So, how much is it with the discount you were talking about?"

He named a figure that would have busted Darla's budget but that made Connie smile. "And throw in the veil?"

"I'll give you the veil at cost."

She considered that a moment and then nodded. "Sure, let's do it."

While Connie hurried off to the dressing room, Daniel gave Darla and Jake a knowing look and buffed his fingernails on his ruffled shirt. "Do I know my brides, or do I know my brides?"

"I'm impressed," Darla conceded with a smile. "If I ever decide to get married again, you'll be my first stop."

"Second," he told her. "It's ring, dress, venue, caterer, and flowers, in that order . . . unless you ask the florist. He'll tell you flowers come right after the dress. But I would be thrilled to be—"

A woman's piercing scream cut him short, the earsplitting cry followed by an unmistakable "Oh my Gawd!"

"Connie!" Darla and Jake chorused, exchanging worried looks.

Accompanied by Daniel's gasp and the surprised cries of the other bridal-dress party, the pair rushed in the direction of the dressing room. Despite Jake's longer legs, Darla was in the lead, though the curtain separating the changing area from the display room momentarily slowed her progress. Once she'd grappled her way past the length of rose-colored velveteen, she halted.

The fitting area was slightly more utilitarian than the front of the store. A broad hallway ran parallel to the showroom and separated it from the half-a-dozen curtained dressing rooms. The drapes on the center two rooms were pulled open to show that they were unoccupied. Those on the remaining four alcoves were partially open. Connie, still in her wedding gown, stood beside the nearest one, her red-lipsticked mouth open in a wide O.

"What's wrong? Are you hurt?" Jake demanded, having caught up with Darla.

Connie shook her head, veil floating about her as she pointed toward the dressing room. "Oh my Gawd, it's awful! I can't look!"

"Can't look at what?" Jake persisted.

Connie took a deep breath and then shrieked, "There's a dead girl in the dressing room!"

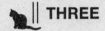 **THREE**

DEAD! SURELY NOT, DARLA THOUGHT IN DISTRESS. IT HADN'T been that many months ago—the day she'd learned about Connie's engagement to Reese, to be exact—that she had stumbled across a dead body herself. What were the chances that the same thing would happen to Connie? But from the look of shock that had drained her olive complexion of its usual high tones, the woman had obviously encountered something untoward.

Before Darla or Jake had a chance to react, however, an unfamiliar and furious male voice erupted from behind the curtain where Connie stood.

"She's not dead, you silly . . . cow," the man declared as he shoved open the drape to confront the three of them.

He had the same blond, spiked hair as Daniel, though the resemblance ended there. Taller and leaner than the latter, he possessed sharper facial features in contrast to

Daniel's rounded cheeks. *Daniel's partner*, she assumed, *and not exactly Mr. Customer Service*.

His pale gaze took in all of them as, spare lips thinned even more by disgust, he repeated, "She's not dead; she just fainted. You get these women all hyped up on being some sort of princess, and after the first couple of dresses they start hyperventilating and take a nosedive. It happens at least once a week. She's fine."

With that curt diagnosis, he stalked off, leaving Darla and Jake to stare after him in astonishment before they pushed past a sputtering Connie to see for themselves.

To Darla's relief, the man was right. The supposed corpse was the same young woman who earlier had been modeling the white satin tuxedo. Now wearing a poufy ball gown featuring a cinched waist and yards of tulle, she lay sprawled on the carpeting like an oversized doll dropped unceremoniously by its owner. Still, her eyes were open, and she was making an attempt to stir while a tsk-ing Liz briskly patted her hand.

"I knew we shouldn't have tried to squeeze you into that one," the shop assistant told the young woman. "But you look real pretty. How about we go for the next size up?"

By that time, the fainting bride's entourage had rushed back to see what the commotion was, shoving past Darla and Jake to crowd around the dressing room. Darla heard a plaintive wail from the fainting bride. "I don't feel so good, Ma."

"Might as well go back to the showroom. Floor show's over," Jake muttered, then grinned a little as she added, "No pun intended."

"Not nice," Darla told her with a reproving shake of her head, though she was having a hard time keeping a straight face herself. Then, as Daniel joined the gaggle of women, she added, "But you're right. We're in the way here."

Connie, meanwhile, had recovered from her momentary shock. Gripping Darla's arm, she nodded in the direction Daniel's partner had gone and declared, "Did you hear what that jerk said? He called me a cow! A c-cow!"

"I'm sure he didn't mean it," was Darla's tactful response to Connie's despairing cry, suspecting that the man had intended a much cruder pejorative and had only just caught himself. Still, the bovine reference must have sounded just as insulting to Connie, given her current "Queen of the Cows" mindset.

Detaching herself from Connie's grasp, Darla went on. "He was probably upset over having another bride pass out on him and wasn't thinking."

"Well, I'm thinking," she huffed as she snatched the veil from her head and started back toward the main shop, Darla and Jake trailing after her. "I'm thinking maybe I don't want to buy a dress here after all."

"Oh no, dearie," Daniel interjected, breaking free of the others to follow after them. "Let's discuss this, shall we?"

They regrouped in the same spot where Darla and Jake had been waiting at the mirrors. With a sidelong wry glance at her that Darla took to mean *I'm bowing out of this one, kid*, Jake strode over to the small table to retrieve her abandoned champagne. Sighing and longing for her own glass, Darla instead tried to reason with the fuming future bride.

"Here's the thing, Connie. I know you're mad, and you have every right to be, after being insulted like that," she assured the other woman while turning a pointed look to Daniel. "That's just what Reese, er, Fi, would expect you to do, raise an alarm like that if something looks wrong. You just went a little overboard and scared the heck out of the rest of us."

"Yeah, well, how was I supposed to know the dumb broad

hadn't croaked?" Connie hotly countered, flinging the veil onto the wicker sofa where Darla had been sitting. Flailing behind her to find the gown's hooks and zipper, she added, "She looked dead to me."

"I'm sure it was a terrible shock, and no one is blaming you for anything," Daniel agreed, though Darla wasn't so sure. By now, the would-be corpse bride's family was filing back out into the showroom, and the nasty looks they were shooting in Connie's direction were potent enough to take out a lesser woman.

Daniel, meanwhile, was nimbly refastening the hooks she'd managed to undo. Then, hands on her shoulders, he spun her back around so that she was facing the mirror. Catching up the veil again, he deftly placed it back atop her head before giving an approving nod.

"Do let me apologize for my half brother," he said, sounding repentant now. "Poor Vinnie, he's had a recent nasty brush with death himself, and he's not been quite the same since. I do understand your outrage at his over-the-top attitude—and, believe me, I will have a word with him about it—but I simply can't let you walk out the door without buying this gown. It is too, too perfect for you."

Then, like any good salesman, he zipped his lip and stepped back to let the dress do the talking for him.

"Well." Connie hedged and preened a little at her reflection.

Darla exchanged a knowing glance with Jake, who was comfortably settled back in her seat and obviously content simply to watch the action. She had seen the covetous look in Connie's eyes when she'd first stood before the mirror wearing that dress. No way was she not going to buy the gown. The question was, how much was Connie going to make Daniel suffer before they agreed on a price?

"Well," the woman repeated with a shrug, expression cagey, "it's nice for off-the-rack, I guess, but all that yelling just spoiled it for me. I don't think I could ever wear it again without remembering that terrible experience."

"Maybe another discount would help erase the memory?"

His expression equally cagey, Daniel named a new price for the gown, which Connie promptly answered with a dollar amount well below. Daniel countered with another price, as did Connie. This continued for another few rounds, until Darla felt like she was watching some strange backward auction. And then, finally, Connie nodded.

"Yeah, I guess that's fair. I'll take the dress."

While she and Daniel headed off to seal the deal and get Connie back into her street clothes, Darla sagged into the empty seat beside Jake.

"What an ordeal. Reese owes me big-time for this. I'd forgotten how bad it is to go wedding dress shopping, especially when you're not the bride."

"Eh, it could have been worse," the older woman pointed out. "There could have really been a dead girl in the dressing room."

"True." Darla lifted her champagne glass, which held a final inch of bubbly, and went on. "I hereby offer retroactive apologies to all my friends and family who went dress shopping with me. I promise, I'll never do that again."

"I'll drink to that," Jake agreed as she lifted her own glass. "That's why I went the easy way and wore my trusty old prom dress when I got married."

Darla choked on her champagne. "Wait! What?"

Setting down the glass with a clatter, she stared at her friend. This was the first she'd heard of that situation. "Married! You were married? When? To whom?"

Jake gave her now-empty glass a rueful look. "Oops. I

forgot I tend to get gabby when I drink this stuff. I don't suppose you can pretend you didn't hear what I just said?"

Not a chance, was Darla's first thought. Jake had always been notoriously closemouthed about her personal life. Darla only knew snippets of her friend's past, with said past limited to the time after the ex-NYPD cop had suffered her career-ending injury a few years earlier. Darla had no desire to pass up the opportunity to learn more about Jake's mysterious former life, up to and including the fact that she'd once been married.

Aloud, however, she virtuously said, "No worries. If you don't want to talk about it, then I won't say another word."

"Thanks, kid. And do me a favor . . . don't mention it to anyone else, either. Maybe someday I'll share the gory details, but right now with all this wedding dress hoohaw I'm about girl-talked out."

And so, while waiting on Connie, they instead spent the next several minutes chatting about the upcoming holidays. Though it was getting close to two years since Darla had taken over the bookstore from her late great-aunt, she still had to remind herself that Thanksgiving and Christmas no longer meant getting a week or two of vacation time from the job. Rather, running a retail establishment meant that she'd be there for the duration, closing only for the actual holidays. Her next real break wouldn't come until after the new year.

"All right, girls. All I gotta do is pay, and I'm all done here," Connie called as, once again wearing street clothes, she headed toward the register tucked discreetly near the bridal shop's main door.

Jake got to her feet, and Darla did the same, gathering up her knee-length, navy blue down coat and handing Jake her fleece-lined black leather duster. Not that either of them would feel the cold on the short walk to Connie's favorite watering hole, Darla told herself with a smile. Though since she did have to go back to work afterward, she planned to limit herself to a single drink.

By the time they joined Connie at the register, she had already signed her charge card receipt and was holding a pink business card die-cut into the shape of a wedding bouquet.

"I'll put the alteration appointment into my cell right now," she assured the man, glancing back and forth to the card as she deftly punched the keys of her oversized phone. Then, with a satisfied nod, she said, "All set. And, listen, here's my reminder tone, since we're going with traditional music at the wedding."

She pressed a key, and the first few notes of "Here Comes the Bride" pealed from realistic-sounding wedding bells.

Jake raised a brow. "I'd have gone with Billy Idol, myself."

She hummed a few notes of the 1980s hit "White Wedding" for Darla's benefit while Daniel helped Connie into her leopard-print coat and began escorting them toward the front door. Darla, meanwhile, smiled at her friend's enthusiastic rendition.

"I definitely could see you doing the old step-and-pause up the aisle to that. Me, I like tradition." And she was a bit surprised that Connie fell into the same camp. Darla pictured her marching to the altar to something trendier—a Katy Perry song, or maybe Alanis Morissette's spoof of Fergie's "My Humps."

Darla's smile broadened as she pictured *that*. But before she could make that quick aside to Jake, the man she'd dubbed Mr. Customer Service—apparently, the "Vin" in Davina— abruptly reappeared.

"Ms. Capello," Vinnie began with a self-deprecating smile as he smoothly inserted himself between them and the door. "Please let me apologize for my earlier behavior. I must explain that it was a shock for me, as well, seeing that poor woman lying there. You see, I recently found my own father deceased in his bed, and the scene in the dressing room brought back rather unpleasant memories. I'm afraid I took out my emotional distress on you."

At the man's approach, Connie had assumed a peeved expression that Darla had been certain would explode into a session of "going all Jersey" on him. Instead, Connie's anger dissolved into a look of concern.

"Oh, you poor man," she replied, giving him a consoling pat on the arm. "Believe me, I know just how you feel. A few months ago, someone died during Darla's block party, and I saw them take away the body. It was awful."

Probably not as awful as seeing your parent lying there dead, Darla thought, mentally wincing at the other woman's insensitivity. To his credit, however, Vinnie did not point out the obvious. Instead, he gave a sober nod.

"How terrible for you. And I completely understand why the sight of our poor bride lying there unconscious upset you so much. I hope this will convey how sorry I am for my boorishness."

With the slick moves of a street magician, he whipped one arm from behind his back. Now, Darla could see that he held a small bouquet consisting of a single white lily and a pale blush rose. The two perfect blooms were backed by a wisp of fern and tied with a mint green ribbon to make an admittedly charming arrangement.

Well played. She silently congratulated the man. Though, given his seemingly volatile manner, he likely kept a few of those bouquets available to placate customers whom he'd ticked off. A glance over at Jake, who was rolling her eyes, confirmed that Darla wasn't the only one who suspected as much.

Connie, however, seemed touched by the gesture.

"How lovely!" she exclaimed as he presented the flowers to her with a flourish. "How can I not forgive you after this?" She turned and winked in Daniel's direction, adding, "Especially since your partner gave me such a great deal on the gown."

"I had no choice," Daniel replied with a small smile that, all at once, made him look uncannily like his half brother. "I couldn't bear to let anyone else buy that dress except you."

With that, the two shop owners opened the plum-colored front doors and ushered them out into the literal cold.

"Ugh, I hate this time of year," Darla lamented, pulling on her leather gloves as a biting blast of chilly wind promptly whipped around them. "It's not even Thanksgiving, and already it's almost as cold here as Dallas gets in January. I'm telling you, my blood's too thin for New York winters."

Jake, who'd pulled on an oversized pair of fuzzy black earmuffs that matched her gloves, merely chuckled. "You say that every time it gets below sixty degrees. C'mon, kid, time to toughen up."

"Yeah, I'll remind you of that next summer when you're complaining about no air-conditioning," Darla grumbled back, though she smiled as she said it.

Whipping a plaid knit scarf from her coat pocket, she looped it over her head so that it covered her hair and ears, then tied it beneath her chin. Not the most fashionable look, she thought with a grimace as she glimpsed her undeniably frumpy reflection in Davina's elegant display window. But when it came to cold weather, comfort trumped style.

Then she frowned. Beyond the window display of bridal mannequins draped in a flurry of winter white tulle, she glimpsed a portion of the shop beyond. She could see that Vinnie and Daniel had returned to the same spot near the register. She could also tell that their earlier unctuous smiles were gone. Instead, both men appeared furious as they silently gesticulated in obvious argument.

Which is why they say family shouldn't go into business together, Darla wryly reminded herself. Aloud, she said through chattering teeth as she sidestepped a pile of yesterday's slush, "Connie, I hope wherever we're going for happy hour is close by. I'm going to turn into an icicle in about three more minutes!"

Connie, looking stylish in a leopard-print cloche that matched her jacket, was busy protecting her flowers from the cold wind by hunching over them. With an awkward glance over her shoulder, she replied, "Oh, didn't I tell you? While I was changing, I called Fi to tell him about the dress. He's going to take an early dinner break and meet us at your bookstore, instead, so I can show him all the pictures of the gown I took. So, rain check on the drinks, okay?"

Darla exchanged disbelieving looks with Jake, not sure what surprised her more: Connie blithely going back on her promise, or the fact she'd convinced Reese to break with tradition and view the dress ahead of the ceremony. Though, likely, Connie didn't consider that a bridal shop selfie or two constituted actually "seeing" the gown.

With a shiver, she replied, "I don't mind the rain check, but I could have done without walking a dozen blocks through the modern ice age. Why didn't you just have Reese pick us up at Davina's?"

Connie shot another look over her shoulder, heavily tweezed black brows rising. "He wouldn't get there for a while, and I didn't want to sit around looking at all those other wedding gowns."

They trudged on, and Darla reminded herself that if Connie could make the trek without complaint while wearing three-inch heels, then so could she in her flats. But by the time they reached the stoop of the bookstore, where Reese's car was illegally parked, she could barely feel her toes and fingers. She held the shop door open just long enough for Connie and Jake to slip in after her before shutting it with a jangle of bells behind her.

Brrr was Darla's first thought. With all the energy-saving initiatives that she and James had put into place—specifically, lowering the thermostat!—the shop didn't feel that much warmer than outdoors.

Her second and quite arbitrary thought was that Reese looked surprisingly good in businessman's tweed. Still wearing his long hound's-tooth-checked overcoat, the detective was leaning up against the counter chatting with James. As the three women rushed in from the cold, the latter gave them all a friendly nod while Reese straightened to greet them.

"Hi, Darla . . . Jake," he said with a smile. Connie got a "Hi, babe," accompanied by a loud smack on her lips as she snuggled up to him. "You girls have fun looking at dresses?"

Then, noticing the flower spray Connie still clutched, he released her and took a step back, hands raised.

"Whoa, what's this? I thought you were going to show me pictures of a dress. You didn't call me here so we can run off to A.C. to get married right now, did you?"

The glare his fiancée shot him was the same look that Hamlet used on Darla when she was late filling his kibble bowl.

"I'll have you know, the flowers are from a very nice man at the bridal shop," Connie exclaimed. "And no way am I going to elope to Atlantic City when I just bought the world's most gorgeous dress that looks like a million bucks on me. Everybody's gonna see me in it, or else. So there."

"Hey, it was just a joke," he replied, though Darla heard a genuine note of relief in his voice. Then, when Connie's glare burned still brighter—*no need to crank up the temperature after all*, Darla decided—he hurriedly backtracked. "I mean, not that I wouldn't do it—you know, elope—if you really wanted to, but I agree with you. I think everyone ought to see you in that dress, too."

Then, while a placated Connie linked a possessive arm through his, he turned to the others. "So, you two look half frozen. What, did you broads walk all the way from the dress shop? I woulda picked you up if you'd said something."

"Yeah, we kind of thought of that after the fact," was Jake's wry reply as she pulled off her fuzzy earmuffs and started in on her gloves. "And, FYI, Connie still owes us a happy hour on your dime."

"How about we do coffee for now?" Darla suggested, still feeling a little fuzzy from the earlier champagne. She'd already shrugged off the down coat and was untying the unbecoming scarf while trying to finger-comb her auburn hair into some semblance of order. "Reese, you want me to fix you a cup?"

"No time," he replied with a shake of his head. "I told Connie before it was bad luck, but she's insisting I take a quick look-see at her dress pictures. Then I gotta drive her home so I can get back on shift. But I'll take you up on the java next time I'm around."

"You and your silly superstitions," Connie countered, giving a dismissive little laugh as she released his arm. She pulled her phone from her coat and started scrolling through it, then held up the cell so he could see.

"Here's the front view. Don't my boobs look great? Come on, take a look. Besides, it's not like you're seeing the actual dress. It's just a picture and—A-a-CHOO!"

Connie's unexpected sneeze made all of them jump. She blinked and promptly sneezed again. Then, dabbing at her nose with the back of her free hand, she waved the cell phone about as if to disperse something.

"Id's dat stupid cad," she exclaimed, her usual nasal tones abruptly sounding downright stuffy. "I'b allergid to—A—CHOO!"

"Bless you!" Darla said as she glanced around for Hamlet. The oversized black cat was nowhere to be seen; still, that didn't mean there wasn't sufficient cat dander floating about to set off Connie's allergies.

Echoing her thoughts, James said, "You might be interested to know, Ms. Capello, that there are seven documented cat allergens—specifically, proteins—the major one being secreted primarily via the subject cat's saliva. It is that protein you are allergic to, and not the dander, per se. And as the protein is microscopic, it clings to everything. We are considering installing a HEPA filtering system for our customers who—"

"Protein, smotein," Connie interrupted him . . . or, at least, that's what Darla assumed she said, since the woman's speech was even stuffier now than a moment earlier. "All I know id dat I godda ged oudda here."

"I'm so sorry," Darla told her. "Go get some fresh air. We'll see you and Reese—er, Fi—another time."

Reese had already given them all an apologetic nod and was hurriedly escorting his fiancée to the door. At Darla's words, however, Connie halted and turned.

"Oh, yeah," she replied. "I forgod do dell you. I wad do comb bag domorrow ad look aroud de andique shob negd door. I need sombding old for de weddig. Cad you comb wid me?"

Which Darla interpreted as, Connie planned to check out

Bygone Days tomorrow for the "something old" for the bride—meaning Connie—to carry at the wedding, and she wanted Darla to accompany her to find it. And while the last thing she wanted to do was run more wedding errands with the woman, guilt over the whole cat-allergy thing tilted the balance in Connie's favor.

"Sure, why not?" Darla agreed, managing to sound upbeat. "I'm off in the morning tomorrow. Maybe you can stop by around eleven or so, and we'll find you something cute there. I know Mary Ann will have some good ideas, and I'll do a little checking online for suggestions, too."

"Eleben," the woman confirmed with a sniffle.

Reese nodded. "Thanks, Red—er, Darla."

Once the door had closed behind the pair in a blast of cold air, Jake chuckled. "Better watch it, kid. Next thing you know, you're gonna end up a bridesmaid at that wedding after all."

"Not a chance."

With a rueful smile, Darla carried her coat over to the vintage wooden rack that stood near the small door leading out from the bookstore to her private hall. Hooking her outerwear onto the coat rack—which she'd just happened to find at Bygone Days—she explained, "This is my last 'girly thing' with Connie until the wedding. The place is right next door, so I'd look kind of like a jerk if I told her I couldn't do it. It'll take, what, thirty minutes and then I'm done."

"You are finished," James corrected her. "Your pot roast is done."

"Finished . . . done. Whatever it is, I am," Darla agreed. "And now, I'm going to thaw out with a cup of coffee before I get back to work. Jake, do you want to join me up in the lounge?"

The PI shook her head as she started for the door.

"Thanks, but I'd better head downstairs and catch up on my paperwork. I've got a couple of clients in the a.m. and I need to finish my reports for them. But text me tomorrow after you go shopping with Connie and let me know if she stumbles across another dead body," she finished, grinning a little as she gave those last two words finger quotes.

Once the door had closed after her, James turned and gave Darla a quizzical look. "Dead body?"

"No dead bodies, just an honest mistake," she replied as she took her place behind the register.

Briefly, she explained about the fainting bride-to-be, and the aftermath that resulted in a substantial discount for Connie. She left off the part where she'd accidentally found out that Jake had been married once before—presumably right out of high school, given the prom dress reference. Though, knowing James, he might already have the scoop on that particular bit of gossip. But she'd promised Jake she'd keep her mouth shut about it, and so she would.

James, meanwhile, was nodding his head.

"Hmm," was his thoughtful response to the Connie anecdote. "I will have to keep that trick in mind the next time I make a major purchase. I was considering replacing my old refrigerator with one of those glass-door models."

"Let me know when you go shopping, and I'll be glad to play the not-a-corpse," Darla cheerfully answered.

What was left of the afternoon moved by fairly swiftly. Robert was upstairs cleaning up the coffee bar for the evening—their current schedule left it open until closing only on Fridays and Saturdays—while James worked on his collectible book online auctions and Darla handled the customers. It was almost closing time when the front door jangled open again, revealing a coatless and breathless Mary Ann.

"Oh, Darla, thank goodness you're here," she burst out, rushing in with hands aflutter. "Hamlet must have gotten out somehow, because I just saw him running from building to building! I've spent the past fifteen minutes trying to catch him, but he's too fast for me. Quick, you need to call him back before he freezes out there . . . or worse!"

FOUR

"MARY ANN, CALM DOWN," DARLA EXCLAIMED, HURRYING from around the counter to meet the old woman. "I promise you, Hamlet's safe and snug inside. Look, here he is."

She pointed toward the children's section, where Hamlet snoozed atop the green beanbag chair that was one of his favorite napping spots. Hearing his name mentioned, he slit open one emerald green eye to see what the fuss was all about; then, obviously deciding he had nothing to add to the discussion, he gave a snoring little snuffle and closed his eye again.

"Oh, dear me," Mary Ann replied with a shake of her gray head. "I feel so foolish. And here I was so certain it was Hamlet. I suppose it was just another black cat."

"You're not foolish at all," Darla reassured her. "Black cats all look alike when they're bouncing about. I'm sure whatever cat you saw has probably already made its way safely home."

James nodded his agreement. "But you are correct, Mary Ann. This can be a dangerous time of the year for lost pets, as well as ferals. If you do see this cat again, let me or Robert know so we can contact our friends in animal rescue. They have the means to trap and hold cats like that somewhere safe until they can locate their proper owners."

Darla smiled and gave James a mental thumbs-up for that. She knew that the bookstore manager was a primary sponsor of a small local rescue group . . . the same group that had helped connect Robert with his Italian greyhound, Roma. Maybe for the upcoming holidays, the bookstore could spearhead a donation campaign for the organization. Making a swift mental note to talk to James about that, she turned again to the old woman and frowned in concern.

"Mary Ann, I swear your lips are blue! Come sit, and I'll have Robert send down a pot of hot tea for you."

"Well, maybe I'll take a cup, if it's not too much trouble."

They didn't head toward the stairs leading up to the coffee lounge. Instead, tucking Mary Ann's cold hands beneath her arm, Darla led the woman to a cozy corner in the main store where a bistro table and two chairs awaited them.

"Do you want black tea with cream and sugar, or do you just want a nice cup of Earl Grey?" she asked, recalling Mary Ann's usual preferences.

The old woman smiled as Darla helped her into the chair. "I think I need something on the stout side, so black tea with cream and sugar would be lovely."

Nodding, Darla sat as well, and used the pen and pad sitting on the table to write out the order. Then, tearing off the top sheet, she pressed an ornate call button on the wall beside them that summoned an old-fashioned dumbwaiter that was an original fixture of the brownstone. Once the doors to the miniature elevator opened, she placed Mary

Ann's order on a plate inside and then sent the dumbwaiter back upstairs again so Robert could retrieve the order and then send it down a few minutes later.

"Such a clever idea, my dear," Mary Ann observed, as she always did.

Darla nodded. Actually, the mini bistro area had been James's ingenious solution for catering to the customers who couldn't manage the stairs up to the coffee lounge. She'd seen customers ranging from seniors to moms pushing strollers take advantage of the system. A framed menu posted on the wall gave a list of the lounge's offerings while also instructing customers on how to order. The basic tea and coffee accoutrements—sugar, sweetener, and so on—were already neatly arranged on the table in a white wicker holder.

While they waited for Mary Ann's tea to arrive, Darla asked, "You remember Detective Reese's fiancée, Connie Capello? I don't know whether you met her at the July Fourth block party or not. They didn't stay long."

When the old woman shook her head, Darla reassured her, "Well, I suspect you'll have a few chances in the future to meet her. I'm planning to throw a little party for her and Reese over at Thai Me Up"—the local Thai food place run by her friend Steve Mookjai—"the Saturday before Thanksgiving. You and Mr. Plinski will be invited. But, anyhow, Jake and I went wedding dress shopping with her today."

She spent the next couple of minutes entertaining Mary Ann with talk of the various dresses until the dumbwaiter had made its return trip. When the doors opened, waiting on a red, cork-lined tray was a fat white pot of steaming water from which dangled a tea bag string and tag. Alongside it sat a rose-patterned teacup and saucer and a white mini pitcher of cream.

While the elderly woman began preparing the tea to her

liking, Darla said, "When we got back this afternoon, Connie remembered that she needed something old for the wedding. You know, *something old, something new, something borrowed, something blue*."

"*And a sixpence in her shoe*," Mary Ann finished with a nod.

"Exactly. So Connie asked me to go with her to your shop tomorrow around eleven. I told her you'd have some great ideas, and—Mary Ann, what's wrong?"

For, to Darla's shock, the old woman had set down her teacup and was dabbing at her eyes with a paper napkin.

"Mary Ann, are you all right?" she persisted, her concern growing as the other woman made no effort to hide her distress. "Is Mr. Plinski ill again? Is there a problem at the store?"

"No, no, I'm just being silly, and thinking about weddings just makes it worse."

Dabbing at her eyes once more, Mary Ann took a fortifying gulp of tea and summoned a tremulous smile. "My dear, may I confide in you?"

"Of course."

She took another sip of tea, and Darla gave her an encouraging nod. It occurred to her, however, that she might know the reason for her elderly friend's distress. Hadn't Jake said earlier that Mary Ann and her brother were at odds over Mary Ann's renewed friendship with her high school boyfriend?

In the next breath, Mary Ann confirmed Darla's guess. Putting down her cup and squaring her shoulders, she began, "Things are quite a muddle these days between me and Brother. He's furious that I've renewed my acquaintance with my high school beau, even though being with Hodge makes me happier than I've been in years."

"But shouldn't he be glad you're happy?" Darla asked in

concern. "It's terrible to say, but if something happened to Mr. Plinski, wouldn't he want to know you wouldn't be alone?"

"Pfft, he'd rather see me alone than with Hodge . . . which is difficult to understand, since the two of them once were best friends." Mary Ann took another sip of tea, her expression now sour. "It's so strange. He claims that Hodge did something quite terrible back when we were young that I know nothing about, but he refuses to tell me what it is. And now he's trying to forbid me from seeing Hodge again. Darla, I don't know what to do!"

"Have you tried asking Hodge if he knows why Mr. Plinski resents him so much?"

The old woman nodded. "Hodge swears he can't remember doing anything that could have caused such a rift back then. Truly, it's most confusing. And until Brother can give me a good reason otherwise, I'll keep seeing Hodge as long as I want to," she finished with a defiant jut of her small chin.

Darla gave her a thoughtful nod.

"Just be smart and keep your eyes open," she advised her elderly friend. "Mr. Plinski seems to have a pretty level head on his shoulders. I can't believe he'd hold a grudge for, what, almost sixty years, if what happened wasn't kind of bad."

"Hmmph. If it was that bad, he should have told me sixty years ago."

With that, Mary Ann finished off the rest of her tea and stood.

"Thank you, dear. This was just what I needed," she said, and Darla knew she meant the unburdening as well as the hot drink. "Do bring Connie by tomorrow. Oh, but wait, I won't be there," she added, looking suddenly flustered. "I, er, have an appointment with a gentleman who wants to consign his mother's estate, but I know Brother will have some clever suggestions for you."

"Not a problem. I'm sure Connie and I will manage."

Then, despite Mary Ann's protests, Darla insisted that the old woman borrow her down jacket for the short walk back to her brownstone.

"Please, as a favor to me." Darla said to mollify her. "My mother would never forgive me if she found out I let you go out in the cold without a coat. Don't worry, I'll pick it back up when Connie and I come over in the morning."

And since it was already dark out, Darla also insisted that Robert leave a few minutes early so that he could escort Mary Ann. First, however, she told the youth about the black cat that Mary Ann had seen outside the brownstone.

"From what she says, it's Hamlet's twin. I really hate to think about it out there in this weather, so keep an eye out. If the poor thing is a stray, maybe we can coax it inside and hold it until your rescue friends can take it to a foster home."

"Sure thing, Ms. P.," he eagerly agreed as he grabbed up his backpack and jacket. "And I'll put a little bit of Roma's food outside my door tonight in case it comes back."

Once he and Mary Ann had rushed out into the chilly evening, Darla carried the tea things upstairs to the lounge and did a final wash-up. When she returned downstairs a few minutes later, she saw that Hamlet had abandoned his beanbag and now was sitting on the counter near James. Both had their noses practically pressed to the computer monitor.

"What's wrong? Does someone's cart have the wrong shipping again?" she ask, referring to their online shop for rare and collectible books that she and James had recently launched as an experiment.

James shook his grizzled head. "Actually, I have found an interesting situation with the algorithm for my automatic pricing. Take, for example, this 1871 edition of Nathaniel Haw-thorne's *The Marble Faun*," he said, pointing to the listing on the screen. "I originally listed the set at one hundred sixteen dollars, which is a more than fair price, given its condition. I found two other online shops with comparable volumes of this title all priced within a dollar or two of our offering."

"But our price says three hundred forty-nine dollars," Darla countered with a frown. "Did one of our competitors hack us?"

"Not in the traditional sense. But apparently they have software pricing programs that are similar to ours, all of which monitor everyone else's prices. When our software sees that Rare Bird Books' copy is a dollar higher than ours, it raises our price accordingly. This then prompts the soft-ware belonging to Books in the Attic to raise their price, too," he explained.

Darla nodded. "Right. The intent is to keep us all on an even footing, so to speak."

"Exactly. And the software should have parameters to limit the number of price changes to a single unit. But if a setting is off, that could open the door to a virtual repricing war that would continue until one of us notices and puts a stop to it, or until everyone's prices reach ludicrous heights. On the bright side," he finished, "at least the algorithm is not dropping the prices."

Darla grimaced. "I wouldn't mind selling the Hawthorne for three hundred fifty bucks, but going the opposite way could be pretty brutal. Is that the only book you know of where the pricing is off?"

"I shall have to go over our listings in the morning and see if I discover any other errors. And I did have such high hopes for this program."

"Check with the software manufacturer," Darla suggested. "Maybe they have a patch you can download to fix the bug."

Leaving Hamlet and James to shut down the computer, Darla did her usual pre-closing walk through the store to check for wayward books and stray customers. She found none of the latter but picked up a couple of the former—a French cuisine cookbook and a sports bio—that had been left behind on one of the chairs scattered about the shop for browsers. Which, while something of an annoyance, was preferable for inventory purposes to being shelved back in the wrong spot.

She halted, however, at the sight of an oversized paperback book lying smack in the middle of the self-help aisle.

She retrieved it and looked at its cover. "*The Fool's Guide to Wills and Estates*," she read aloud. And then, feeling suddenly unsettled, she glanced around for Hamlet.

The cagey feline had developed a habit of communicating with her by means of book titles from volumes he would surreptitiously pull from the shelves when she wasn't looking. Of course, said communication only happened after some sort of disaster or another . . . such as an unexplained death. Darla frowned. Fortunately, nothing like that had happened in months. So why the book snagging?

Hamlet chose that moment to stroll up the aisle to join her, tail waving gently as if to show he just happened to be walking past. *Nothing to see here, nothing to do with the book*, he seemed to be saying. She was just about to agree and chalk the incident up to coincidence, when it hit her.

"Aha! Sorry, Hammy," she told him with a smile as she waggled the book at him. "Your whiskers are crossed on this one. Connie thought she saw a dead body at the bridal shop this afternoon, but it turned out it was just a woman who'd fainted. No one's going to be reading wills and settling estates around here. So, no sleuthing necessary on your part."

By way of answer, Hamlet flopped on the floor, green eyes narrowing into slits. Then he flung one hind leg over his shoulder and began licking the base of his tail—his classic "kiss off" gesture when offended.

Darla's smile broadened.

"Back atcha, Hammy," she said without rancor as she reshelved the book and started back toward the register. But when the cat remained stubbornly in place, so that she had to step around him, she said, "I'm sorry, I shouldn't have made fun of you. Every great detective blows it one time or another, and today was just your turn. Now, come along. It's time to close shop and head upstairs for some supper."

At that last magic word, the cat paused in midlick and then sprang up, his sulk forgotten. Trotting past her, he tossed a look back at Darla as if to say, *Get a move on, human, I'm hungry.*

By the time Darla reached the front counter, Hamlet was already sitting at the side door, attention focused on it as if he could open it by sheer force of his will. James, meanwhile, had gathered his things and was headed to the front door.

"I shall be here at nine tomorrow to open," he said, reminding her. "And, depending upon how busy we are tomorrow afternoon, I was hoping to finish my shift two hours early."

"You mean, leave at four? Sure, if we're not slammed, you might as well take a little comp time. You've definitely earned it."

"Thank you. I have a pressing errand that cannot wait."

"What, an early night on the town with Martha?" she asked with a smile.

"In a sense. I am in need of a new light fixture for my dining nook, and she has agreed to help me pick out a suitable replacement."

Darla's smile became a grin. "Uh-oh, shopping for fixtures together. You know that's the first step down that slippery slope that leads to cohabiting, don't you?"

Her store manager gave her a stern look. "I certainly know no such thing. I simply value Martha's opinion in matters of home décor. Please do not read anything more into our outing than that."

"Sorry, I was just kidding." She swiftly backpedaled. "I guess I've got a touch of Connie's wedding fever on your behalf. I didn't mean to make you feel uncomfortable."

"Apology accepted."

She and James made their good-byes, and she let him out the front door, pausing for a quick look near the stoop lest an errant flash of black signal that Hamlet's doppelganger had returned. Seeing no sign of the stray, she shut and locked the door again. It might be cold out, but the weather hadn't yet turned bitter. If it found a snug corner, the cat with its built-in fur coat should be able to last quite nicely through the night.

"All right, we're headed out," she told the original model. She flipped off all but a single light over the register and then joined him at the side door. After setting the alarm, she slipped out into her hallway with Hamlet and then locked the store door behind her. A single lamp on a side table against the wall provided just enough light for them to make it safely up two flights to Darla's apartment above.

But rather than flying up the stairway as usual—and narrowly avoiding tripping Darla—Hamlet instead made a beeline for the windowed door leading out to her private stoop and the street. Rearing up on his hind legs, the cat stretched to his full length so that he was able to peek beneath the lace curtains to the busy street beyond.

Curious, Darla followed after him.

"Did the stray come back?" she whispered as she bent next to him and peered beneath the curtain, too.

The street below was partially lit from a nearby street-light and the headlamps of passing traffic; still, with the row of brownstones looming on both sides of the street, the side-walks were already fully shadowed though it was only just nightfall. Darla squinted in the darkness, looking for an even darker shape slinking low to the ground that might indicate the homeless feline's presence.

And then, even though she was half expecting it, she caught her breath as she saw a shadow move over the Plin-skis' stoop next door and halt.

Definitely not a cat.

That was what had startled her, she realized an instant later . . . the fact that the shadow wasn't a tiny black flash, but stretched long and was vaguely human-shaped. As for whoever cast it, he was himself hidden by even darker shad-ows. Not that it was odd for someone to be walking past, she reminded herself, particularly this early in the evening. But what *was* unsettling was the fact that whoever stood outside their buildings wasn't moving.

Abruptly, Darla wished she'd thought to turn off the hall-way light before taking a peek out the window, lest someone notice her and Hamlet peering out. Though surely the unseen person was doing nothing more sinister than a bit of after-hours window shopping. Didn't she and Mary Ann both keep their store windows deliberately uncurtained in hopes of tempting any late-night lookers to return during business hours? Darla had never considered the policy much of a risk, since the sills were above head height. Besides, she had installed a security system complete with exterior cameras the year before, after an unsettling incident that had made her wonder if the bookstore was haunted.

But, for some reason, she couldn't shake the feeling that whoever now stood outside Bygone Days wasn't simply curious as to the latest window display. Perhaps it was because the shadow was unwavering, as if the shadow-caster was spying on the building . . . maybe waiting for someone to enter or exit.

Just as she was contemplating throwing open the door to startle whoever it was into running off, a sudden yellow flame flared in the darkness. The spark was promptly extinguished, replaced now by the tiny red glow of a cigarette ember. Then the shadow moved on past the Plinskis' building and out of sight.

Darla managed a self-deprecating laugh.

"So much for strangers lurking," she told Hamlet as she stood. "Whoever it was just stopped to light a cigarette. Now, let's go have our supper."

This time, it took a bit longer for the magic word to take effect. Darla was halfway up the first flight before the cat finally left his window post and joined her on the stairs.

"Nosy boy," she fondly told him as he trotted on ahead. "If you're still curious, after you eat, you can try out that new windowsill perch I bought you and watch the front of the building all night long."

Sure enough, once he'd finished off his kibble in the kitchen, Hamlet headed to the living room. There, he leaped with silent grace onto the carpeted kitty roost attached to the sill of the window overlooking the street. When Darla finally called it a night around 10 p.m., Hamlet was still crouched there, nose inches from the glass.

She flipped off the living room light, leaving the cat an inky silhouette against the silvery glow of the window.

"Still keeping an eye out?" she asked him.

He silently turned, and in the darkness a pair of yellow-green orbs shined back at her, giving him a distinctly sinister look.

"Whoa!" she said with a chuckle. "I'm fine with a regular old guard cat. You don't have to go all hell-kitty on me. How about this? If it's not too cold in the morning, we'll take a quick walk up the street and see what's what. Will that satisfy your curiosity?"

She caught a faint, momentary gleam of sharp white teeth, courtesy of the kitchen light behind her, before he turned back to the window again.

Darla smiled a little as she left him there and started down the short hallway to her bedroom. Had that been a sneer, or a grin? No matter, she felt oddly safer knowing that Hamlet, her guardian cat, was on the job while she was busy snoozing.

And when she woke suddenly sometime after midnight from a strange dream of wedding dresses and cigarettes, she sighed and settled comfortably back to sleep to the sound of Hamlet purring softly on the foot of her bed.

FIVE

"OH MY GAWD, THIS PLACE IS SO FREAKIN' CUTE," CONNIE exclaimed the next morning with a pop of her chewing gum as she and Darla entered Bygone Days. "It's like Nana's attic, only better. Oh, look at that dress form wearing a poodle skirt and tight sweater."

While Connie went over to check out the fifties outfit, Darla spared a fond look around the place. This was no snobby antiques emporium stuffed with European antiquities that only the wealthiest could afford. Instead, Bygone Days specialized in eighteenth- and nineteenth-century Americana, though more recently they had added a substantial inventory of collectibles from the early 1900s up to the Swinging Sixties. The faintly musty scents of old wooden furniture and vintage clothing and linens always made Darla feel at home in the crowded shop.

The shop was blessedly toasty inside; still, she blew on her hands to warm them. Since she'd simply run from her front stoop next door to the antiques shop, she hadn't bothered with a coat. Rust-colored corduroys topped by a forest-green-and-white ski sweater and worn with ankle-high brown leather boots warded off the worst of the cold. In fact, the only other casualty besides her hands were her ears, since she had braided her hair into a single auburn plait that hung over one shoulder, exposing her lobes to the elements.

But she forgot that momentary discomfort as she started browsing about the place, which never looked quite the same any time she stopped in for a visit. Now that it was verging on Thanksgiving, the Plinskis has switched out their previous Halloween display for something more autumnal. Their front display counter now held items ranging from harvest memorabilia to Pilgrim-themed collectibles. A mid-century covered pie dish in the shape of a pumpkin caught her eye.

Perfect for my upcoming Thanksgiving dinner, she told herself, noting with satisfaction that it even had a pumpkin pie recipe printed right on the plate. Double-checking the price, which was surprisingly reasonable, she did the obligatory inner debate and then picked it up.

Sold!

"Mr. Plinski," Darla called, peeking down the nearest aisle as she remembered that Mary Ann had said she'd be gone until after lunch. Seeing no sign of the shop owner, she tried again. "It's me, Darla. My friend Connie and I are just going to look around for a bit. If you have any brilliant ideas for something old for a bride to carry at her wedding, let us know."

She heard no response, but wasn't surprised. Despite his protestations to the contrary, the elderly man was half deaf. If he was in the back room unpacking new inventory, chances were he hadn't heard them come in.

Still clutching her pie dish, Darla went over to join Connie, who'd doffed her leopard-print coat.

The woman had done Darla one better in the après-ski look, Darla had to admit. Instead of sensible corduroy and knit, Connie wore tight black ski pants topped by an open-weave, hip-hugging yellow sweater, with a creamy lace camisole plainly visible beneath. Unlike Darla's practical short boots, Connie's were spike-heeled, black suede versions into which her ski pants were tucked, giving her that vaguely superhero-costume look.

The poodle skirt already forgotten, Connie had moved on to vintage millinery. Now she was busy trying on a Jackie Kennedy–style baby blue pillbox hat over her teased black hair.

"Whaddaya think?" she demanded, preening at her reflection in the miniature cheval mirror on the display counter. "Cute, huh? I could wear it when I change for the reception."

"Ooh," she added before Darla could answer. "I have a great idea! You could buy it, instead, but I could borrow it to wear for the wedding. So we got old, blue, and borrowed . . . you know, one-stop shopping," she finished with a nasal laugh at her own cleverness.

"Well, why don't we look around a bit more," Darla suggested, trying not to roll her eyes at Connie's attempt to cheap out with the traditional wedding rhyme. "The pillbox hat *is* pretty clever, but I did a little checking online this morning. Things like old lace hankies that you can tuck into your bra or sew into the lining of your gown are good for 'old.' And some brides take vintage brooches and pin them to the ribbons of their bouquets."

Connie shrugged. "I don't know. That all sounds pretty boring, know what I mean? I want something different."

"Okay, then, how about this? You can find a nice bit of antique lace and sew a cute bow onto your garter."

"Oh, yeah, the garter," Connie replied with a sly smile.

"Forget the white lace. I bought a sexy one made with black and red lace and silk . . . you know, like a burlesque queen would wear. Fi is gonna love it."

"I'm sure he will," Darla agreed, trying not to wince at the mental image of Connie parading around on her wedding night in nothing but the garter.

Clutching the pie holder more tightly, she added, "Anyhow, there are lots of things you can choose for something old. It doesn't even have to be something you wear. Maybe a nice silver cake knife to use for cutting the wedding cake. Or a pretty candleholder for the head table. So why don't you start down that first aisle, and I'll start at the far side? If you see anything promising, just yell."

"Yeah, okay."

With seeming reluctance, Connie removed the pillbox hat and returned it to its stand. Then, following Darla's suggestion, she started down that row again, while Darla went to the far side of the shop to begin her browsing.

But she found herself doing a little overdue soul-searching instead. She'd been in an emotional funk ever since the Fourth of July block party, when violence had struck the neighborhood. She had almost fallen victim to the same killer herself, and only Hamlet's timely intervention had saved her. But rather than being grateful that she'd dodged that metaphorical bullet, she had found herself swamped by the occasional wave of hopeless fear that made it hard to get out of bed in the morning.

Survivor's guilt, combined with PTSD, both Jake and Reese had diagnosed, urging her to speak to a counselor. When an equally concerned James had chimed in with the same suggestion, she'd finally broken down and visited a psychologist who'd given her a combination of sympathy and tough love, but mostly allowed her to talk. After a few sessions over the summer, she'd pretty well come to terms with what had happened, and the fearful thoughts had soon diminished. But what lingered was a certain emptiness that even her store and her friends couldn't fill.

At the end of the day, she wondered, just what was she missing from her life?

She'd finally asked that question of Jake, who'd had a blunt reply.

You've got the career thing covered. What you need right now is a guy, she'd decreed. Then, as Darla began a sputtering protest, the PI had clarified, *I don't mean for the old "you complete me" BS. I'm talking, you need a decent guy you can go out to dinner with, run off for the weekend with, maybe even do the dirty with. I'm not saying you have to go get married or anything. You just need to have a little grown-up fun for a change.*

And then, when Darla had testily countered that Jake didn't seem to be following her own advice, her friend had grinned and winked. *Hey, kid, let's just say I'm not a blabbermouth who goes around telling her friends every personal detail.*

After sputtering over it a bit longer, Darla had agreed that Jake had a point. The problem was, the one so-called nice guy she'd found had turned out to be not so nice, after all. And dating Reese hadn't worked out much better. Although there had been a definite spark between them—okay, maybe it had been a definite glow of a possible spark—after a couple of uncomfortable evenings out, they had come to the mutual decision that they were better friends than romantic partners.

Even so, she'd been a bit stunned by the unexpected announcement of his and Connie's engagement. And while the rational part of her brain agreed that Connie was far more suitable a fiancée to Reese than she could ever be, the emotional side had still felt a silly if undeniable twinge of jealousy. But by the time Darla had worked through her other issues, she had finally come to realize that the emotion she was feeling regarding Reese and Connie was nothing more than hurt vanity.

Darla paused as she spied an old chalkware wedding cake topper inside a glass case. It was uncannily appropriate, with a dark-haired bride and blond groom atop an ivy-wrapped platform. The tiny couple stood beneath a bower of white silk flowers—now slightly tan with age—from which hung a tiny porcelain bell. Of course, given its condition the topper couldn't go on the cake, but it would be adorable on the same table alongside it. Darla squinted to read the tag. It was circa the nineteen-forties, she saw, which more than qualified for something old, and the price was less than the pillbox hat.

Putting the cake topper on her mental list to tell Connie about—since she and Connie were apparently the only customers for the moment, she didn't worry about losing it to another shopper—Darla moved to the next aisle. But the image of the tiny bride and groom stuck with her, and she found herself picturing another cake topper, this one with a chestnut-haired groom and an auburn-haired bride.

She grimaced at the memory. They'd had to special-order the topper so that the bride's hair would be the right color. He had insisted on it, just as he'd insisted on new matching towels in the bathroom. And just as he'd insisted on buying a brand-new bedroom suite to replace her well-loved furniture that she'd bought one piece at a time at auctions and consignment stores.

Too bad you didn't make sure your mistress matched your wife, she sourly thought. If he had done so, Darla's coworker in accounting might never have realized that the woman—the blonde—that she had seen her married boss kissing in a darkened nightclub wasn't his wife, who happened to be Darla.

And Darla wouldn't now be mentally rehashing any of these unpleasant memories in the middle of Bygone Days if her slimeball ex-husband hadn't chosen this morning of all mornings to send her an email out of the blue.

Darla grimaced again. She had almost deleted the message unread. Her finger had hovered over the "Delete" key a good minute before she decided to open the email in case it contained news about his family (she still quite liked several of her ex-in-laws), or on the chance there were some legal loose threads concerning their divorce. Instead, the email had been what she'd feared it might be . . . a nonchalant request to make nice.

She had read the message several times, just to make sure she wasn't missing some sinister nuance. By the fifth go-round, she had the email memorized.

Hey, Darla, long time, no speak. I heard you are up in Brooklyn running your great-aunt's bookstore now. Quite a change from the old corporate world, huh? Anyhow, I'm going to be in your neck of the woods the week after Thanksgiving on business. I was thinking maybe we could get together for supper or something. You know, let bygones be bygones. No pressure, just friends. If you can break free one night, let me know and I'll put you on the schedule.

And then, in what she guessed was an attempt at humor, he'd signed it

Your favorite ex-husband,

followed by

P.S., I'm buying.

Her first reaction had been to mutter a stream of bad words that caused Hamlet's ears to prick up in surprise. Her second had been to type out a hasty reply beginning with *Dear Slimeball*, followed by the same bad words that Hamlet had disapproved of, and ending with *Not in your wildest dreams.* Bygones, indeed!

But discretion had intervened before she had hit the "Send" button, and she'd deleted the message instead. True, her ex had been the one in the wrong—way in the wrong!—but there was no reason she should stoop to his level. And so she'd decided to wait a day to respond.

Which would be in the negative, of course.

Now, Darla shoved aside that unpleasant blip on her radar and returned her attention to the errand at hand. She had finished perusing her current aisle but had found nothing else wedding worthy besides the cake topper. Maybe Connie had had better luck.

She was just about to call to Connie to see how she was faring in the search, when a piercing scream nearly made her drop the pie plate.

And then a now-familiar cry came from Connie.

"Oh my Gawd, there's a dead guy behind the counter!"

After a swift moment of shock, Darla rushed to the rear of the shop in the direction of Connie's cry. What had she stumbled across now? Maybe one of the mannequins that Mary Ann sometimes used to display vintage dresses had toppled over in a corner. Whatever it was, if it was dead, Connie's shrieking darn well should have awakened it again!

A moment later she reached Connie, who stood near the sales counter, manicured hands clapped over her mouth and overly made-up eyes wide.

"Connie, what's wrong?" Darla demanded. "What did you see?"

Connie slowly removed her hands from her red lips and extended a quivering forefinger. "It's a dead body."

"Where? Oh!"

Darla rolled her eyes. Connie was pointing behind the modern computerized register, where Mr. Plinski sat in a wood-framed wingback chair upholstered in red brocade. His slippered feet were propped on a horsehair hassock. With his eyes closed and chin tucked to his chest, and a vintage needlepoint pillow propped on his lap, he did rather look like a display, Darla thought with a glimmer of amusement.

"Shh," she told the other woman in a stage whisper, unable to suppress her smile. "That's Mary Ann's brother, Mr. Plinski. He's just taking a nap. Lucky for you, he's half deaf, so you didn't startle him awake with all your yelling."

"No," Connie persisted in a small voice, pointing again. "Look how white his skin is. I tell you, he's dead."

Darla took another swift look at the man, and her smile abruptly faded. The old man did look strangely pale, but surely that was just a trick of the light. His chest was moving . . . wasn't it?

Trying to tamp down a sudden surge of foreboding—*he's fine; it's just Connie's imagination going wild*—she set down her pie dish on the counter.

"Don't move," she told Connie. "I'm going to try to wake him."

Tiptoeing around the counter—*don't want to startle him awake*, she tried to tell herself—Darla eased her way over to the wingback chair and bent closer to the man. Up close, the waxen stillness of his features was even more apparent, the gray stubble of his unshaved cheeks surprisingly dark against the slack flesh.

No, no, no, she told herself, feeling her chest tighten abruptly. "Mr. Plinski," she croaked through a suddenly constricted esophagus. Then, clearing her throat, she tried again.

"Mr. Plinski," she said, trying to keep the desperation from her voice. "It's me, Darla from next door. Please wake up."

She put out a tentative hand, praying this was all a terrible misunderstanding and that the old man would stir as soon as she gave him a gentle shake. But when she lightly touched his scrawny shoulder, she knew.

"Connie," she choked out, tears springing to her eyes. "Call Reese and tell him we're at the Plinskis' shop. Tell him Mr. Plinski is . . ."

She trailed off, unable to say the word aloud. Connie, meanwhile, had pulled her phone from her bag and hit a key.

"Fi," she said a moment later in a small voice, "Can you come get me? Something really bad has happened. Yeah, talk to Darla, would ya?" she said, and handed over her cell.

By now, Darla had edged back around the counter, away from the silent figure in the red brocade chair. The old man had seemed to have shrunk in on himself, becoming little more than a husk, while the round needlework pillow propped on his lap seemed a mocking reminder of transience.

Gather ye rosebuds while ye may, it read, the doleful words encircled by a stitched garland of red roses. She couldn't help but remember the rest of the poem from high school.

Old Time is still a-flying:
And this same flower that smiles to-day
To-morrow will be dying.

Shivering a little at that last word, she put the phone to her ear. "Reese," she managed, "I've got some awful news."

In a halting voice, she relayed what had just happened. When she'd finished, she heard him sigh.

"Sorry, Red. He was a nice old guy. Don't worry, I'll make all the calls. How's Mary Ann holding up?"

"Mary Ann!" Darla gasped, her heart sinking even further, if that were possible. "How could I forget? Reese, she's not here. She had to meet a customer about a consignment. What should I do? I can't tell her this over the phone."

"I'll take care of that when I get there. Are there any other customers in the place with you?"

"No. Just us."

"Good. Don't touch anything. Put the 'Closed' sign out so no one else can come in, and then wait up by the front door for me. Any idea when Mary Ann is due back?"

Darla shook her head, even though she knew Reese couldn't see her. "I'm not sure, probably after lunch. She took a car service out, so the same people will probably pick her back up. Hurry, would you?"

"Be there in ten," he assured her. "I'll make all the calls as soon as I hang up."

Darla pressed the "End" button and handed the phone back to Connie, whose gaze was studiously directed to the front of the store. "Reese wants us to wait up front until he gets here," she told the woman. "We need to make sure no other customers come in."

Connie nodded but made no move to comply until

Darla—whose own gaze was also fixed anywhere but the red brocade chair—gave her a small shove.

"Okay, I get it," she whined, rubbing her arm where Darla had nudged her. "All I can say is that Fi better—"

Before she could finish the thought, a jangle of bells that signaled the shop door opening cut her off. *A customer!*

"I told you!" Darla said with a gasp. "Quick, we have to intercept whoever it is and tell them the shop is closed."

Not waiting to see if Connie was following, Darla rushed down the aisle toward the front of the store. She'd have to tell this newcomer something—gas leak in the store, perhaps, or maybe a hazardous cleaner spilled. Anything that would hurry them right back out the door. But as she reached the door and saw who was there, she gasped again.

"Mary Ann!"

"Why, Darla, I wondered if you and your friend might still be here," the old woman said with a smile as she paused to remove her bright red wool scarf and camel-haired coat. "Was Brother able to help her find something nice?"

"No . . . that is, we're still shopping. I mean . . ."

She trailed off, praying she could keep her composure. Somehow, she had to stall the old woman where she stood until Reese got there.

"Your dress is lovely," she temporized, indicating the old woman's winter white brocade suit, a Jackie O style that Darla assumed was one of her vintage finds along with the pillbox hat. Managing a smile, she continued. "A little fancy for going out to Queens and talking to some guy about used furniture and whatnots, isn't it?"

To her surprise, Mary Ann blushed. "Oh, it's just something I threw on. I like to dress up every so often."

Then she babbled on. "And I must say the poor fellow was totally out of his element trying to deal with his late mother's estate. Apparently, she had been something of a world traveler and collected all sorts of indigenous art. We had another similar estate a few weeks ago, with a son trying to sell off his father's lifelong collection of ephemera. Some of it was shockingly valuable, and some of it, well, frankly needed to be recycled. You just never know. But back to today's appointment . . ."

She went on to describe a few pieces she'd seen, while Darla shot a despairing look at her watch.

Reese, where are you?

Fortunately, Mary Ann was in a talkative mood, which saved Darla from having to keep the conversation going herself. Still, if Mary Ann insisted on stirring from her current spot, she'd have no choice but to tell the old woman what had happened. But even as she mentally scrambled for another delaying tactic, Connie abruptly walked up behind her and planted herself squarely in front of the old woman.

"You're the sister . . . Ms. Plinski, right? I'm Connie Capello." She put out a hand. "Soon to be Mrs. Fiorello Reese."

"Oh, yes, the bride. How nice to meet you." Mary Ann twittered with pleasure while Darla tried not to panic.

Don't say anything. Don't say anything! she mentally commanded Connie, well aware that the woman was a loose cannon when it came to expressing herself. Unfortunately, her back was now to Darla, so that there was no possibility of pantomiming zipped lips. She could only pray that Connie had the good sense not to blurt out the distressing news.

But the telepathic command didn't work. Once they'd exchanged a ladylike shake, Connie gave the old woman's wrinkled hand a consoling pat. In a flash, Darla knew what Connie was about to say . . . knew she had no way to stop her.

"It's such a shame we're meeting under these circumstances." Connie said, sadly shaking her head. "I am so very sorry for your loss."

"My loss?" Sliding her hand from Connie's grip, Mary Ann turned a puzzled look from her to Darla, who could only stare miserably back. "I'm not sure I understand."

"You know, your brother," Connie continued. "It was a terrible shock to us all, especially me. I mean, it's not every day you find—"

"Connie!" Darla shrieked, finally finding her voice. "Don't. Say. Another. Word."

"What?" Connie stared back at her, expression peeved . . . and then understanding dawned. "Oh my Gawd, you didn't tell her yet, did you?"

"Tell me what?" Mary Ann demanded, fear abruptly coloring her tone. Hugging her coat tightly to her, she persisted. "There's something wrong, isn't there? Where's Brother?"

"Why don't we go over to the bookstore," Darla suggested. "I'll have Robert make us coffee, and—"

"Don't treat me like a child—or, worse, like a bumbling old fool." The elderly woman cut her short in a strong if quavering voice. "I'm perfectly sound of mind and capable of withstanding whatever I must. If there's something I should know, tell me right now."

"You're right, I'm sorry. We—Connie and I—found Mr. Plinski sitting in his chair behind the counter. It looks like after you left, he decided to take a nap and just never woke up." Darla paused for a steadying breath; then, blinking back tears, she finished in a rush. "Mary Ann, I'm afraid your brother is dead."

|| SIX

"HOW IS MARY ANN HOLDING UP?" JAMES ASKED ONCE
Darla returned to the bookstore for a short break after sitting
with the old woman for the past hour. "You did not say much
about her mental state before. Should I go over and make
my condolences, or wait a bit?"

"Actually, Reese is busy questioning her right now, and
then he wants to talk to Connie and me. I suppose they need
some sort of timeline for the medical examiner, or something. But I know she'll want to see you. After all, you've
been friends for, what, almost eleven years?"

"Since I have been working here at Pettistone's. She and
Bernard are—were—both very fine people."

"Yes, and I—"

Darla broke off abruptly as she realized what James had
said.

"Bernard? Mr. Plinski's first name is Bernard?" At his
nod, she gave a small laugh. "I've been wondering what his

name is forever. You know how Mary Ann always called him 'Brother,' and everyone else called him 'Mr. Plinski.'"

"Or 'Mr. P.,' in the case of young Robert."

Darla nodded. "Right, and after a point it seemed like too much time had passed to just go up to him or Mary Ann and ask his first name. So he was always Mr. Plinski to me."

Then, her momentary amusement fading, she sagged onto the stool behind the register and said in weary admiration, "I swear, that Mary Ann is a trouper. I think I was a bigger mess than she was. She never broke down, not even after Reese walked her back to where we found Mr. Plinski—Bernard—so she could see for herself he really was gone."

Fortunately, Reese had pulled up to the store just as Darla was telling Mary Ann about her brother's passing. She had feared that the old woman might break down into hysterics, maybe even faint. But she'd done none of that, save for a slight buckling of her knees and an almost inaudible "Oh, dear me."

Sparing only a quick nod for Darla and his fiancée, Reese had helped steady Mary Ann, giving her a few words of encouraging comfort before handing her back over to Darla's care. Then, leaving the three women at the door, he had strode to the back of the store to check out the situation for himself.

Connie had not been pleased.

"Well, hello to you, too," she'd muttered once Reese was out of earshot, giving her gum an irritated smack. In the next moment, however, she'd dragged over one of the ladder-back chairs from a nearby display so Mary Ann could sit. The three of them had huddled there for a time: Mary Ann, sitting ramrod straight in the uncomfortable seat with her eyes closed; Darla, settling one comforting hand on the old woman's shoulder while discreetly brushing away her own occasional tear with the other; and Connie, tapping a leopard-print-shod foot and checking her phone.

As the wait dragged on for medical personnel to arrive and pronounce the elderly man officially dead, Darla had taken that opportunity to borrow back her down coat and rush back to the store for a few minutes. She wanted to let James know what was going on, in case he or Robert spied the activity on the street. But the youth had been busy upstairs, and so she had left the responsibility to James before heading back to the antiques shop again.

Now she asked James, "How about Robert? How did he handle the news?"

"Not very well, I fear. I told him you had decided to close the store for the rest of the day, and that he could return home, but he preferred to remain here. He is upstairs in the coffee lounge doing some cleaning."

James shook his grizzled head and sighed, adding, "The next few days will not be easy for him. It would not be amiss to say that he looked upon Mr. Plinski as a grandfatherly figure."

"I know," Darla soberly agreed, "And since neither of them ever married, I think that he and Mary Ann thought of Robert as a surrogate grandson."

For, like James, the youth had known the Plinskis since before Darla had inherited the bookstore. He'd started out as a customer buying Victorian mourning jewelry and vintage clothing that fit in with his goth lifestyle; then he'd served as an unofficial assistant helping the elderly siblings with some of the heavy lifting during their busy seasons. He had continued that role even after taking a full-time job at Pettistone's, doing occasional chores in return for a significant discount on rent in their garden apartment, where he lived.

It *would* be hard on him, she told herself. Maybe it was a good thing Robert would be going off to stay with his father for a week.

"I need to send a quick email to a vendor," Darla said as she slid the stool over to the computer. "As soon as I get that out of the way, I'll go upstairs and talk to Robert. I'm going to see if Mary Ann wants to stay with me tonight, and I think it would be a good idea for him to have supper with us so he's not down in that apartment all alone."

She made quick work of the correspondence while James reshelved a few errant books. Then, climbing off the stool and allowing herself a nervous stretch, she told her manager, "Oh, and thanks for telling Robert and Jake about Mr. Plinski. It was hard enough telling you after having to break the news to Mary Ann."

"I was glad to be of service," James replied. "Under the circumstances, you should not have been forced, as they say, to do all of the heavy lifting. And I agree that closing the store for the afternoon was a proper response. I am finding it rather difficult, myself, to concentrate on work in the wake of this distressing news. However, perhaps we should volunteer to assist Mary Ann by notifying our mutual friends about what has happened."

"We can get Jake to help with that," Darla agreed. "She was waiting for things to settle down a bit with Reese and all his people before going over there, anyhow. And I'll be sure to let Mary Ann know that if she needs help with any of the arrangements over the next few days, one of us will be glad to step in."

Leaving James to check his online book sales, Darla

made her way upstairs to the empty coffee lounge. She found Robert there slumped in one of the bistro chairs. Hamlet was perched at full length on the table near him. With his front paws tucked beneath his chest and long tail wrapped tightly about him, he looked like a small black sphinx as he studied the young barista through narrowed green eyes.

Darla did a little studying herself—of Hamlet, not of Robert. Had the cat predicted Mr. Plinski's death with his book snagging the day before? Or had it been nothing more than a sad coincidence? Hamlet didn't seem inclined to elaborate on the subject, however, but instead kept his focus on Robert.

Dismissing her uncertainty for now, Darla pulled out the chair opposite the pair and sat. "Hey, how are you doing?" she softly inquired of Robert.

The youth lifted red-rimmed eyes to meet hers, the black kohl he normally wore now smeared as if he'd rubbed a hand across it. His expression was haunted—not in an angsty teen attempt to appear put-upon, but in true adult grief.

"I don't believe it," he said in a choked voice. "I mean, I know Mr. P. was old and stuff, but I just talked to him this morning and he was fine. How can he be dead?"

"Oh, Robert, I know it sounds cliché, but it was his time. Sometimes people just wear out," she told him. "I saw him, and it looked like he'd gone to sleep. He was in his own store doing what he enjoyed, so if you have to die, that's probably the best way to go."

"Yeah, I guess."

He pulled a paper napkin from the holder on the table and wiped his eyes, smearing the kohl even more. Then, giving Hamlet a pat, he rallied a little.

"He could have, you know, had to go off to one of those

old-people homes and die there. So this is okay, I suppose. But I'm sure going to miss him. He was really smart and all."

"Yes, he was. And remember, Mary Ann is going to need us, so we need to be thinking of her, too. I'm going to see if she'll stay with me or Jake, at least for tonight. Can I count on you to join us for a while and help keep her company?"

"Yeah, sure, Ms. P. I'll need to check on Roma first, though . . . you know, feed her and walk her."

"How about you bring the pup up to my apartment with you after you're done? I know that Mary Ann likes her, and maybe some of Roma's doggie antics will help take her mind off things for a bit."

At Robert's eager nod, she finished, "I'll text James with the plan when I've confirmed with Mary Ann, and he'll let you know what's going on when. I'm heading back over to Bygone Days now. You can stay here with James and Hamlet as long as you like."

She gave Hamlet a scritch and then left the stoic feline to serve as confidant to the youth. Once downstairs again, she told James as she headed toward the door, "This shouldn't take long with Reese. There's not much to tell."

Making another swift, coatless run through the freezing outside air, she hurried back to the antiques store. A funeral home vehicle was now parked on the street in front of the building, causing the afternoon traffic to have to swerve around it. She shuddered, and not just from the cold. She'd hoped to miss this part of the process, seeing the old man wheeled away.

A uniformed officer she recognized from earlier stood just inside the shop's doorway. He nodded to her to come inside, and she gratefully rushed in out of the cold. She heard a murmur of male voices, and then Reese strode over to her.

"Darla." He greeted her with a nod. "Let's step over here so we can talk."

"Where's Mary Ann?"

"I sent her down to Jake's. We're not ready to release the place yet, and I didn't want her stuck in the middle of all this."

Darla frowned. The way Reese was talking, it was almost like he was treating the place as an actual crime scene, rather than simply dotting the i's and crossing the t's necessary for a natural death. Certainly, nothing she'd seen had made her think anything suspicious was going on. Couldn't he stop being a cop about things just this once?

"And Connie?" she persisted.

His words took on an impatient note. "I got her statement already, so I called a car for her and sent her home. End of roll call?"

Darla shot him an angry look . . . because if she didn't get mad, chances were that she'd burst out in tears instead. "Just checking on my friends," she clipped out. "I want to be sure all of them are doing okay under the circumstances."

"Sorry, Red." His attitude momentarily softened. "I get it. Believe me, I hate like hell having to be here. Why don't you sit"—he gestured to one of the two ladder-back chairs that had been moved into the aisle in an impromptu conversational group—"and we'll get this over with."

She sniffled, nodded, and then sat.

He pulled out a notebook from his jacket pocket. "What time did you arrive here at the store? Tell me what happened, starting from the minute you walked in the door."

Darla complied—leaving out, of course, her whole inner debate about her ex-husband's email and how she should respond to it.

"Connie was the one who found him," she said when she got to that part, to clarify. "I heard her scream, and I ran over to see what was wrong. I don't know if she told you what happened in the bridal shop yesterday, when that girl fainted. I thought she was just being dramatic again, until I took a good look at him."

She couldn't tell from Reese's expression if Connie had filled him in on the bridal shop incident or not, but it likely didn't matter, for all he said was, "Did you touch Mr. Plinski . . . move him, at all?"

Darla nodded. "I-I touched his shoulder to see if he was sleeping. But when I realized he wasn't . . ."

She trailed off momentarily to take a steadying breath. "When I knew he was dead, I backed away and told Connie to call you. Neither of us touched anything after that. We were headed to the front door like you told us, when we heard the bells ringing. Mary Ann walked in. I tried to keep her talking until you got here, but Connie accidentally blabbed, so I had to tell her—Mary Ann—everything."

He nodded. "It's okay; you did good. Now let's talk about what you saw around Mr. Plinski. There was some kind of weird ceramic dish that looked like a pie sitting on the counter. Any idea what that is?"

"That was mine," Darla told him, smiling a little. "I was planning to buy it and I set it down there when I went to check Mr. Plinski."

"Fair enough. Now how about that pillow on his lap . . . was it there when you found him?"

"Yes."

Darla sobered again as she nodded. How could she ever forget that uncannily prescient example of needlework propped on the old man's knees like a grisly billboard? But why would Reese care about a pillow?

"You're sure about that?" he persisted. "You didn't maybe pick it up off the floor and prop it on his lap before you realized, well, you know."

"No. Why, what's important about it?"

But rather than answering that question, he asked her something even more disconcerting. "What do you know about Mary Ann's friend, Rodger Camden?"

It took her a moment to figure out just who Reese meant.

"You mean Hodge? All I know is what Mary Ann told me last night. He was her boyfriend back in high school, and apparently, there was some sort of falling-out between him and Mr. Plinski. She broke up with him, and they just reconnected a couple of months ago."

"Mr. Camden initiated this reunion?"

"Actually, she found him. From what Mary Ann told me, she hadn't seen the man for decades until she got some kind of wild hair and tracked him down on social media. And they've been a couple again ever since."

"Uh-huh," he replied, pausing to scribble a note. Then, fixing her with a bland blue gaze, he asked, "And you've met Mr. Camden?"

"Just once, when she brought him by the bookstore to introduce him. But she wasn't making a huge production about it." *Not like a certain future Mrs. Fiorello Reese*, she thought with a mental roll of her eyes.

"So, this falling-out thing. What did Mary Ann tell you about Mr. Camden's relationship with Mr. Plinski?"

"Nothing, really. She indicated there was some sort of bad blood, but I think it was just an old high school rivalry." By this point, suspicion was taking hold. Frowning, she added, "Reese, is there something about Mr. Plinski's death you're not telling me?"

"Just covering all the bases," was his noncommittal reply.

Then, in what seemed to her a deliberately casual manner, he added, "You still have those exterior security cameras at the bookstore?"

"Sure, why?"

"Just checking. I was kind of surprised when Mary Ann told me she didn't have any cameras here in the shop. I thought most antiques stores had a whole bank of cameras to watch for shoplifters."

She nodded. "Most of the ones I've been in do. I asked Mary Ann about it one time. She said she and Mr. Plinski thought having cameras all through the store was too unfriendly. Most of the really valuable things were either in cases, or else too big to sneak out with, and she said she'd rather lose a few cheap collectibles than make her regulars feel like she didn't trust them."

"Too bad," he muttered, and it occurred to Darla that what he was looking for was a recording of the events leading up to Mr. Plinski's death. The idea made her shudder . . . made her wonder why he seemed to be making a federal case of an old man's passing from natural causes.

"Reese, you're really starting to make me nervous," she told him. "What's with all these questions? I mean, poor Mr. Plinski was eighty years old. Is it really so strange that he might have had a stroke or heart attack?"

"You know the drill, Red. We cops don't make the determination as to cause of death."

He'd explained this more times than she'd cared to remember over the past year and a half—something to the effect that, unless the departed died with a doctor holding his or her hand, the death was treated as suspicious until determined otherwise. But surely the cause of death here was more than obvious.

And yet Reese was asking about security cameras . . . and about Mary Ann's friend Hodge.

Abruptly, Darla recalled the shadowy figure she and Hamlet had seen outside the antiques store the previous night. At the time, she'd dismissed it—him?—as a passerby grabbing a smoke. Could somebody—Hodge?—have been scoping out Bygone Days for some reason? She tried to recall what she could of the unknown person's size and shape. It could have been Hodge. On the other hand, it could have been half the people in Brooklyn. Either way, it made no sense that some late-night skulker was tied into Mr. Plinski's death.

She debated a moment longer about mentioning what she'd seen, and then decided against it. Reese would probably just dismiss her misgivings as her and Hamlet's imagination, having little respect as he did for Hamlet's sleuthing instinct.

Instead, she asked, "Anything else, Detective?"

Reese gave her a slanted look as he flipped the notebook shut. "That's it for now, but I might want to look at those camera recordings later. Will you be there?"

"I shut the store down for the day. James and Robert are still there doing busywork, but I don't think any of us are up to dealing with customers. Before I go back, though, I'm going to stop at Jake's place and talk to Mary Ann. I think she should stay with me or Jake tonight."

"Good idea." He stood and gestured her toward the door. "Do me a favor, would you, and don't say anything to her about me asking you about this Camden character. She might get the wrong impression, know what I mean?"

Or she might give Hodge a heads-up that he is on Reese's radar, was Darla's thought. But she would go along with his request and wouldn't tell the old woman anything. Mary Ann had enough to deal with without worrying that her boyfriend had attracted the detective's notice.

Darla gave Reese an absent nod as she plunged again into the cold. At least Mary Ann would be in good hands with Jake, since the ex-cop-turned-PI had experience in dealing with the recently bereaved. Hurrying past the wrought iron railing with the sign "Martelli Investigations" bolted to it, she ran down the few steps to Jake's garden apartment and swiftly knocked on the door. Barely waiting for the other woman's "Come in," she rushed inside and shut the door behind her.

Jake's garden apartment boasted an open floor plan similar to Darla's, with a single large space serving as a combination living room, dining room . . . and now, as the office for Jake's detective agency. The place was a study in Mid-Century Modern that always reminded Darla of old television sitcoms. From what Jake had told her, the apartment's previous tenant had left behind a mishmash of old furniture dating from that era.

Rather than hauling it all to the curb, however, Jake had embraced the style. She'd methodically continued the decorating in that same vein with finds from various thrift shops, changing up a piece here or there when she got bored with it. From the chrome dinette table with a red Formica top that served as her desk, to the mod floor-to-ceiling lamp with its three shades that looked like melted red plastic bowls, the décor had a funky kitschy look that usually made Darla smile.

No one was smiling now, however. Handkerchief to her eyes, Mary Ann huddled in a turquoise leather tufted club chair—one of Jake's more recent acquisitions—looking smaller and frailer than Darla had ever seen her. Jake was walking out from behind the trifold red lacquered screen that divided the living area from the galley kitchen, a steaming blue-flowered teacup and saucer in hand. She gave Darla an acknowledging nod and then addressed Mary Ann.

"Sorry, the only tea I have is the bedtime kind," she said, indicating the tea bag perched on the saucer as she set the beverage on a glass-topped end table. "I hope that's okay."

"Fine, dear," the old woman murmured, tucking away her handkerchief. She dunked the tea bag into the hot water and then glanced Darla's way.

"Oh, hello, dear. Have you finished talking with Detective Reese?"

"We're finished," Darla told her, not wanting to worry her by mentioning that he still wanted to review the bookstore's security camera recordings. "I'm not sure how much longer they'll be investigating, though. But Reese agrees it would be a good idea if you stay with me or Jake tonight."

"We already talked about that," Jake interjected. "She'll stay here tonight, and we'll see how things are in the morning."

Darla nodded. That way, Mary Ann wouldn't have to navigate the two flights of stairs up to Darla's apartment. But that still left the matter of Robert. While the old woman sipped at her tea, Darla gestured Jake over.

"Robert's pretty upset over all of this," she murmured. "I didn't want to send him home all alone to his place, and I know he wants to talk to Mary Ann. Before I knew the plan, I was going to have him and maybe James join me and her for supper. But if you don't mind, maybe we can move the gathering over here. I can whip up a quick casserole to bring over."

"Sure, kid, that sounds fine. I've got some stuff in the

fridge we can add to it. And a couple of bottles of wine if we need some fortifying."

She sighed, looking weary all at once. Darla reminded herself that Jake, too, had known the Plinskis for several years.

"I'd appreciate the company myself," the PI conceded in a low voice. "This has been tough on all of us, and I'm afraid things will get morbid if it's just me and Mary Ann trying not to talk about what happened."

"Great. Let me run back to the apartment and start throwing things together. We'll all meet back here at, what, five?"

"Sure, but give me a few minutes first to run over to Mary Ann's place and see if Reese will let me pick up some things for her tonight. She gave me a list, and I've got her spare keys."

While the PI made a quick exit, Darla took a seat on the short leather sofa across from Mary Ann and gently asked, "Can I get you more hot water, or anything else?"

"Really, my dear, you don't have to treat me like an invalid," she replied in a quavering voice. "This is a terrible shock, but at my age I've outlived plenty of friends and family. This is hardly my first brush with death."

"I know, and I'm sorry. I promise, I'm not trying to patronize you," Darla told her in chagrin. "But I'm glad you're taking Jake up on her offer to stay here tonight. I'm going to cook us supper and bring it over here. Robert will come with me . . . James, too."

"That'll be nice, dear."

Mary Ann took another sip of tea, then abruptly set her cup back into its saucer with a clatter.

"Oh, Darla, I don't know what to do," she cried. "I didn't want to say anything in front of Jake, because she would feel obligated to say something to Detective Reese. But I'm so worried about Hodge. I think Detective Reese thinks he had something to do with Brother's death."

Then, before Darla could respond to that, the old woman added in a voice so quiet she could barely hear it, "And, Darla, I'm afraid he did, too."

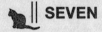 **SEVEN**

DARLA STARED AT MARY ANN IN SHOCK.

"What do you mean, you think Hodge had something to do with Mr. Plinski's death? Are you trying to say your brother didn't die of natural causes?"

Swiftly she summoned a mental picture of the old man as she'd last seen him lying lifeless in his chair. There had been no sign of violence—no blood on his shirt, nothing wrapped around his neck—which eliminated stabbing or shooting or strangulation. And she'd seen no wound on his scalp, so no one had conked him over the head. What could Mary Ann mean?

"Of course, Hodge would never have hurt Brother on purpose," the old woman replied, vigorously shaking her gray head. "But I'm afraid I mentioned to Detective Reese that Hodge might have paid Brother a visit the other morning while I was, um, busy elsewhere. Hodge had been threatening to have it out with him over whatever caused problems between them all those years ago. I begged him not to do it. I even warned him that Brother had a bad heart. You remember, only last year he had that trouble . . ."

She tearfully trailed off, and Darla recalled the night she'd seen the elderly man being hauled away from the Plinskis' brownstone in an ambulance. She had been afraid at that point that Mary Ann's brother had breathed his last, but he'd rallied and come home the following day. But it was obvious that Mr. Plinski's health had been precarious. Could an argument with an old enemy the day before have been the final stressor that caused his heart to fail? Was that what Mary Ann feared?

She gave her friend an encouraging pat on her hand.

"Even if your brother was still upset over an argument, you really can't blame Hodge for that. I'm sure you're worrying for nothing."

"I hope so, my dear. But I don't know what I'm going to do about any of this. My entire life is topsy-turvy now."

She lapsed into silence and concentrated on her tea. Darla simply sat quietly across from her until Jake reappeared a short while later. The PI was carrying a canvas tote bag that obviously had come from Mary Ann's closet, for it proclaimed *Yes, I Was a Hippie* in Day-Glo mod lettering. Darla smiled a little as she pictured a twenty-something version of the tiny gray-haired woman dancing about a meadow wearing bell-bottoms and a lacy top, with flowers woven into her long streaming hair.

Jake's expression was pensive as she handed Mary Ann the tote. All she said, however, was, "I found everything except the green embroidered slippers. I hope that's okay."

The old woman nodded and clutched the canvas bag to her. "I'll be perfectly fine, dear, don't worry. But if you don't mind, I'd like to lie down for a time."

Darla made her quick good-byes; then, while Jake escorted Mary Ann to her tiny spare bedroom, she hurried outside again to make the swift run up her private stoop. She paused there, however, to spare a quick look toward Mary Ann's brownstone. To her relief, the funeral home van had left . . . presumably, Mr. Plinski with it. Reese's vehicle and a marked patrol car remained, no doubt finishing up any final police business. With luck, they'd soon be gone as well, and then Mary Ann could go about the sad task of mourning her brother.

But as her chilly fingers fumbled with the key, she caught a flash of black from the corner of one eye. She whipped around in time to see a long black tail slip around the stoop of Bygone Days and then vanish.

The Hamlet doppelganger?

Hopefully so, and not Hamlet taking an unauthorized leave from the brownstone! Still, Darla couldn't help but worry a bit about the big cat's safety until she'd entered the bookstore from her private hall and saw him lounging atop the counter watching James. The latter, in turn, was on the computer intently studying the screen. She didn't have to ask where Robert was, for the smell of roasting coffee filled the air. Apparently, he had decided to channel his emotions into practical activity.

"I'm back," she said unnecessarily. "And we have a small change of plans for tonight."

Giving Hamlet's sleek black fur a ruffle, she told James of the new supper venue and the fact that Mary Ann would be spending the night with Jake. When she finished, the manager nodded his understanding.

"I will let Robert know. I think it best that she does have company, at least for this one night. If you think about it, she has lost someone who has been close to her for more than seven decades. One does not adjust to a bereavement like that overnight."

"No," Darla agreed, "one does not."

With that grim pronouncement, she reached beneath the counter for her purse. "Hammy, you want to come upstairs and help me cook?" she asked the cat. "I'll even let you do a little taste-testing, if you want."

Hamlet blinked, yawned, and slowly stood, seeming to understand that the usual routine had been disrupted. But he and Darla had barely reached the side door when she heard her manager make a sound of surprise.

Turning, Darla asked in concern, "What's wrong, James?"

"I have been working on that software malfunction I told you about yesterday. I thought I had it repaired, but it seems not. The pricing for the 1871 box set of *The Marble Faun* has made another unexpected jump. It is now over eight hundred dollars."

"Wow. Talk about inflation."

"But that is not all." James frowned at the computer screen. "Someone who is apparently local to us has since selected the Buy It Now option and requested an in-person pickup. We have sold the set."

"Wow," Darla repeated. "Quick, send him the invoice before he tries to unbuy it."

James slanted her a look reminiscent of Hamlet at his sternest. "Really, Darla, would you wish me to take knowing advantage of a customer? *Honor virtutis praemium.*"

Which Darla knew—but only because her manager had quoted it to Robert a time or two—meant, *Esteem is the reward of virtue.* Shrugging, she said, "I suppose not. But what about *caveat emptor*? Besides, no offense, but maybe they know something about this particular edition that you don't. Maybe that's a really good price for the set."

James allowed himself the slightest hint of a superior smile.

"I think not. The price that our fine computer software suggests for this set would be in line for an 1860 first edition, first printing. A later printing of that same first edition would be worth somewhere in the range of two to three hundred dollars. What we are offering is a late-nineteenth-century reprint. It is still a two-volume set, as is the original, but it sells for considerably less than the later first-edition printings."

Ever the pragmatist when it came to dollars and cents, Darla nodded.

"I understand, but business is business. Your listing is filled with pictures, and you've stated very clearly what is for sale. Send them the invoice, and give them a chance to take a good look at the set when they come to pick it up. If they realize they're overpaying, you can refund their money . . . no harm, no foul. If they still want to pay that much after they've done their due diligence, then wrap that puppy up and send them on their way."

"Very well. But, for the record, I still must protest this tactic."

"Protest noted," she said with a wry smile. "But protesting doesn't pay the utility bills."

Leaving James to send his correspondence to the customer, Darla headed up to her apartment. For once—apparently also realizing that the mood was somber—Hamlet did not play his usual game of "Try to Trip the Human" as they took the stairs. Instead, he padded sedately at her side. Once inside, however, rather than taking his usual perch along the back of the horsehair couch, or dangling off the cushion of one of the ladder-back chairs, he made a beeline for the front window.

While Darla went about preparing her casserole and a couple of side dishes for that evening, she periodically glanced into the living room to see Hamlet still entranced with the view outside. Was he looking for the other black cat, she wondered . . . or was he keeping tabs on possible sidewalk skulkers? Or, worse, was he on feline alert lest the funeral home van return for someone else?

Unsettling as the sight of him was with his nose pressed to the glass, at least guard duty was keeping him out from underfoot, she decided as she went about her tasks. Needing the distraction, she turned her television to a home improvement show marathon. The background sounds of thrilled homeowners walking into their made-over rooms lightened the atmosphere a bit. She only sniffled a time or two as she sliced and diced, and those times she pretended the onions were to blame.

By a few minutes until five, when she took one final look as she was wrapping up the food to go, she saw that Hamlet had abandoned his post. He'd moved instead to her desk and was sprawled at full length across her open laptop keyboard.

"Hammy, get down, you're going to ruin my computer!" she said, scolding him.

When he merely stretched—showing four paws' worth of exposed claws in the process—and then settled comfortably again atop the keys, she rushed over to shoo him off. "Really, Hamlet, the repair guy is going to laugh me out of the store if I bring this computer back to him again stuffed with cat fur. Now, scoot!"

Hamlet scooted, but at his own pace. Once he'd abandoned his makeshift bed, Darla blew the loose sprinkling of fur off the keys and then hit "Enter" to take the laptop out of sleep mode. Fortunately, the computer seemed no worse for having served as a feline futon. And she could only shake her head as she saw that the cat had somehow managed to pull up an Arthurian website while he was snoozing.

"Dreaming about being king?" She smiled as she closed the website window that featured a series of paintings by N. C. Wyeth that had illustrated a classic version of the Round Table legend. "How about you be king of the food bowl and go eat your supper?"

He turned a cool green squint on her, obviously not appreciating the humor . . . but equally obviously not ready to pass up a meal. Turning the television to his favorite nature channel to keep him company, Darla left Hamlet munching his kibble while she carried her meal down to Jake's apartment.

James and Robert were already there, along with Roma, when Darla walked in. The gray-and-white Italian Greyhound curled sweetly in Mary Ann's lap, her delicately pointed muzzle tucked beneath the old woman's arm as she petted the little pup. Robert had pulled a footstool up beside her chair and was softly talking to Mary Ann. Jake and James were quietly chatting, as well. Both jumped up to help Darla with the food.

"Smells great, kid," Jake told her as she took the casserole. "Let's put this in the oven to stay warm, and I'll pour you some wine."

"How's Mary Ann doing?" Darla murmured as the trio headed into the kitchen.

"She is bearing up well," James said. "We have learned that apparently Bernard's final instructions specify he is to be cremated, so there will be only a small memorial service whenever Mary Ann is ready. In the meantime, we will all do what we can to support her while she decides whether to keep Bygone Days operating."

"She's thinking about closing the antiques store?"

Though, of course, that made sense, Darla told herself. Mary Ann was already well past traditional retirement age, and now she no longer had her brother and business partner to support her. She'd have to hire someone to help her run the store, an expense she likely couldn't afford. But if she liquidated the business, maybe even rented out the space to someone else, Mary Ann could see a nice income stream to keep her comfortable in her retirement.

"Whatever she does," Darla said aloud, "I just hope she doesn't rush into it. You know what they say about making life-changing decisions when you're under stress."

Then, remembering Mary Ann's earlier concerns about Hodge, she added to Jake, "Have you heard from Reese yet? He was acting kind of mysterious the whole time he was talking to me. I kept getting the feeling he thinks there's something strange about Mr. Plinski's death."

"You know the protocol, kid," the PI replied, expression bland. "The ME has to confirm the cause of death, and Reese isn't going to talk about his findings until that ruling is made."

"Well, I was there, and it looked pretty darned obvious to me what happened."

She accepted the glass of Chardonnay from Jake and trooped with her and James back into the main living area. For the next hour or so, they let Mary Ann reminisce about her brother, finally breaking to replenish the tissue supply and partake of Darla's casserole, which everyone agreed was excellent.

"I've made this same chicken tortilla dish for years," she said with a dismissive wave as everyone—even Mary Ann— had seconds. Secretly, however, she was pleased that the southwestern-style meal had gone over so well. "It was my go-to recipe every time my ex and I had friends over for supper. Though usually we served Mexican beer, and I'd make stuffed jalapeños as an appetizer to go with it. But Jake's antipasti went just fine, instead."

"And I heard no complaints about the white wine," Jake said with a grin as she topped off everyone's glass with more Chardonnay . . . except for Robert, who was drinking flavored water. "And once everyone is finished, I just might have some chocolate ripple ice cream in the freezer if anyone wants some."

They continued at the table in companionable conversation for a while longer, with Robert excusing himself to take Roma for a brief walk. The pair returned a few minutes later, and as the youth stripped off his heavy wool coat, he gave a hearty sneeze.

"Bless you," Darla exclaimed, adding, "Don't tell me you ran into the mystery cat out there, and you're allergic to it, just like Connie."

Robert shook his head even as he achooed again. "Nobe," he declared, his voice stuffy. "No sign ob it. I just wogged past some dude out dere who was smokig, ad it made be sneeze. I'm fine."

And as he predicted, a few moments later he was back to his usual voice.

Further discussion on the mystery cat went unsaid, however, as Jake brought out the promised ice cream and began serving it.

"While it does seem counterintuitive to eat ice cream in the winter," James observed as the PI offered him a scoop, "Russian folklore holds that eating or drinking something cold will actually warm you more than consuming hot food or drink. And scientific studies have backed up that claim. Eating or drinking something very cold causes your blood vessels to tighten which, in turn, makes you feel warmer."

"Good to know," Darla said with a smile. "Now I have a good excuse for stocking up on all the seasonal ice cream flavors like pumpkin pie and peppermint stick."

She was halfway through her bowl when her phone chimed to indicate an incoming message. She pulled the cell from her pocket and sneaked a glance at her screen, then felt her stomach clench. The sender was Reese, and the message was a terse Can you show me those surveillance recordings tonight?

She glanced about the table. Everyone else was still involved with their ice cream and chatting about other folklore that had scientific basis, so she quickly returned the detective's text.

At Jake's now. When?
Can you meet me in 10?
OK. Knock at the front door and I'll let you in.

Shoving the phone back into her pocket, she stood and said, "Sorry, y'all, but I have to duck out. I just got a text from Reese. He has a couple more questions, so I'm meeting him at the store. Jake, I'll pick up my dishes in the morning."

"Anything that we should be concerned with?" James asked, while the rest—even little Roma—fixed her with equally questioning stares.

Darla shook her head even as she deliberately didn't look at Mary Ann.

"He didn't say exactly what he was looking for," she told them, which was technically true. She was simply guessing what he had in mind, and she'd been wrong about that before. "I'm sure he's just wanting to clear up a few things for his report."

"What about Brother?" Mary Ann asked in a quavering voice. "Does Detective Reese know . . . ?"

She trailed off, but Darla knew she was asking, *Does he know the cause of death? Does he know when his body will be released?*

Before she could answer, Jake interjected in a soothing voice, "Reese won't be able to tell anybody anything at this point, but try not to worry. I'm sure everything will be resolved tomorrow, and you'd be the first to hear. These things just take a while sometimes."

"I'm sure it's nothing," Darla added. "I'll stop back by here in the morning and give you any news."

Reminding Robert and James that they'd be conducting business as usual tomorrow, she gave Mary Ann a quick hug good-bye and hurried back to her place. She'd be wearing a rut in the sidewalk pretty soon, with all this back and forth, she thought with an ironic shake of her head. But at least she didn't have far to go. It was a little after seven, and the sun had set, so the only illumination came from the nearby street-lights and passing traffic. But the light was sufficient for her to make her way easily along the walk.

Reflexively, she glanced about for the mystery cat. If it was there, it had blended into the shadows. A couple walked past her, murmuring softly and intent only on each other, followed by a bundled-up jogger. No smokers went by, how-ever, and the faint breeze moving between the buildings on either side of the street had long since dissipated the sec-ondhand smoke that had caused Robert's sneezing fit.

She entered the brownstone through her private door and went into the store through the side entrance, punching her alarm code into the keypad there. As per her usual routine, only the light over the register remained on. Since the computer was right there, she didn't bother turning on any other lights. Instead, she booted up the computer, pulling up the security camera program.

Her original installer, Ted—he of the imaginary finger pistols and bluffly friendly manner—had come back by a few months earlier with the opening of the coffee bar to make a few tweaks to the security system. In addition to an upgrade to color video, she now had a full view of the upstairs lounge as well as a larger portion of the bookstore's two downstairs rooms. A rear exterior camera covered her courtyard and the narrow alleyway beyond, while the front exterior camera gave a view of her stoop and a portion of the sidewalk to either side.

And because she'd also sprung for infrared cameras, the system's night vision was almost as clear as daytime, meaning she clearly saw Reese pulling up in his unmarked car a moment later. She had the front door open before he'd even made it up the front steps.

EIGHT

"IT'S COLD AS THE KNICKS OUT THERE," THE DETECTIVE greeted her, referring to the New York City basketball team that had been on a losing streak of late.

Darla smiled a little as she shut the door behind him. "Back in Texas, we say it's cold as a witch's tit in a brass brassiere."

"Nah, it's not that cold yet. Wait until December." Then, settling into official cop mode, Reese asked, "Where's the camera setup?"

"Over at the register."

She walked him to the counter and pulled up a second stool so they could sit side by side at the computer. "I'll pull up the screen so we can see it live, first," she said, pressing a key.

The main screen divided itself into six miniature screens: two exterior and four interior. "It'll record up to four weeks' worth of video before it starts overwriting the old files," she continued, "so I just let it run. Everything is location- and time-stamped."

She pointed to the narrow banner at the top of each screen. The time, broken down to seconds, was displayed in digital numerals. Alongside the time was the date and one of six camera locations: front door, courtyard, coffee bar, register, front room, back room.

"This way you don't have to search through hours of nothing if you want to see what happens overnight. You can narrow the recording down to a particular camera and time fence," she finished, slipping into her old business-speak with that last.

He nodded. "Mary Ann said she left her place at nine this morning. Let's take a look at what your front door camera caught starting at that point in time until eleven, when you and Connie showed up at Bygone Days."

"And we're looking for . . . ?"

She trailed off, wondering if he would actually admit that he had his suspicions about Hodge. He hesitated a moment and then replied, "For Mary Ann's sake, I'd like to eliminate Rodger Camden as any sort of suspect. No, I'm not saying he or anyone else killed Mr. Plinski." He hurriedly clarified as Darla stared at him, wide-eyed. "Like I told you before, I'm covering all the bases. That's kind of what we cops do."

He shook his head, and she could almost hear his patronizing thought . . . *Civilians.*

Ignoring that, Darla asked, "But what makes you think he was there today? Mary Ann told me he might have stopped by her place yesterday while she was gone, but she didn't say anything about this morning."

"Call it a hunch," he told her. "So help me out here. You're still sure you'd recognize this Hodge person if you saw him? Mary Ann texted me a pic she'd taken with him on her cell phone, but she only caught half his face, so I'm kind of at a disadvantage here."

He pulled out his own cell and swiftly scrolled through his pictures. "That him?"

The picture Mary Ann had taken was typical of someone new to the selfie game, with the distinctive "fishbowl" look that exaggerated their noses and added several chins. Hodge had indeed been caught halfway out of the screen, but his snowy hair and Ronald Reagan–like rosy cheeks were unmistakable.

"Yep, it's him," she confirmed. "We only met once, but he's a distinctive-looking guy. I'm pretty sure I'd know him anywhere else."

So saying, she began typing in the parameters for the video review. But as Reese leaned in nearer to watch, she found herself uncomfortably aware of just how closely they were sitting to each other. Back in the antiques store, with a man's dead body not far away and several emergency personnel within speaking distance, she'd barely taken notice as they'd sat knee to knee. But alone with him now, here in the half-lit bookstore, she felt oddly like a teenager on her first date.

She scooted her stool away just a little, pretending she was trying for a better view of the screen. Maybe it was the hush around them that added a certain sense of intimacy. Or maybe it was how the scent of his leather coat was mixing with the faint spicy smell of his aftershave to form a cliché masculine perfume that—just like in romance novels—was strangely compelling.

Reese, on the other hand, seemed totally oblivious to any such nuances.

"You think you can hurry this along, Darla? I told Connie I'd pick her up for dinner to make up for this morning."

"Right," she replied, her momentary lapse into fancy bursting, as James would say, like the proverbial soap bubble.

Now the computer screen was back to a single image, with the time stamp across the top indicating nine that morning. Forgetting anything but the color images on the monitor, she leaned closer to watch the action.

Her street was still surprisingly busy at that hour . . . though, of course, since she was usually in her apartment or downstairs in the store by then, she never really paid close attention to the morning traffic patterns. Pedestrians and vehicles were moving at a regular enough clip. Had she set the software to motion-activated recording, the video still would have replayed at a relatively constant pace.

But, as she'd previously pointed out, the view from the front camera extended to only ten or so feet to either side of her stoop. If Reese indeed suspected Hodge of having been in Bygone Days at the time of Mr. Plinski's death, the man would have had to come from the direction of Darla's shop to be caught on her video.

"Can you fast-forward it a little?" Reese wanted to know.

Darla nodded and adjusted the settings. Now the video played at the pace of an old-time silent movie. Twice, the detective had her stop and replay so they could study a particular passerby. Both times, a closer look confirmed that the figure in question wasn't Hodge.

Darla glanced at the time stamp. They'd reached ten o'clock with no sign of him, until Reese abruptly said, "Wait."

Darla stopped the video as Reese pointed to a tall, bundled-up figure whose pale hair was visible above his turned-up collar. "Can you zoom in?"

Darla nodded, feeling her stomach suddenly clench as she focused the scene in closer. Now the man's face was a bit pixilated even though it was more distinct. A broad nose that looked like it had been broken a time or two was clearly visible, as were the rosy cheeks made brighter by the cold.

Reese, meanwhile, had pulled up the photo on his phone again. He glanced from one screen to the other and then nodded.

"That's him," he said, jaw hard. "That's Rodger Camden."

DARLA SAT ON HER HORSEHAIR SOFA, WRAPPED IN ONE OF GREAT-AUNT Dee's old afghans and watching Hamlet bat a tailless catnip mouse across the rug. Reese had left the bookstore an hour ago, but not before he'd received a cell phone call that left him looking even grimmer than before. All he'd said about it, however, was, *Connie's gonna be pretty ticked off when I cancel dinner on her.*

They'd debated a few minutes on the best way for her to get him a file of the twelve hours of the security recording prior to eleven on the day in question. Once they agreed she could save it on a thumb drive that he could pick up in the morning, he headed out into the night. She hadn't asked if he was going to talk to Hodge or Mary Ann, and he hadn't volunteered the information. Though, of course, he would have that conversation . . . but surely only to clear Hodge of any responsibility in Mr. Plinski's death, she tried to reassure herself.

Why, then, did she feel like she'd somehow betrayed Mary Ann by sharing the recordings?

"If I hadn't volunteered to let Reese watch the video, he still could have slapped me with a warrant, and he'd have ended up seeing it, anyhow," she told Hamlet, unable to keep the defensiveness from her voice. "And even without the video, you know he was going to talk to Hodge. I knew it when Reese asked about him this afternoon."

Hamlet blinked, then returned to his cat game, obviously not willing to weigh in on the matter. Not getting any help from that quarter, Darla debated calling down to Jake's place. She could tell her friend what had transpired, and then leave it to the PI to forewarn Mary Ann about the situation. But Jake would likely revert to cop mode and not tell the old woman anything, so no need to put either of her friends on the spot.

With a small groan of dismay, she tossed aside the afghan and stood. It was almost nine, still too early to call it a night, yet her thoughts were far too troubled to take up any pre-bedtime project. Even reading a book or turning on the television seemed more effort than she could manage.

Deliberately, she pushed herself past that mental stagnation and launched into a few warm-up exercises she'd learned from her previous martial arts classes. Maybe shaking up her body a bit would help settle down her mind.

"Ugh, stiff," she muttered as she went through the routine. Obviously, she was out of practice. Time to head back to the dojo with Robert again.

But as she finished a final series of crunches and got to her feet, she noticed that Hamlet had abandoned his cat game. Instead, he again was stretched at full length against the front window, peering out to the street beyond. Curious, she hurried over and joined him.

The street traffic below was relatively busy; indeed, given that it was a Friday night, things would be lively until well after midnight despite the cold weather. And though they were three levels up, she knew that with the room lit she and Hamlet could still be seen from the sidewalk. Not a good strategy if she wanted to spy, she wryly told herself. With that, she reached over and flipped off the lamp, so that the room was equally dim as the half-lit street.

"Who're you looking at, Hammy?" she softly asked him. "Is the mystery kitty running around again?"

Hamlet gave a little *meow-rumph* that could have meant anything, the tip of his long black tail gently whipping back and forth as he concentrated on whatever it was that he watched. Darla squinted down into the night with him for a while longer, until it occurred to her that she had something almost as good as cat vision to call upon.

"Let's see what the camera sees," she told him as she went over to her laptop and booted it up. A few moments later, she had her security software showing live video of the stoop and surrounding area. As before, the black-and-white views courtesy of the night vision camera were crisp enough that she could have been watching a movie.

"No cats here," she said after a few minutes of studying the street view. And no skulkers, either. Everyone who had passed seemed intent on his or her destination. Not like last night.

"Wait. I wonder . . ."

With those murmured words, she switched the software over to the playback mode. If she and Reese had been able to catch Hodge walking past her store that morning, maybe she could spy last night's smoking skulker and finally satisfy herself that he—or she—was simply an innocuous passerby.

Repeating the earlier drill she'd done with Reese, Darla pulled up the previous night's video. She started the recording fifteen or so minutes prior to her best guess as to when she and Hamlet had noticed that unknown person loitering about.

For the first several minutes, the videoed sidewalk remained empty. Darla frowned, tempted to fast-forward through but not wanting to miss any glimpse of the figure. If her memory was accurate, the skulker had stood almost directly in front of the Plinskis' brownstone, meaning he—or she—would only just be visible on Darla's security camera.

Hamlet, meanwhile, had noticed her focusing on the computer. Abandoning his window post, he came over to help her conduct the review, lightly leaping up onto the desk and peering rather nearsightedly at the laptop screen.

"Let me know if you see anything," she told him with a wry smile. But barely had she finished the words when the cat abruptly swiped an oversized black paw at the corner of the video image.

"Wait." She echoed Reese's earlier command as she hit the "Pause" button. Sure enough, someone had moved into view from the direction of Mary Ann's place. A look at the time stamp confirmed that this had to be their so-called skulker.

"Good catch," she said, praising the feline. With her nose almost as close to the screen now as Hamlet's, Darla hit the "Play" button again.

This time, she let the video run in slow motion. The figure stood leaning quite casually against one of those fancy, waist-high metal trash containers installed curbside. She was almost certain the figure was male, though dressed as he was in a heavy winter coat, it was hard to be one hundred percent certain. What was even more maddening was the fact that he was just on the edge of camera range so that—rather like Mary Ann's selfie—only half his face and body were visible.

Darla zoomed in as the video played on. Because of the cold, the figure wore a scarf wrapped around the lower portion of his face, making identification even more difficult. With the camera angle, all she could tell was that he had a nose, though it seemed to be a substantial one. The person could be Hodge . . . but then again, he could be almost anyone else, too. And, once again, she couldn't figure out why someone would linger in the cold like that for no good reason. The person had to be watching for—waiting for—something.

"Move over," she muttered at the image. Maybe when he lit his cigarette, his angle would change enough to accommodate the camera and give her a better look at his face.

The figure remained in place a few minutes longer. She marveled a bit at his fortitude given the weather; though, of course, if he was a native New Yorker, the temperature would have likely seemed no more than a bit brisk to him.

And then, finally, she saw the flare of a lighter. Now, the figure leaned further into the frame as he drew on the cigarette. She saw a distinctive shock of pale hair just before the lighter flicked closed and the figure spun and walked out of camera range.

"Darn it," she muttered, rewinding and replaying that snippet of video a couple of times more. "What do you think, Hamlet? Is it Hodge, or not?"

For, despite the relative clarity of the recording, the angle of the figure combined with the fact that he was mostly out of camera range the entire time made it impossible to confirm his identity. And while the man's size and his white hair were telling, that was hardly enough to point to Hodge as the skulker. And it occurred to her that she had no clue if Hodge was a smoker or not, though she didn't recall him smelling like an ashtray or smelling like he'd bathed in aftershave to cover up the evidence.

Hamlet offered no opinion either way. Instead, he lightly leaped back down again and trotted over to the sofa. There, he sprawled along its back, legs dangling on either side so that he looked like a cat-shaped antimacassar . . . the old-style doily meant to keep gentlemen's hair oil from staining the sofa fabric.

Shaking her head in amused dismay, Darla shut down the computer again and rejoined Hamlet on the couch.

"Why don't we let Reese handle the police stuff on his own?" she told the cat. "He's the professional here, not us. We should be concentrating on how we can help out Mary Ann these next few days." And so she leaned back against the sofa listening to Hamlet's rumbling purr and went through a mental list of things to do.

Notify the local friends and neighbors as James had suggested: *check*.

Bring Mary Ann a few hot meals so she didn't have to cook: *check*.

Get rid of that red brocade chair so Mary Ann didn't have the constant unsettling reminder of her brother's last few minutes on this earth: *double check*.

She'd forgotten to ask Reese when Mary Ann could have her place back, but hopefully she might return in the morning if she was ready to do so. And if Mary Ann wanted to open up the shop again, Darla could send Robert over for a few hours each day to help out the old woman, since he'd worked part time there before.

She was mulling over a few possible thoughts for the memorial service when her cell phone abruptly rang. The unexpected sound made her jump and sent a startled Hamlet leaping off the sofa and darting back toward the bedroom.

Darla hurriedly reached for the phone, noting as she did so the caller ID. *Jake*, she saw in dismay. Why would the PI be calling, unless something had happened to Mary Ann?

She hit the "Talk" button and, not even bothering with a hello, breathlessly asked, "What's wrong? Is Mary Ann okay?"

"She's sleeping now," Jake replied, her tone sounding grim. "The glass of wine she had, combined with all the stress, pretty well knocked her out. With luck, she'll sleep until morning. I'll wait and tell her then."

"Tell her what?"

"Reese called me a few minutes ago. Apparently, they've got a cause of death for Mr. Plinski."

"Heart attack, right?"

She heard the PI's sigh through the phone and braced herself for the news. But what her friend said next nearly caused her to drop her cell phone.

"The cause of death was reflex cardiac arrest as a direct result of suffocation," Jake corrected. "Specifically, homicidal smothering. Bernard didn't just die, he was murdered. And Reese is bringing in Mary Ann's friend, Hodge, for questioning."

║ NINE

"LET ME BE SURE THAT I UNDERSTAND THIS," JAMES CHOKED
out the next morning as he paused in the midst of stowing
his belongings beneath the front counter. "You are saying
Bernard Plinski was murdered? How?"

"He was smothered with a pillow," Darla told him, still
not quite believing it herself. "Whoever did it used the
embroidered one that was still in his lap when Connie and
I found him."

"And the medical examiner has confirmed this?"

Darla nodded.

"Apparently, Reese was suspicious from the start because
Mr. Plinski's dentures had come loose, and his tongue was
bitten," she explained. "And there was some bruising around
his mouth that couldn't be explained by a stroke or heart
attack. Because of that, Reese managed to convince the
ME's office to move Mr. Plinski's autopsy to the head of the
line. The lab found his blood and saliva on the pillow, so

along with all the other autopsy results, that pretty much clinched the deal."

"Extraordinary!" James mused. "And we were all so certain that Bernard had suffered a heart attack."

"Actually, he did. Being smothered triggered a cardiac event, so technically, he did die of a heart attack. And that's the only saving grace in this whole horrible situation," she added with a shudder. "From what Jake said, that meant his death was probably pretty swift. If it had been the smothering that killed him, it could have taken three or four minutes for it to be over with."

"Horrible, indeed," James agreed, his expression sorrowful. "But what is this about Detective Reese thinking Mr. Camden had anything to do with it?"

"All I know is that he was brought in for questioning last night. It turns out there's video of him from our security camera showing him headed to Mary Ann's shop that morning after she left, but before Connie and I got there. Reese is supposed to pick it up sometime this morning. Here, just in case I'm tied up with a customer, it's in the register," she said and opened its drawer to show James it was stowed in the twenties slot.

Her manager, meanwhile, was frowning. "But being caught on video—the wrong place at the wrong time—is hardly evidence of murder."

"Agreed," Darla said with a sigh. "But what worries me is that there doesn't seem to be anyone else who could have done it. Nothing was taken from the store, so apparently they've ruled out some random robbery as a motive. And Mary Ann swears her brother had no enemies."

"Indeed. Though I suppose that the concept of enemies is a relative one. I daresay we have all left an angry soul or two in our path at some point and not even realized it."

With that lapse into the philosophical realm, James finished putting away his things and then went about his usual pre-opening routine. Shaking her head, Darla did the same.

At least she'd again been spared explaining this new and far more disturbing development to Robert. Since it was Saturday, and the coffee bar usually did brisk business early, he had been waiting on the stoop for her when she'd come down to the bookstore thirty minutes earlier. One look at the youth's distraught face, and she knew he'd already paid a visit to Jake's and heard the news.

"This is, like, too freakin' crazy," he'd angrily muttered as he'd stomped his way into the store and up the steps to the lounge.

Darla had had no argument to refute that sentiment. She'd let him go on his way, knowing he needed some time to process the shocking news and hoping the routine of the workday would help somewhat. She hadn't yet dared call Jake to see how Mary Ann was handling this latest revelation, though she knew that at some point she would have to reach out to her elderly friend.

But what in the world did one say to someone whose only sibling had been murdered?

With the register up and running, and paperwork in place, Darla busied herself with rearranging a few shelves that had been left disarrayed from the day before. In the process, she found propped against the old mantelpiece a copy of Arthur Miller's *The Crucible*, which had somehow migrated out of the classics section.

Or, given the fact that Mr. Plinski's death had been ruled a homicide, had Hamlet been doing a bit of random book snagging again?

She frowned. In the past, the plucky feline had used his book-snagging skills to help snare killers. But even if

Hamlet *was* weighing in on the situation, what did this classic play have to do with a supposed high school rivalry?

She glanced around for the cat, who had kept himself scarce since breakfast that morning. Just like her, he'd not had much sleep the night before . . . she, because of Jake's phone call with the shocking new developments regarding Mr. Plinski's death, and he, because her tossing and turning in bed hadn't allowed him his usual undisturbed spot atop her comforter. Chances were the feline was holed up somewhere taking a little snooze. She finally spied him lounging on the foreign language shelves, eyes tightly closed as he snored gently.

Seeing him sleeping there, she spared the cat an indulgent smile. No doubt finding the book was simply a coincidence. She'd added the wayward volume to her stack of books to reshelve, when she heard James say, "Our auction customer has agreed to stop by today."

"Are you talking about the *Marble Faun* buyer?" Curious, Darla set down her stack of books and headed to the counter, where her manager was going through his email.

James looked up from the screen and nodded. "Yes. He will be here sometime around noon today . . . and, to quote, *with cash in hand.*"

"Great. I can't wait to see how this works out. What's the guy's name, in case I'm up front when he comes in?"

"He did not say. He is using one of those free email accounts, and he apparently calls himself BookBuyer75."

Darla frowned. "Odd. I'm sure it's no biggie, especially since he's a cash buyer. But all the dealers I know always have a full-blown signature file attached to their messages."

"Precisely. I agree, this is a bit unusual. I will do a web search on his nom de guerre to see if I can find any further information on him."

While James played Internet detective—to no avail, he finally admitted—Darla opened the bookstore and ushered in her usual Saturday morning coffee addicts. Things stayed busy enough that she was able to forget for a while the previous day's tragedy. But every so often, Mr. Plinski's slack face flashed through her mind, so that she had to stop and compose herself before she could continue waiting on her customers.

When she had a moment, she ran upstairs to check on Robert. He was doggedly keeping the coffee drinks flowing, but from the grim set to his mouth she could see he was having even more difficulty than she coping with what had happened.

She returned downstairs to find that, while she was talking with Robert, Reese had stopped in for the thumb drive. *Typical*, she grumbled to herself. He probably deliberately timed it that way so he could slip in and out without having to talk to her.

She also took time to check off one item from her mental list, calling some of her and Mary Ann's mutual friends in the neighborhood to tell them the disturbing news. It was still early enough in the day that, while some had heard via the grapevine about Mr. Plinski's death, not everyone had seen the story that morning that confirmed it was murder.

Such nice man, and so terrible thing to happen, Steve Mookjai had sadly told her. *I send my daughter over with food for her.* And then, pragmatically, he had asked, *Will you still want engagement party for Detective Reese and Miss Connie next week?*

Darla assured him that the gathering was still on, that Reese had guaranteed his fiancée that he'd be there for it, no matter what. Then she'd hung up to make a couple more calls.

When the usual lull hit a bit after eleven, she found James and told him, "If you can hold down the fort, I should go see how Mary Ann is doing. Jake shouldn't have to carry the whole burden of watching out for her. It's important that Mary Ann knows she can turn to us, too."

"I agree. Do let Mary Ann know that Robert and I are both at her disposal."

"I'll be back as soon as I can," she told him. She pulled a jacket off the coat rack at the side door, heading into her private hall and then out the front steps. A flash of black fur greeted her as she stepped from stoop to sidewalk.

The mystery cat! Once again, she'd seen little more than its tail but, as best she could judge, the stray appeared smaller and less hefty than Hamlet. A female, perhaps?

"Here, kitty," she called as the sleek black feline disappeared behind the bookstore's stoop, as if headed to Jake's place. "Don't worry, I won't hurt you. It's too cold for a kitty to be running loose."

But, search as she might in the vicinity of the steps, she saw no further sign of the cat. Obviously, it shared more than just its inky coat color with Hamlet. Like him, the stray seemed to have a talent for padding through walls. Reminding herself to put out water and a bit of kibble for the cat later, she pulled her coat more closely about her and hurried down the stairway leading to Jake's place.

Pausing for a quick knock, she opened the door—Jake left her front entrance unlocked during business hours—and hurried inside.

"Hey, kid," Jake said, looking up from her seat at the chrome dinette table. She was wearing a celery-green corduroy shirt over an incongruously cheery knit turtleneck printed with what Darla, squinting, saw were cartoon bears on skis. Quite the change from the PI's usual black and jewel tones.

Pulling off her black-framed reading glasses and tossing them onto a stack of printouts, Jake gestured Darla to the seat across from her. "How are you holding up?"

"I'm fine," she replied. "I'm more concerned about Mary Ann. I thought I'd check in and see how she's doing. Is she resting again?"

"She's back at Bygone Days. Reese released the building again, so she decided she might as well open the store."

"What?" Darla stared at her in disbelief. "That's crazy. Why did you let her go?"

Her friend quirked a brow. "She's a grown woman, and she's of sound mind. What should I have done, tied her to the bed and made her hang out with me all day?"

Yes, was Darla's first reaction, though obviously Jake had a point. If the old woman wanted to open her store, that was her prerogative. Still . . .

"Sorry, I didn't mean to jump on you like that," she replied. "I mean, Mr. Plinski's barely been dead a day. I guess I didn't expect Mary Ann would just pick up and carry on like normal."

"Actually, it's probably the best thing she can do. You know, get back into a routine."

Jake picked up her glasses again and idly chewed on the tip of one earpiece.

"People handle grief differently, kid," she reminded Darla. "You know that. Mary Ann's from a generation that does the whole stiff-upper-lip thing . . . won't ask for help . . . won't admit they hurt. All we can do is keep an eye on her and be there when she needs us. Because, eventually, she will."

Darla nodded. "You're right. She should do what she needs to do. But I think I'll still stop by and see how she is, and let her know I'm bringing by another casserole for her."

She paused and added, "I might have overstepped, but I

did call a few people this morning to let them know what happened so they wouldn't have to read it in the papers or online."

"Did you tell them about the pillow . . . I mean, that it was the murder weapon?" Jake quickly asked, looking suddenly concerned.

Darla thought back and then shook her head. "Not with our friends. I tried to make it as short and sweet as I could. I'm pretty sure all I said was that he died of a heart attack when someone tried to kill him, but I don't think I said the actual word 'pillow.' But James and Robert both know. Why?"

"That's probably one of those things Reese will be holding back from whatever account of the murder goes to the media. You know, to weed out the crazies that always like to wander into the station and confess to the latest crime. So all of you need to keep that on the QT for now."

"I'll warn both of them as soon as I get back," she promised. "Anyhow, Steve Mookjai said he's going to send by some food later, and Hal and Hank Tomlinson want her to know they're available for any lifting or moving."

"Right, the guys from the dojo," Jake said. "It's good you called them. That's the kind of help she'll need, not someone wrapping her in cotton batting and sticking her on a shelf somewhere."

Darla hesitated again, and then asked. "What about Hodge? Did anything happen after he went in for questioning?"

Did anyone arrest him? was the question she wanted to ask, but she couldn't quite bring herself to do so.

Jake shrugged. "As far as I know, talking was all that happened, so I assume he's back home again. That is, unless Reese really does think there's a case against him."

"Poor Hodge," Darla found herself declaring. At Jake's

quizzical look, she explained, "I know I only met him once, but I just can't believe he could murder someone. If he had any true feelings for Mary Ann, he couldn't hurt her brother."

"I'm inclined to agree, kid. Problem is, we've got motive and opportunity with Hodge, and no other suspects lined up. And don't forget, there was plenty of time between when Hodge was caught on your security camera heading to the shop and when you and Connie arrived there for him to have done the deed and taken off again."

"I know, but even with that whole bad blood thing with Mr. Plinski, I'm not convinced he's guilty. And I have a feeling Mary Ann isn't, either." Pushing back her chair, she stood. "I'll head over to her place now, and then I need to get back to the store. We have a cash buyer for a collectible book, and it sounds like the deal is going to be interesting."

She halted with hand on the knob, however, and shot her friend an amused look. "Okay, I have to ask before I go. What's with the bear shirt? It's not your usual thing."

Jake smiled. "Let's just say it's my little tribute to Bernard."

Darla puzzled over that one a few moments as she trotted back up to street level and turned down the sidewalk toward Bygone Days. But by the time she reached the antiques shop, she recalled that "bern" was derived from the Germanic word for "bear." She smiled a little at that. Mr. Plinski probably would have appreciated the sentiment.

As Jake had predicted, the sign on Bygone Days' door was turned to "Open." Steeling herself, Darla turned the knob and went inside. The usual faint jingle of bells accompanied her entrance. She glanced around her, aware that nothing had changed in the shop, itself. Yet somehow it felt emptier than it had a day ago.

Toward the back of the store, however, she could hear

faint conversation . . . Mary Ann's soft quaver, and a male voice that sounded familiar.

"Mary Ann," she called as she pulled off her jacket. "It's Darla."

Not waiting for a reply, she headed down the side aisle in the direction of the register. As she rounded the endcap, she saw the old woman perched behind the counter on a low-backed bar stool upholstered in fifties orange-sherbet vinyl. Her brother's red brocade chair was gone, Darla realized in relief.

But Mary Ann wasn't alone. Doug Bates, owner of Doug's DOUGhnuts—the local independent doughnut shop—was leaning against the counter chatting with her. At Darla's approach, he straightened and gave her a friendly smile.

Nearing fifty, and packing almost that many extra pounds, Doug favored multiple gold chains and a tan that would put a Hollywood starlet to shame. His genial, blond good looks always brought to Darla's mind an image of how Reese might look in another decade or so, if he gave up the gym for a daily dose of doughnuts. For once, the man wasn't wearing his baker's white drawstring pants and double-breasted chef's jacket. Instead—no doubt as a concession to the chilly weather—he wore jeans and a thick sweatshirt with his shop logo on the front. His usual black-and-white checkered newsboy cap was on his head, however.

"Good to see you, neighbor," he said in greeting as she drew closer. Gesturing to a large pastry box that also bore his logo, he continued, "I brought over some doughnuts if you want to sample one. Of course, I brought my famous apple fritters just for Mary Ann. She and Bernard always liked them best."

"They are wonderful," the old woman agreed with a

tremulous smile. "Brother would have had one for breakfast every day if I'd let him."

She broke off momentarily for a quick snuffle into her handkerchief, and Darla and Doug exchanged looks over her bent gray head. Doug had suffered a tragic loss of his own over the July Fourth holiday, so he could readily sympathize with what the old woman was going through. He gave Darla a little head shake that she translated to mean *Don't push it*, and she nodded back her agreement. But it would be difficult not to hover over her for a time.

"I'm sorry to be so weepy," Mary Ann quavered once she'd wiped her eyes again. "It's just hard knowing after all these years I'll never see Brother again."

"There's nothing to apologize for. Everyone understands," Darla assured her. "But are you certain you're up to putting in a full day at work?"

"She needs to keep her mind occupied," Doug answered for her. "Right, Mary Ann?"

The latter nodded. "If I don't stay busy, I'll dwell on all this unpleasantness. The nice gentleman from the funeral home will be phoning later this afternoon, so I'll need to be prepared for that."

"If you need any of us to be on those calls with you or go with you somewhere, we'll do it," Doug assured her.

The old woman gave his stubby hand a fond pat. "I'm so fortunate to have good friends like you and Darla and the rest," she told him. "I know that—oh, a customer." She broke off as the shop door's bells jangled. Popping up from the bar stool, she straightened the wrinkles from her blue corduroy shirtdress and headed toward the front.

"Tough break," Doug said with a shake of his head once she was out of earshot. Moving around the counter, he took the stool Mary Ann had just vacated. "Someone his age, you expect old age to get him. But cold-blooded murder . . . that's awful hard to wrap your head around."

Now it was his turn to grow momentarily teary as he obviously applied that same scenario to himself. Darla gave him a sympathetic nod as she recalled the brash and colorful dance instructor who had been a neighborhood fixture, as well as Doug's girlfriend. Her loss had been shocking, to say the least. "I understand. We all still miss Penelope, too."

After giving him a moment to compose himself, she checked to make sure Mary Ann still was dealing with her customer. Then, needing someone to use as a sounding board, she lowered her voice.

"I don't know if you heard, but Mary Ann's gentleman friend, Hodge, was taken in for questioning about the murder. I can understand wanting to cover all the bases, but I think Reese ran off the rails with this one. No way is Hodge a murderer."

Doug cocked his head, his expression quizzical. "I don't know the guy, so I can't say. But you know how it is on those TV shows. It's always the nice guy, the one you least expect, who done it."

"Seriously, Doug? You know this is real life, don't you?"

"Hey, I'm just playing, whaddaya call it, devil's advocate," he shot back. "Who else woulda had a good reason for killing the old guy? Nobody stole nothing, so it wasn't some druggie or street thug. And I'm pretty sure he wasn't having an affair with a married woman whose crazy husband found out about it. Whaddaya know about that Hodge character, anyhow?"

"I only met him once," she admitted, "but he seemed like a decent sort. And the way Mary Ann talks about him, she's pretty happy getting her old high school boyfriend back. I'm sure she doesn't believe he killed Mr. Plinski, either. What reason could he have for doing it?"

The baker circled his thumb over his forefinger and middle finger in the universal gesture indicating cash. "Money's always a good motive."

Now it was Darla's turn to give *him* a quizzical look. "They're doing okay, I think, but it's not like the Plinskis have a big stash of gold hidden in the storeroom."

"Yeah, but they're sitting on a small fortune with this building."

Darla considered that and then nodded. Her own property was worth a pretty good chunk of change, so long as she could afford the taxes every year. "I suppose so," she conceded, "but you can't exactly steal a building."

"Sure you can. With her brother out of the way, it would all be Mary Ann's. And it'd be pretty easy for some smart guy to convince her she needed another man to take care of her. Stand up in front of a judge, and five minutes later half that building would be his. And if anything happened to her, well . . ."

He trailed off with a meaningful look, and Darla stared at him in alarm.

"That's pretty cold-blooded," she softly exclaimed, careful to keep her voice low lest Mary Ann overhear. "You don't really think that could be true, do you?"

"You never know, maybe he's done this kinda thing before. You know, like a merry widower. Google the guy, and you might find he's got a whole line of late wives."

Darla frowned. Hadn't Mary Ann mentioned that Hodge's wife had recently died? Of course, at his age, it wouldn't be odd to lose a spouse. Unless, as Doug had implied, said late spouse was the latest in a series of deceased wives.

And then, unbidden, a mental image flashed in her mind of the book she'd found lying on the bookshop floor a few days before: *The Fool's Guide to Wills and Estates.* Could Hamlet have come to the same conclusion about Hodge's possible intent?

Even as she strove to dismiss that incident as pure coincidence—was Hamlet now a mind reader as well as a super kitty sleuth?—she heard Mary Ann's excited voice as she came walking down the side aisle. Darla suppressed a smile as she saw the old woman carrying a vintage turkey-shaped tureen the size of a farmers' market pumpkin. She was followed by two giggling young women wearing very short down jackets over very tight ski pants.

"Darla, these young ladies are going to make their very first Thanksgiving dinner for all their friends," she said with an approving smile. "They're going to put dried flowers in this old tureen for their centerpiece. Won't it be cute?"

"I'm sure it will be," Darla agreed, giving the girls a warm nod. She hadn't made her own first Thanksgiving dinner until after she was married, and it had been only a marginal success. A nice turkey flower arrangement probably would have made the food seem tastier.

Doug took advantage of the distraction to come around the counter and give Mary Ann a quick peck on the cheek. "Gotta go. Doughnuts to fry and glaze. I'll check in on you tomorrow."

Grabbing the heavy wool jacket he'd parked atop a midcentury stereo cabinet, he gave Darla a wave and started toward the front of the store. Darla watched him go, debating whether she should follow after him to hash out his Hodge theory. But she'd come to the store to check on Mary Ann.

She waited while her elderly friend rang up the girls' purchase, which was surprisingly more affordable than she'd supposed. Wondering if she should ask Mary Ann if she had another turkey tureen tucked away somewhere, Darla watched her carefully wrap the purchase in white paper. As the girls left with free doughnuts in hand and promises to return for more tableware for their next dinner party, Mary Ann gave Darla a satisfied look.

"It's so good to see young people enjoying the nicer things," she declared. "And there is nothing better than sharing happy times with friends."

"Agreed," Darla said, returning her smile. Then, sobering, she went on, "I was surprised when I stopped by Jake's to find out you'd already reopened the store. But I guess Doug's right that it's better to keep occupied. I just want to be sure you know that you can ask for anything, and one of us will be glad to help."

"I know that, my dear. Actually, Douglas was kind enough to move Brother's chair to the storeroom and bring this one out," she said, giving the vintage bar stool a pat. "I couldn't bear to have him put it out on the street corner, but I couldn't imagine seeing it sitting there empty every day. Maybe down the road I'll reupholster it in some cheery fabric and bring it out again."

"Good idea," Darla agreed. Then, changing the subject, she said, "About Hodge being taken in for questioning—"

"He didn't do it!" Mary Ann exclaimed, her wrinkled lips flattening into angry lines. "Hodge doesn't have a violent bone in his body. If anything, Brother would have attacked him. He's wanted revenge all these years."

"Revenge?" Darla stared at her in surprise. "For what?"

"I didn't know about it until the night before Brother died, when he finally told me the whole story about what happened when we were in high school."

The old woman hesitated, as if screwing up her courage,

and then plunged on, "When I was fifteen years old, my parents went to prison, and it was Hodge who sent them there."

"Your parents went to prison?" Darla stared at the old woman in disbelief. "And what do you mean, Hodge sent them? He wouldn't have been old enough then to be a police officer."

Mary Ann gave her a sad nod.

"No, he wasn't . . . but he was old enough to tell the FBI that my parents were Communists."

|| TEN

"YOUR PARENTS WERE COMMUNISTS?"

After her initial shock, Darla mentally counted back. Since Mary Ann had been a teenager in the early 1950s, that would have been during the time of Senator Joseph McCarthy, which tied in to the Communist theme. Truly, the old woman's explanation was getting stranger by the moment. "But surely Hodge was mistaken about that. Weren't there a lot of false accusations back then?"

"Oh, no, he was quite right. Mom and Pop actually *were* Communists."

Mary Ann gave a wry smile as she settled on her orange bar stool again.

"Don't look so surprised, my dear. Many everyday people were involved in the Party in those days. My parents were labor union members and believed in all sorts of idealistic causes. They passed out leaflets and waved protest signs, but they didn't do any harm. Of course, I had no idea until

I was very much older that they were going to Party meetings when they went out at night. I thought they were going to the corner bar to have a drink with their friends. But Brother knew . . . and, somehow, Hodge found out."

"But why would Hodge care, especially if he was your friend? Like you said, they weren't hurting anyone."

"Darla, you have to understand, it was a different time . . . and I'm not talking about *Father Knows Best*. I'm sure you learned in school about the House Un-American Activities Committee and the so-called Red Scare."

At Darla's nod, the old woman continued, "I can remember watching the trials on television and being terribly frightened, myself. And much of this unpleasantness happened after the Korean War, so some people truly did fear that Communists might show up in their own backyards. That's what happened with Hodge. His father died fighting in Korea, and so Hodge was doing what he thought was his patriotic duty in reporting my parents. Remember, he was only seventeen years old at the time."

"So what about your parents? Did you have any idea why they were in prison?"

Mary Ann shook her head. "I never even knew that was where they'd been. I was at school the day they were arrested. They told Brother to tell me that they had to make an ocean trip back to Poland because they received a telegram that my *babcia*—my grandmother—who still lived there was very ill."

"So you didn't get to say good-bye to them. Didn't you wonder about that?"

"Of course," she replied, voice wavering a bit at the memory. "I found it all very strange and upsetting, but since Brother told me that was what happened, I suppose I accepted it. We even received a telegram from Poland a few weeks later to assure us that that Babcia was on the mend but not well enough for them to leave. Of course, Brother had arranged for a relative in Warsaw to send the telegram."

"So how long were they away?"

"Fortunately, it was only six months before they came home again. By then, the tide was beginning to turn against Mr. McCarthy, so the government reversed many of the convictions, including theirs." She smiled a little. "The first thing I did was ask my mother where my present was from the old country. She told me somebody had stolen the sack while they were disembarking from the ship. As far as I knew, that was that, and life continued on again as it always had. Although my parents did stop going out at night."

"And what happened to Hodge?"

"He quit speaking to me at school the day after my parents left, and I had no idea why. Brother told me he'd probably found another girlfriend and was too cowardly to tell me. But Brother admitted the other night that he'd tracked down Hodge to tell him that I didn't know what actually happened, and that Hodge better keep his mouth shut about it, or else."

Mary Ann paused and sighed. "I guess Hodge figured he'd done enough damage, and so he never even hinted at the truth. By the time my parents came back, Hodge had already graduated and gone off to college somewhere. Of course, I was heartbroken for a while—remember, I was only fifteen—but I got over it. I never saw Hodge again after that until I found his profile online and contacted him."

"So he doesn't know yet that you finally learned what he did."

The old woman shook her head. "No. And I don't think I'll tell him, unless someday he asks me outright about it."

She reached again for her handkerchief and snuffled into

it for a moment. Then, raising her head, she said, "Perhaps I did try coming back to the store too soon. I believe I'll close for the rest of the day and go upstairs to rest. Steve Mookjai's daughter brought by a whole tray of food right before you stopped by, so I don't even have to cook my dinner."

"Do you want me or James to check in on you after work?"

"No, dear, I don't want to be any trouble. Though perhaps Robert can stop by for a few minutes. I'd like to discuss the estate sale with him. I'll need an assistant at the actual event, so I thought perhaps he'd like to earn a little extra pocket money . . . but only if you can spare him from the bookstore, my dear."

"Just tell me the dates, and I'm sure we can work something out," Darla assured her.

Giving the old woman a hug, she retrieved her coat from the stereo cabinet and headed out. A glance at her watch showed that it was already noon. If she was lucky, she'd be back in time to see the mysterious BookBuyer75 come purchase his copy of *The Marble Faun* and, hopefully, at the upper price level.

And, quite fortuitously, when she stepped through her private side door into the store, she saw that a white-gloved James was already in conversation with a man who presumably was that customer. He stood at the counter in profile to her, wearing a puffy green down jacket that made him look almost as broad as he was tall. The black ski cap he wore low on his brow obscured most of his features from the side, save for a prominent nose. Still, for a moment she thought she recognized him from somewhere.

But she didn't have time to dwell on that possibility. From his stiffly hunched body language, she could tell that the transaction wasn't going well . . . as in, a plum sale falling through, she thought in disappointment.

"It's the wrong book," the buyer was saying as he frantically leafed through one of the volumes, voice raised to just below a shout.

He grabbed the second book from the slipcase and gave it an equally frantic examination. "It's wrong," he repeated. "You've got to have another set, right?"

"I beg your pardon," James replied, polite as always, though Darla could hear the undertone of irritation at the man's obvious disregard for the book's age. "This is the set we advertised, and the only one in-house. If you are not going to purchase it, I must request that you cease manhandling it."

By way of response, the man all but slammed the book onto the counter. "That's not it. That's not the one."

"Enough, sir," James declared, pointing toward the front door. "I am asking you to leave the premises immediately."

But the man had already swung about and was stomping away.

"What in the heck?" Darla asked as she hurried to join James at the counter. "Should we go after him?"

"And force him to apologize? Frankly, I think we are well rid of the fellow."

James gave his head a wry shake as he checked the abused book for damage. Apparently satisfied that it had suffered no injury, he resleeved both volumes and then stripped off the thin cotton gloves he wore when handling the collectible stock.

"Fortunately, no harm was done. But that was quite the strange encounter. The man came in and did not wish to discuss the price. The minute I placed the set before him, all he did was paw through the pages as if he were searching for something. You saw the rest."

Frowning, Darla pulled on the gloves James had left on the counter and picked up the slipcased set. The characteristic aroma of old books swept over her . . . the faintly musty, faintly vanilla scent that always emanated from their pages. James had once explained to her it had to do with the chemical compounds in the glue and ink and paper that broke down with age. No matter the explanation, she always found herself remembering the old library in her grade school, a place where she'd spent many a happy hour.

She gave the set a once-over, sliding out each volume for a quick look. For their age, their condition was remarkably fine, with the gold embossing on the spines and slipcase almost as shiny as the day it was stamped.

"I suppose he realized this wasn't the first edition he was expecting," she said as she put down the set and removed the gloves. "But he should have known better if he was a true collector. Talk about an over-the-top attitude."

James nodded. "I suspect he was not so much an antiquarian book collector as he was in search of this particular work. You know quite well that some volumes have a sentimental value—stories that one was read as a child, or books one's parents owned, or even a favorite volume one read every summer in the local library."

Darla nodded. "I hope he finds what he's looking for, as long as he stays far from here. I guess you can go ahead and relist this one."

"I shall. And that does remind me, I still have a few boxes of books I obtained from Bernard that I need to appraise. Several volumes came from their store, and others were leftovers from the recent estate sale that the Plinskis managed. After a cursory look, I do not believe there is anything of significant value, but most are quite decorative. They will probably go into our Yard o' Books pile," he said, referring to the pretty if relatively worthless volumes that they sold to decorators and real estate stagers.

He retrieved the *Marble Faun* set and carried it over to the locked, glass-fronted case where the shop's more valuable books were displayed. Darla checked in with a couple of customers in the rear room who were happily browsing. Assured they didn't require immediate assistance, she left them under James's watchful eye and went up to the coffee lounge to check on Robert.

As she reached the top step, however, her barista was there blocking her way. "Shhh," he softly greeted her. Pointing, he added, "Hamlet's got a visitor and, like, I'm not sure he's real happy."

"What? Who? Oh!" Darla softly exclaimed as she looked in the direction he indicated.

For a moment, she'd assumed he meant Roma . . . but this was no leggy little gray pup that was perched on the farthest bistro table. Instead, standing nose to nose with Hamlet was his mirror image.

"The mystery cat," she said with a gasp as she took in the sleek black feline that—other than being a bit shorter and slightly less muscular—could have been his twin. "How did it get inside?"

Robert shook his head.

"Maybe she came in with a customer. Or, you know how Hamlet has all his secret passages. She could have, like, snuck into the building and been hiding in the storeroom," he added, gesturing to the small room off the lounge where James warehoused the extra stock.

Hamlet, meanwhile, had begun to growl, the sound resembling the rumble of a diesel truck warming up. As for the interloper, it—she?—puffed out her silky fur and gave a couple of tiny hisses that exposed a bright red tongue. They stood another instant that way, with matching emerald gazes locked.

Then Hamlet let loose a hiss of his own . . . a hiss that Darla had, in the past, compared to the sound of a cobra on steroids. At that, the smaller cat leaped up in a veritable explosion of black and made a beeline for the storeroom.

For a moment, Darla feared that Hamlet would give chase. Instead, he settled back on his haunches and gave his front paw a lick as if to say, *My work here is done.*

Darla and Robert exchanged uncertain glances. Then Robert asked, "Should I, you know, go looking for it?"

Darla shook her head. "If it—she—were still in the storeroom, I'm sure Hamlet would have gone after her and cornered her. Like you said, she probably found some of Hamlet's secret passages, and she's already back outside again."

She shot Hamlet a stern look. The passages in question had been a point of contention between Darla and the wily feline since she'd first moved in. Darla knew that her and Mary Ann's nineteenth-century brownstones had once been a single house. Over the years, however, the original structure had been internally split into two separate living spaces.

Unfortunately, much of the remodel had been surprisingly careless, perhaps since members of the same original family had continued to live on both sides until well into the twentieth century. Darla had found evidence of cubbyholes, papered-over closets, and various cat-sized openings, all of which allowed Hamlet to stealthily slip from floor to floor. He'd even found his way outside before and had once shown up in Mary Ann's store.

Darla had finally thrown up her hands, deciding that if Hamlet had safely done his appearing and disappearing act for more than ten years, then she wasn't going to fret about it. But she certainly hadn't expected any feline interlopers to use his same unorthodox exits.

"It's a good thing there weren't any customers up here to witness the cat fight, or we'd probably be getting a visit from the health department," she said with a wry smile. "But since this cat seems to be sticking around, maybe we should borrow a trap from your rescue group friends and try to catch her."

Robert nodded. "I can call them. They could scan her for a chip, and if they can't, like, find her owner, they'll get her all vetted and put her up for adoption." Then his kohled eyes grew wide. "Hey, maybe Ms. Plinski would want her. You know, for company and stuff."

"Well, you can find out if she'd want to be put on the adopters list when you see her later. Mary Ann asked me to ask you if you'd stop by after work."

"Yeah, sure. I was planning on doing that, anyhow."

She left Robert wiping down the table that had hosted the feline fireworks and started downstairs. Hamlet, looking quite pleased with his cat self, padded alongside her. The rest of the afternoon proceeded without incident, for which Darla was grateful. She'd considered sending Reese a text to see if he would share any more information about Hodge's situation, but ultimately she decided against it. He always hated when she second-guessed him, not that she blamed him. Besides, he'd probably gotten his share of grief from Connie the night before about canceling on another dinner date.

The thought of the future Mrs. Fiorello Reese reminded her that the woman's plans to purchase "something old" had been superseded by the police investigation. If Mary Ann opened the store tomorrow, she'd stop in and purchase the cute cake topper for Connie as her engagement party gift. That way, if Connie didn't find something else on her own, Darla's present would cover that part of the wedding rhyme. And, if not, Connie would have something fun to put on the bridal table.

And Darla reminded herself that she could also see if the vintage pie dish she'd picked out to buy before things had gone terribly wrong was still available.

ROBERT HAD ALREADY LEFT FOR THE DAY, AND DARLA WAS BEGINNING the usual closing routine, when she heard James call to her from upstairs.

"I'll be right up," she shouted back. "Let me lock up, first."

She did the quick check for stragglers, politely rousting a middle-aged businessman who'd spent the past hour in the back corner reading a graphic novel. Once she was certain no one else remained, she flipped the sign to "Closed" and locked the front door, and then headed upstairs.

She located her manager working at the table in the storeroom.

"Sorry, I had to kick out a 'library patron,'" she said, her explanation earning a faintly censuring look from him.

Darla gave him an unapologetic smile. The ironic phrase was one she and Robert had privately coined for customers who had no qualms about camping out in the store and reading without buying anything. Fortunately, some of those same "patrons" did eventually make a purchase. And Hamlet had a habit (which Darla never quite got around to scolding him for) of staring down the nonbuyers until they either whipped out their credit cards or else left the store posthaste.

"So what was the emergency?" she asked him.

James pointed to a cardboard box marked "Estate1507" sitting amid three neat piles of leather-bound and dust-jacketed books.

"Since I had a bit of time, I decided to sort through the books I obtained from Bernard. Many of the volumes proved to be more valuable than I had anticipated, especially for those collectors who specialize in fine bindings. But as I got to this last box, I found something rather . . . unexpected."

He reached into the box and pulled out a red, clothbound book of indeterminate age, with a publisher's stylistic gilded marking imprinted onto its front cover. Then he turned it so that she could read the spine. A gold-stamped, almost heraldic design featuring stylized flowers and vines covered three-quarters of the space, with the book's title and author stamped there in gold, as well.

Slowly, Darla read it aloud.

"The Marble Faun by Nathaniel Hawthorne."

"An interesting coincidence, is it not?" James said as he carefully flipped open the front cover. "As you can see by the date, though this edition dates from the turn of the century—1912, to be exact—it is a much newer copy than the one we had for sale. And the facing title pages are exquisite."

He turned to them, and Darla nodded her appreciation. Rather than simply listing the pertinent information in fancy script, the two pages featured prints resembling Chaucerian-style woodcuts. The left page featured a quote from the Elizabethan courtier Philip Sidney, while the facing page gave the title, author, and publisher.

The endpapers were equally charming with an almost Art Deco feel to their swooping vine-and-leaf design. In one corner, lightly written in pencil so faint as to be almost unnoticeable, were the words *V. Modello*—doubtless, the previous owner's name.

"Delightful," she agreed. "So, how much would this book be worth?"

"Twenty, perhaps twenty-five dollars."

At Darla's look of disappointment, he explained, "You should know by now that the mere fact of age has little to do with a vintage book's value. Someone writing in it who is not the author or a famous personage lowers the value even more. Moreover, the endpapers do not appear to be original to the book. But I am sure we will find a buyer who will appreciate its overall artistry."

"Actually, I think we already have," Darla told him with a smile as she held out her hand. "I've always had a soft spot for Hawthorne, and with all the hoopla over the book I think I'd enjoy having this copy. Write me up for twenty dollars in the morning."

"As you wish," James replied, returning her smile as he handed the book over. "In my view, it is not his finest work—I assign that honor to his short story 'Rappaccini's Daughter'—but it does have its elegant moments. I will be interested to hear your opinion once you have finished reading."

"I'll put it on my bedside table and start on it tonight."

With that, Darla tucked the book under her arm and preceded James down the stairs. Once she'd let him out the front door, she shut down the register and called for Hamlet.

"Supper time . . . and I promise, you won't have to share it with any strange cats."

Apparently satisfied by that last, Hamlet came trotting out and followed her to the side door. With the lights off, door locked, and alarm set, the pair headed upstairs to Darla's apartment.

But she'd barely reached the first landing when her cell

phone vibrated, and a series of chirps indicated an incoming text. She paused there and, shuffling her new book and her purse, took a look at her phone. The short message was from Jake and, she saw, copied Reese. It read:

Can U meet me & Reese @ Greek place @ 7?
Interesting Hodge update.

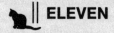 **ELEVEN**

"SO, I GUESS YOU'RE WONDERING WHY I INVITED YOU ALL here," Jake said, smirking a little as she gestured around the Greek restaurant where they were sitting.

Darla merely rolled her eyes at the cliché, but Reese shot Jake a sour look.

"It better be good," he warned her. "I had to put off my dinner with Connie for a couple of hours to be here, and she's pretty ticked off.

"I think you'll find it interesting."

She paused for a sip of ouzo and a stuffed grape leaf. Darla helped herself to one of the dolmas, too, though she'd opted for white wine rather than the anise-flavored aperitif. As for Reese, he was driving, so he'd stuck with a soda and had already downed two of the appetizers.

Jake finished chewing and then, with another sip, set down her icy drink, her expression now determined.

"First off, Reese, I didn't plan to stick my nose in your

case," she told him. "But Mary Ann stayed with me last night. You already know that the rest of us—me, Darla, James, and Robert—hung out at my place to eat Darla's excellent casserole and keep Mary Ann company. She had a second glass of wine after everyone left and, well, let's just say the old girl ended up pretty tipsy."

Darla gave Jake a surprised look, trying to picture their elderly friend getting—as Darla's dad would have put it— *drunk as Cooter Brown*. Understandable under the circumstances, but just about as shocking as it would be to see James tie one on!

Jake, meanwhile, continued, "So I let her talk. I figured it would do her good, know what I mean? But right before I sent her off to bed, she said a couple of things that struck me as odd."

"If this has to do with Rodger Camden," Reese mumbled through a mouthful of tzatziki dip smeared on pita bread, "we did a pretty thorough background check on him. You wanna know the name of his sixth grade teacher, I can tell you."

"Yeah," Jake countered, "but did you know that Hodge got Mary Ann's parents arrested for, quote unquote, un-American activities back in the fifties?"

"Yeah. It came up."

He finished swallowing and said, "Mr. Camden gave us the whole scoop about calling the feds on the Plinskis' parents about sixty years ago. Water under the bridge. Next."

"Okay, so you knew that," Jake replied, obviously disappointed. Still, she persisted, "But that's not much of a motive for Hodge to want to see Bernard dead."

Before Reese could reply, Darla lowered the stuffed grape leaf she was about to pop in her mouth. "How about the fact that he doesn't know that Mary Ann already knows about it?" she chimed in.

Then, earning a surprised look from her companions, she asked, "What? Mary Ann told me the whole story this morning. Maybe Hodge's motive was that he wanted to make sure Mr. Plinski didn't try to get back at him by spilling the beans to her and ruining their relationship again."

And what about Doug's "merry widower" theory?

She hesitated, remembering that she was on Team Hodge, and decided to keep her mouth shut about *that*. Instead, she said, "But that's just off the top of my head. Bottom line, I don't think Hodge did it, and neither does Mary Ann."

Reese gave a snort of disgust. "Yeah, well, how about we agree to disagree on this one. Shocking as it might sound, we've actually got some pretty good circumstantial evidence that points to Mr. Camden's guilt. There's a couple more things I can't talk about, but let's just say we didn't drag him in to chat just because."

While Darla worried a bit over that last, Jake took a sizable swig of her ouzo, set down the glass, and said, "All right, what about this? Did either of you know that Bernard had a gun stuck under the counter at Bygone Days, and a couple of weeks ago he'd threatened to shoot Hodge with it?"

"What?" Darla and Reese chorused.

But when Darla would have persisted, Reese put up a restraining hand. "Let me ask the questions, Red," he clipped out. To Jake, he said, "What's he got, and where is it?"

"Don't worry, it's an antique," the PI replied, "so he wasn't breaking any laws. From what Mary Ann described, I'd guess it was a Winchester, probably an 1894 lever-action. He had it stuck up underneath the counter. I don't even know if it's loaded."

Reese sighed. "I'll stop by on Monday and talk to Mary Ann about it."

"That's up to you," Jake replied, "but here's where I'm

going with this. We've got Mary Ann's statement that Bernard threatened Hodge not long before his murder. Bernard might have been old, but he wasn't a slouch. If their argument that last day had gotten too heated, he'd probably have pulled out that rifle and gone all Lucas McCain on Hodge before Hodge could do anything. So I'm thinking that even if he and Hodge got into it, Hodge isn't the guy. I'm thinking maybe Bernard's actual murderer is still out there."

Darla allowed herself a fleeting smile as the "Lucas McCain" name clicked. She'd watched her share of nostalgia television, and she couldn't help but be amused the thought of Mr. Plinski imitating *The Rifleman* of 1950s TV Western fame.

She sobered, however, as she saw that Reese wasn't buying what the PI was selling. He shoved another stuffed grape leaf into his mouth, washed it down with half his glass of soda, and then pushed back from the table.

"You know what I think? I think you and Darla should quit Monday-morning-quarterbacking me. Just because no one's brought any charges against the guy yet doesn't mean he's off the hook."

His cell phone chose that moment to vibrate, signaling that he had a text message. He pulled the cell out of his jacket pocket and read the text, then softly swore.

"Bad news?" Jake asked.

"Yeah, you might say so."

With that cryptic response, he grabbed his tweed overcoat and stalked out of the restaurant without a good-bye. Jake watched him go and then shrugged.

"What do you put your money on, work or Connie?"

"Not Connie," Darla promptly replied. "He's got a special sound for her texts, and that wasn't it. But he sure didn't look happy."

"He's probably got the higher-ups on his back about something. That, or he's just ticked off he didn't spot Bernard's rifle while he was giving the store the once-over."

"Well, it's not too surprising he missed it. I mean, who would expect a nice little old man like Mr. Plinski to be packing?"

Though, if this had happened back in Texas, Darla wryly thought, the cops would have been surprised *not* to find a weapon of some sort stashed beneath the counter. She added, "I'm sure he'll get over it."

"Yeah."

Shaking her head, Jake reached for the dinner menus and handed one to Darla.

"I don't know about you, but stuffed grape leaves and pita bread won't do it . . . especially if I plan to have one more of these," she clarified with a gesture at the chilly glass of ouzo. "My treat, as long as you promise to entertain me with stories that don't end with someone dying."

Once the waiter had taken their orders, Darla obliged with an account of the mystery cat's confrontation with Hamlet that afternoon . . . complete with sound effects. Jake was an appreciative audience, asking at the end, "So Hamlet has a girlfriend now? I thought that cat was going to remain a bachelor for life."

"We're only guessing she's a girl," Darla said with a smile, "but she's a pretty feisty little thing. Robert is hoping that if it turns out she doesn't have a home, maybe Mary Ann will adopt her."

"Well, every antiques store needs a resident kitty, just like every bookstore does. And she probably will want the company. It's hard coming home to an empty house when you're not used to that."

"We'll see what happens. I put out some food and water

for her before I left, so hopefully she'll eat something and then find herself a snug place to stay for the night. Robert should be able to pick up that trap from his rescue friends sometime tomorrow."

Their food showed up at that point, so for a few minutes she and Jake concentrated on their plates of moussaka. After a few bites, however, Darla was fortified enough to regale her friend with the day's even stranger story—the one concerning BookBuyer75 and the *Marble Faun* online auction fiasco.

"I know we get some odd customers," Darla finished, "but this guy was something else. I was thinking earlier that between him, Connie, and good old Vinnie from the bridal shop, we've got a full slate already for Pettistone's first-ever Actor of the Year award."

"Wait, you forgot Hamlet," Jake said, grinning. "Or do you plan a separate Four-Footed Actor of the Year category?"

"Might as well lump them into one award, though I think Hammy should get a Lifetime Achievement trophy instead. That cat is Mr. Drama in fur pants." Then she sobered. "Is it terrible to be having fun and making jokes like this when Mr. Plinski isn't even buried yet?"

"Remember, he's supposed to be cremated," Jake replied. "And, no, it's not bad. It's normal, and it's a heck of a lot healthier than doing the old sackcloth-and-ashes routine for weeks on end. Bernard was our friend, and I think he'd want us to go right on enjoying life even though he's gone."

"I guess you're right. When I die, I don't want people to be prostrate with grief. Well, I do want them to be at least a *little* sad," she amended with a small smile.

Jake gave a vigorous nod.

"When I croak, I want everyone to have a big party in

my honor and get sloppy drunk and laugh like hell," she said, toasting herself with her second glass of ouzo. "On the other hand, I told Ma I want one of those giant weeping angels on my grave. You know, so when people wander past, they'll figure I was this saintly being in life."

"Jake Martelli, saintly?" Darla shot back, smile broadening. "Wow, talk about acting. I think I'd better nominate you alongside Hamlet for that Lifetime Achievement trophy."

They finished their meal chatting about inconsequentials, deliberately avoiding the topic of Mr. Plinski's murder and possible suspects. Finally, well after eight o'clock, it was time to brave the late fall weather outside.

"You know, I think I need to drag Maybelle out of storage," Darla said as they plunged into the cold night air. She referred, of course, to the decade-old Mercedes-Benz that Great-Aunt Dee had left her, which was parked at a nearby garage. "All this walking around is making this Texas girl stir-crazy. I need to hop in the car and drive somewhere."

"Well, you better hurry before the bad weather comes in."

Then, snapping her fingers—quite the accomplishment with gloved hands—Jake added, "I know, why don't we take Mary Ann out to the place where she's going to be holding the estate sale? I talked to her about it last night, and she's determined to carry on with handling the event. The house is in Queens somewhere, so it's not like we'd be driving all over creation, but it'll get you on the road."

"Actually, Mary Ann said she wanted to talk to Robert about the sale, to see if he could help," Darla replied. "The bookstore's closed on Monday, so that would be a perfect day to for all of us to help her get things set up. Why don't we swing by Mary Ann's place on the way home and talk to her about it?"

They hustled down the darkened streets, which, because

it was Saturday night, were busier than normal. It was closing in on nine when they reached Darla's brownstone. The
usual faint light in the bookstore shined through her front
window, while in her apartment above, a second light burned
brighter. She could see Hamlet sitting there, silhouetted like
a Halloween cat as he kept watch over the street, and she
gave him a fond smile.

Mary Ann's place, a few steps away, was dark, except for
a light burning on the third floor. Darla knew that, unlike
her portion of the building, the Plinskis' place did not have
a separate entry hall and stairs to divide the retail space
from the private areas. Instead, there was a single main
staircase, which they kept roped off from customers. If she
recalled correctly, Mr. Plinski's bedroom plus his workshop
and storage rooms were on the second level. Common
areas—kitchen, living room, dining nook—were on the
third floor, along with Mary Ann's bedroom and a second
guest room. And, of course, there was Robert's garden apartment below street level.

"Good, she's still up," Jake said, pulling out her cell
phone while Darla huddled deeper into her coat. "I'll call
her first to let her know we're here."

"Odd," she said after letting the phone ring for a few
moments. "It went to voice mail."

"Maybe she's taking a bath. Give it a minute and call
again."

Jake waited and then tried again as Darla had suggested,
only to shake her head. "Still no answer. I'm going to try
the front door."

They hurried up the steps, pausing on her stoop to ring
the doorbell. Like Darla, Mary Ann had an intercom in
place, so she could find out who was at the door from the

safety of her apartment. But no tinny voice emerged from that metal box to greet them.

"I'm getting a little worried," Jake admitted with a frown as she rang a second time and got no answer via the intercom. "There's no reason she shouldn't be home, and even if she was asleep, the phone calls and doorbell ringing should have woken her up by now."

"Do you think something's wrong?" Darla asked, feeling a little worried herself. "What if all the stress of the past few days has made her sick? What if she had a heart attack just like Mr. Plinski and can't get to the phone to call for help?"

Jake nodded and reached into her coat pocket, pulling out her keychain.

"I still have her keys from the other night," she said, flipping through the bunch until she reached one that shined bright blue in the gleam from the nearby streetlight.

At Darla's uncertain look, she added with a wry smile, "Don't worry, kid, it's not breaking and entering since we're not planning on stealing anything. Worst they can get us for is criminal trespass, and that's only if Mary Ann presses charges."

Darla hesitated, torn between concern at invading the old woman's privacy and fear of what could happen if Mary Ann truly was ill and they didn't investigate.

Then a worse thought occurred to her. Burglars were known to take advantage of deaths and the bereaved. What if an intruder assumed the place would be easy pickings under the circumstances, and had broken in to steal what he could?

Or, even more chilling, what if the person who'd actually killed Mr. Plinski had come back looking for the old man's sister!

That last possibility settled it for her.

"I'd rather have her mad at us for overreacting than find out later she'd needed help and we weren't there for her," she finally declared. "I vote we go in, too."

"Okay, we'll take a look. But don't panic until we know for sure something's wrong. There's probably a logical reason why she's not answering."

With that, Jake turned the key in the lock and slowly opened the door. She took a quick look inside before glancing back at Darla and shaking her head.

"The alarm system is off," she whispered, ushering Darla inside the shop and closing the door behind them. "Not a good sign. I think something else is going on here."

Darla glanced over at the faintly glowing keypad on the wall, and a shiver went through her. The red LED that typically indicated a security system was armed wasn't lit, while the green "Ready" light glowed brightly. Definitely not a good sign, she silently agreed, trying hard to follow her friend's previous instructions not to panic.

Jake, meanwhile, flicked on the tiny flashlight attached to her keychain. "Wait here. I'm going to take a quick look around, first," she whispered.

Darla nodded as she mentally finished her friend's thought. *To make sure no one is lurking around down here.* She watched as Jake, with her tiny but powerful light, made her cautious way down the aisles. Other than the PI's flashlight, the only illumination came from outside through the windows and from the glowing alarm panel at Darla's shoulder. The usually homey shop had taken on a mysterious air that was deepened by the uneven shadows tossed out by the odd-sized array of shelves that lined the aisles. Even worse were the distorted human shapes that, on closer review, were mannequins wearing vintage clothing. Probably her ceramic pie plate would look equally scary under the circumstances, she told herself grimly.

After what seemed like several minutes but was probably less than one, Jake returned to where Darla waited.

"Nothing looks out of place," she murmured. "I'm going to try something else. You wait right here by the door, and if anything goes south, get out as fast as you can and call 9-1-1."

"Got it," Darla whispered back, pulling her cell phone from her purse so she would have it immediately at hand. She added, "Be careful."

Jake nodded and quietly started toward the stairway. Despite her nervousness, Darla couldn't help but marvel at how the woman's footsteps made no sound against the wooden floor, even though she was wearing her usual clunky Doc Martens boots. The PI definitely could give Hawkeye from *The Last of the Mohicans* a run for his money when it came to tracking.

Once she reached the foot of the stairs, Jake flicked off her small flashlight, but not before Darla saw that the automatic gliding stair lift the Plinskis had installed a while back to help them negotiate the two flights of stairs sat empty. Moving to the far side of the carved newel post, the PI called up, "Mary Ann, it's me . . . Jake. Are you up there? Mary Ann?"

Darla held her breath. A couple of heartbeats later, she heard from the floor above the faintest squeal of an opening door, and then the soft, cautious creak of wooden floorboards.

Not Mary Ann, she instinctively knew, and shivered. What would happen now? Would this stranger come down the steps to confront Jake face-to-face, or would he somehow try to make a break for it? A second door at the rear of the store led out to a mirror image of Darla's own courtyard. If the interloper could make it that far without Jake stopping him, he could be into the alley and out onto the street within moments.

The footsteps kept coming, and Darla could feel her heart beating faster. The footsteps halted at the top of the stairway, and she knew the confrontation was imminent. She tensed and put a hand on the front doorknob, ready to follow Jake's instructions if need be.

Abruptly, the overhead bulbs flashed on in a blinding wave of light, and a man's outraged voice boomed, "Who are you? What are you doing here?"

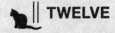 **TWELVE**

AS DARLA WATCHED IN AMAZEMENT, A TALL, WIRY OLD MAN
with rosy cheeks came marching a few steps down the stairway. He was holding a baseball bat and wearing only baggy
white boxer shorts topped by a white tank-style undershirt.

Hodge?

No surprise that he was back on the streets—after all,
he'd simply been questioned in the murder—but what was
he doing at Mary Ann's at this time of night? She eyed the
baseball bat he held with sudden suspicion. What if they'd
all been wrong, and he *had* been the one to kill Mr. Plinski?
And what if he'd switched to a new and far more brutal
weapon than a pillow, and Mary Ann was lying somewhere
upstairs bludgeoned to death?

But that horrifying possibility had barely flashed through
her mind when Darla saw that he was followed by a very
living and breathing Mary Ann.

The old woman was dressed in a lacy white nightgown

with a pink plaid flannel robe belted tightly around her. Her gray hair, which was usually pulled up in a neat, tight bun, drifted loose past her shoulders, giving her an oddly girlish look that belied her many wrinkles. She pushed past Hodge and marched halfway down the stairs, her expression stunned.

"Jake . . . Darla? What in the world are you girls doing in here?"

Darla stared right back at her as realization dawned. Obviously, what was happening between Mary Ann and Hodge was a far cry from murder. She shot a helpless look at Jake, who appeared, for the first time since Darla had known her, to be at a loss for words.

"Uh, we—that is, Darla and I—were worried about you," the PI finally managed. "We, uh, came by to ask if you wanted us to drive you out to Queens on Monday so you could work on that estate sale. You didn't answer your phone or the door, and we thought . . ."

She trailed off, and Darla dutifully took over.

"We're sorry, Mary Ann. We thought maybe something happened to you. We saw your light on upstairs, so we tried calling and ringing the bell. We couldn't just walk off without knowing you were okay, and Jake did have a key, so we . . ."

Darla stuttered to a halt as well, feeling almost like she was sixteen again and facing a parental scolding for missing curfew. And Mary Ann did not disappoint her.

"I see," the old woman clipped out, her reproachful gaze moving from her to Jake and back again. "And I suppose it never occurred to you girls that I might be deliberately ignoring your interruptions? That I might be otherwise occupied?"

"Now, now, Annie," Hodge broke in, laying a large hand

on her thin shoulder. "Don't be so hard on them. They only had your best interests at heart . . . right, girls?"

Darla glanced Jake's way again and saw to her relief that the PI had regained her equilibrium.

"I think we're forgetting the important thing," Jake coolly replied. "Mary Ann's brother—our friend—was murdered just yesterday in almost this very spot. I'm not saying I think you had anything to do with it, but unless and until Reese finds himself another suspect, you're still going to be on his radar. I'm not sure it's a good idea for you to be here, under the circumstances."

"And I think that's something for me to decide," Mary Ann broke in, sounding affronted.

Then, as the three of them stared at her, she continued, "Do you honestly think I would welcome Hodge into my home"—her pale cheeks abruptly pinked at the logical if unsaid corollary, *into my bed*—"if I didn't believe he was innocent? Now, I think you girls better go home and leave us in peace. Oh, and Jake, I will take those keys, if you don't mind."

She took a few more steps down the stairs, held out a wrinkled palm, and waited while the PI unfastened the keys from her ring and handed them over.

"Thank you," she said, closing her fingers over them. "Now, why don't I show you girls out?"

She followed Jake to the front of the store. Darla, meanwhile, stole a look at Hodge to see his reaction to this last. He caught her gaze and gave her a wink and a nod. He, at least, didn't seem offended by their interference, she wryly thought.

She waited, however, until they were outside again, standing at her own stoop, before she told Jake, "Well, talk about a night. We've ticked off Reese and Mary Ann, both. And, on top of that, we've learned there really is sex after seventy. Anything else we should try for before we call it a night?"

Jake gave a self-deprecating snort. "Yep, one for the books, kid. I think we've done enough. Hopefully, both of them will cool off by tomorrow."

Darla nodded. "On the bright side, it looks like Hodge and Mary Ann might find themselves a nice little happily ever after."

Unless Doug's theory about the merry widower was right?

Suddenly shivering, and not just from the cold, she wondered if she should run the idea past Jake. But the PI was already saying, "We're still back to the original problem. Someone murdered Bernard, and if we take Hodge out of the mix, there's still no suspect, and no obvious motive. I tell you, kid, I have a really bad feeling about this."

Darla shot her a look of alarm. "What, do you think the real killer is someone else Mary Ann knows?"

"Maybe. Maybe not. All I know is that I'm going to cancel my appointments for the next couple of days and stick around here to keep an eye on things."

Darla frowned. She knew from both Jake and Reese that the more time that passed after a murder without an arrest, the less likely it became that anyone would ever be charged with a crime. They were already approaching the end of the forty-eight-hour window popularized by true-crime television. If Reese didn't have a new suspect soon, the old man's murder might go unsolved.

Jake must have seen the worry in her face, for she gave her a reassuring pat on the arm. "Don't worry, kid. This is personal for all of us. Between Reese and you and me, I promise we'll find out who really did it and get some justice for Bernard and Mary Ann."

* * *

"SO, WHAT WAS THE FINAL SCORE ON THE BOOKS FROM THE ESTATE sale?" Darla asked her store manager the next afternoon.

James had just come downstairs after spending the last couple of hours in the storeroom evaluating and pricing the volumes he'd shown her the previous night. Now he gave his brown-and-tan hound's-tooth-checked vest a satisfied tug as he addressed her.

"I think we shall make a small profit from our buy," he said, and pulled a list from his inside vest pocket. "My original estimate was fairly accurate. Perhaps half the volumes have a value that is strictly aesthetic, but the remainder do have some small collectible value. I will price them accordingly and we shall see if they sell.

"Oh, and I presume you found the invoice for the copy of *The Marble Faun* that I left on the register for you?" he added. "If you noticed, I did give you the usual employee discount."

"Already handled," she said with a smile. She picked up the document in question from the bin beneath the counter and pointed to the red stamped letters proclaiming "Paid" across it. "You'll find my personal check in the register."

"Very good. Did you have the opportunity last evening to do any reading?"

"Actually, no. My head was in such a whirl with everything that happened after I locked up last night that all I did was crawl into bed and shut off the lights."

She hadn't had time to relate all the details of the prior night's events to James before the first customers had come in. But now, after first checking to be sure Robert was still safely upstairs and no customers were in earshot, she launched into her account. She started with her and Jake's meeting at the restaurant with Reese, and finished with their subsequent visit to Mary Ann's place—leaving out the fact that Mary Ann and Hodge had been in their nightclothes during that denouement.

"I was pretty shocked to see Hodge there, but I didn't really think he'd killed Mr. Plinski, in the first place. And Mary Ann seems convinced of his innocence. But we're back to the original problem. A murderer is still out there."

"Has Detective Reese opined at all about this?"

"I haven't heard anything from him since last night, and I don't know if Jake has, either."

Then she shook her head. "All the stories I'm reading online and in the paper are saying it's looking like a random killing, and maybe that's true. Though I'm not sure if a random-killer scenario is better or worse than someone deliberately ending your life for a specific reason."

"A crime of passion versus a crime of disinterest," James mused. "I am sure philosophers could debate the virtues of both and not come to a decision as to which was the greater sin."

He scrubbed a hand across his bearded chin and sighed.

"I find myself at a loss, as well. But there is one thing I have learned over the years, and that is that one never knows about another's past. It could be possible that Bernard had a dark secret from his youth that came back to haunt him."

"You mean, something worse than Hodge betraying the Plinskis' parents to the government back in the fifties? Oh, wait, I suppose you don't know about that."

By the time she'd gotten James up-to-date on the McCarthy-inspired machinations that had happened sixty years earlier, her store manager was shaking his head.

"As I said, one never knows. I am surprised that the press has not brought up that particular detail. Not to offer spoilers, as they say, but if you do manage to read your new

Hawthorne, you may find some interesting parallels between it and our current situation."

Reading was the last thing on her mind at the moment. She did, however, make a mental note to keep an eye on Hamlet . . . that, along with sitting down when she had a moment and making a list of the books that had she'd randomly retrieved off the floor these past few days. It appeared she'd been a bit hasty the other day in informing the crafty feline that his sleuthing talents weren't needed in this situation.

Obviously, they were. The question was, did Hamlet actually know anything about Mr. Plinski's murder . . . and, if so, would he reveal what he knew?

For the moment, all she said aloud was, "I just wish there were something we could do to help."

"I think all we can sensibly do is what Jake suggested. We should keep the proverbial eye on the situation and make sure that Mary Ann remains safe."

"I'm on board with that, too. In fact, if Mary Ann has forgiven us by then, Jake and I were going to drive her out to Queens on Monday so she can prep for her estate sale."

"An excellent idea. I must admit that, with all you have told me, I am rather nervous at the thought of her being alone."

A customer walked up just then with a couple of books on financial planning. Darla halted the conversation to ring up her purchases, while James excused himself to enter the new books on their auction website.

Afterward, a steady stream of customers alternated between browsing for books and drinking coffee, so that Darla didn't have a chance to chat again with James. And since Robert was keeping equally busy in the coffee lounge, she didn't get the opportunity to learn if Mary Ann had indeed recruited the youth to help with the estate sale.

Finally, around four, there was a lull in the action. Darla was just about to go upstairs when she heard the bells on the front door chime again. She turned back around, only to see a determined Mary Ann Plinski wrapped in an oversized blue shawl headed her way.

Recalling too well last night's less-than-cordial parting, Darla glanced about for reinforcements. Unfortunately, James was straightening stock in the back room, meaning she wouldn't have him as a buffer should Mary Ann want to continue her previous night's lecture. Steeling herself for a chilly reception, she hesitantly greeted the old woman.

"Hi, Mary Ann. Are you looking for Robert? He's upstairs in the coffee bar. I can send him down, if you like."

"Actually, Darla, I'm looking for you." Cheeks growing pink and wrinkled hands tightly clasping the shawl to her, she said, "I really must apologize for my behavior last night.

"No, no"—she interrupted when Darla would have protested—"hear me out. I know that you and Jake were only looking out for my well-being, and I do appreciate that. I suppose I mostly was embarrassed for you girls to find me, well, in flagrante, and so I fear I acted a bit badly. I do hope you can forgive me, my dear."

"Of course," Darla exclaimed, rushing over to give the old woman a hug. "And you certainly had a right to be upset that we just waltzed into your place. But I'm glad to know that you realize we did it for the best of reasons. And I promise, we'll never do that again."

"My dear, I am so glad we've cleared the air. I did stop by to see Jake first, and she was good enough to accept my apology. So I believe I've put everything to rights again."

Then she wrinkled her brow. "Oh dear, I did mean to give her back my keys, but she had to run off to an appointment and so I didn't get the chance." She dug into the pocket of her shirtdress and pulled out the same keys from the night before. "Would you very much mind giving these to Jake the next time you see her?"

"Of course," Darla agreed, pulling out her own ring from beneath the counter and hooking Mary Ann's keys on for safekeeping. "So I suppose Jake didn't have time to say anything to you about taking a field trip tomorrow to Queens?"

When the old woman shook her head, Darla told her the PI's suggestion that they drive her out to the house where she would be holding the estate sale for a customer in the next week.

"It would save you having to hire a car up and back," Darla finished, "plus we can help with some of the grunt work. You know . . . moving things around, setting up tables. And assuming Robert already agreed to help you with the sale, we can bring him along, too."

Mary Ann considered the idea for a moment and then nodded.

"That is an excellent idea. Let me contact the executor right now and make certain the house can be available tomorrow. And, I must admit, I always did enjoy being squired around town in Dee's old car. I feel quite elegant sitting in those fancy leather seats."

After agreeing to call Darla back within the hour, the old woman snugged her shawl more tightly around her and left the store. As the bells chimed after her, James appeared, silent as Hamlet, at the counter.

"I am happy to hear that you and Mary Ann have resolved yesterday's differences. Do I understand you will be helping her set up this latest estate sale?"

At Darla's nod, he quirked a brow.

"I suppose I do not need to tell you to keep an eagle eye out, as they say, for any interesting literary finds. A time or two, Bernard was kind enough to let me do a little early-bird shopping before the general public was allowed into one of his sales, and I ended up with a few respectable buys out of it. I shall be out with Martha most of the morning, but do feel free to text me any photographs of likely volumes. Perhaps we can do that last collection of books one better."

Agreeing to be his official book scout—and thus earning the privilege of borrowing his *A Pocket Guide to the Identification of First Editions* for the day—Darla left James to start the closing process while she went up to the coffee lounge to chat with Robert.

She found Hamlet keeping him company, the cat's cool green gaze focused on the storeroom. "Has Hammy's new friend showed back up again?" she asked the youth.

Robert shook his head. "If she did, she's, you know, keeping a low profile. He's been watching the storeroom like a hawk, but I haven't seen any sign of her."

"Well, I did leave food and water out for her last night. Were you able to get hold of anyone from the Furry Berets Pet Rescue about the cat trap?"

She was speaking of the volunteer group run by a woman named Bonnie Greenwood and dedicated to rescuing stray pets in the Brooklyn area. James was a behind-the-scenes sponsor of the organization, which had been responsible for formally placing Roma the Italian greyhound in Robert's care.

The youth nodded.

"Yeah, I called Sylvie." He referred, Darla knew, to Bonnie's teenage daughter who was also a member of the group. "She said all their humane traps were out, but she might have one by, you know, Tuesday, and she'd bring it to me."

"I guess that will have to do," Darla replied. "Of course, if we're lucky, maybe our mystery kitty will turn out to be tame enough that we can catch her ourselves and put her in

Hamlet's carrier to take her over to them instead. And I guess it's just as well, since we'll be gone tomorrow. Do you want to come with me and Jake to help Mary Ann get set up for her estate sale?"

"Sure. Ms. Plinski asked me about helping for the actual sale, but I told her I had to clear it with you." He paused and gave her an uncertain look. "But I think the sale is Friday and Saturday, and those are our, you know, big coffee days. So I guess maybe I have to tell her no?"

"Of course not. This would be the perfect trial run to see how good a job you did training Pinky as your backup for when you're gone next week," Darla said with a smile.

Pinky—so named for his dyed-pink chin braids and a single pink braid atop his head—was Robert's boyish-looking goth friend who fronted a goth/emo/metal band called The Screaming Babies. Pinky and his fellow musicians had filled in at the neighborhood July Fourth block party when the previously booked band had backed out. While not normally a fan of that sort of music, Darla definitely had been impressed by the young man's fabulous tenor and his band's willingness to play cover songs.

But Pinky seemed perpetually short of cash despite his musical talent. And so he'd been an eager volunteer to train as a backup barista for the inevitable times Robert was ill or on vacation.

Robert gave her an eager nod. "I'll call him now. Even if he has any gigs those days, he wouldn't have to play until late at night."

Leaving him to finish cleaning up the coffee lounge and make his call to Pinky, Darla rejoined James downstairs to let him know what she'd decided.

"I see," her manager replied when she had explained the Pinky substitution. "A trial by fire, of sorts, for the young man."

"Exactly. I'd rather know whether or not he can handle the coffee bar on his own now, before Robert leaves town next week." Darla smiled. "I'm sure Pinky can do better than me. I can whip up a pot of your standard house brew, but I'm not much with the specialty drinks. I'll know for sure if Pinky's on board when we head out to the estate sale location tomorrow. Speaking of which . . ."

Her cell phone was chiming to alert her to an incoming text message. A quick check showed that the sender was Mary Ann.

"We're on for our road trip tomorrow," she told James as she read it and then typed a swift acknowledgment that included Jake. "I'll let Robert know as soon as he comes down."

"It appears that all is settled," James replied as he reached for his overcoat. "I presume you have no objection to my leaving a few minutes early? Good. Then I shall plan to see you again on Tuesday. Remember," he added as he reached the door, "do feel free to call or text me if you find any unusual volumes. Just do not, as they say, bust the budget."

"I'll be a smart shopper," she promised with a smile as he headed out.

A few minutes later, Robert and Hamlet trooped down the stairs together. Darla updated Robert on the plan for the next day, and the youth confirmed that Pinky had agreed to run the coffee lounge for the two days Robert would be out with the estate sale, in addition to covering his vacation days.

"Perfect. And don't worry about Roma being alone all day long while you're working the sale. James and I will take turns checking in on her." Then, lapsing into surrogate-mom mode, she added, "Now, go on home and don't stay out with your friends too late. I'll pick you up at nine along with Jake and Mary Ann."

She let him out the front door; then, with Hamlet supervising, she did the final closing routine and was back out in her private hallway a few minutes later.

"So, Hammy," she said as they climbed the stairs together, "got any ideas for something fun we can do tonight?"

But Hamlet had no suggestions, other than to give her an impatient *meow* as he reached the apartment door ahead of her, the wail signaling that it was way past his preferred time for supper. While Darla prepared his food, she recalled what Jake had said before about needing to find herself a decent guy and have a little grown-up fun for a change. Much as she was fond of Hamlet, spending all her evenings in with him didn't exactly constitute a social life.

But since the decent guy had yet to appear on her doorstep, Darla contented herself with some leftover chicken pot pie for supper and her favorite zombie television show for après-meal entertainment. She and Hamlet both retired to bed soon after, though Darla opted for a little quick reading before she went to sleep. Her copy of *The Marble Faun* was still lying on her nightstand, untouched since she'd not had time the night before to start paging through it.

"Let's give it a try," she told Hamlet, who had come to join her at the foot of the bed. She'd made her way through but a few pages, however, when she closed it with a groan.

"Well, Hammy," she told the cat, "James is going to think I'm a true hick, because I'm already about to give up on this book. Hawthorne spends the whole first chapter having his characters talk about statues of fauns and gladiators and picking on this young Italian guy who looks just like the faun. It's all very lovely and poetic, but it's about to put me to sleep. I guess the whole thing about how writers should start a story in the middle of the action wasn't the fashion back in the 1860s."

Hamlet, who had been lying with eyes closed and front paws hanging off the side of the comforter, gave what Darla was sure had to be a fake snore in response. She laughed. "So it's putting you to sleep, too, huh? Well, don't rat me out to James, okay? I'll give it another try tomorrow night."

Marking her place with a bookmark—James would have a stroke if she dared to dog-ear a page, no matter that she'd paid for the darned thing—she set the book back on her bedside table and flicked out the light. But as she lay back in the dark, she found herself childishly wishing she had a night light there in the room to dispel some of the darkness. For, much as she tried to forget it, Mr. Plinski's murderer was still at large somewhere in the city.

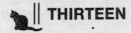

THIRTEEN

"SO, HOW DID I DO?" DARLA ANXIOUSLY ASKED.

It was Tuesday morning, the day after she, Jake, and Robert had helped Mary Ann with her estate sale prep at the house in Queens. In between customers, James had made a quick examination of the dusty box of used books she had acquired during what Mary Ann had cheerfully termed the "pre-sale" . . . though Jake had, with a grin, deemed it the "cherry-picking."

Her store manager peeled off the gloves he'd worn as he inspected the volumes and gave Darla a considering look.

"If this were an exam, I would say that you earned a solid B. And since I am feeling particularly generous today, I might even bump you to a B plus."

"Really? Great," she replied, more than a little pleased by what was, from James, high praise. "How much profit do you think we can make off of these?"

"That depends, of course, on how much you paid."

Darla told him the lot price that she and Mary Ann had settled on, and he nodded in approval.

"I suspect we should be able to average a one hundred percent markup across the board. This 1966 first edition of Julia Child's *Mastering the Art of French Cooking* is a good example. True, it is a thirteenth printing, but it still should sell for around one hundred eighty dollars. And I do like the little homey touch of the cut-out newspaper recipes tucked between a few of the pages," he added with a small smile.

Darla smiled back.

"That's one thing Mary Ann shared with me about books at estate sales," she replied. "She said to always leaf through the books, because people stick all sorts of things in them as bookmarks, or for safekeeping. Recipes, old letters, even money, sometimes. I found a couple of school pictures that looked like they were from the 1960s in one old paperback. I gave those to Mary Ann to return to the estate's executor. And another book had pressed pink flowers of some sort in them that someone had forgotten."

"And you will agree that is much better than some of the things our customers manage to leave on our shelves and in our books here," James said with a faint shudder of distaste.

Darla couldn't dispute that. Despite all of them keeping as close a watch as possible, at least once a week they found fast-food wrappers and empty plastic soda bottles stashed on shelves and—particularly in the children's section— bubble gum stuck on book covers and half-eaten fruit leathers stuck between pages.

"At any rate," he finished, "I would say that you had a successful first excursion into buying collectible books.

Speaking of which, how are you proceeding with *The Marble Faun*?"

"It was tough going the first couple of chapters," she admitted. "But I gave it another shot last night, and it started to grow on me. I mean, it doesn't have the pulse-pounding excitement of today's bestsellers, but I'm getting curious to see what happens next. Right, Hamlet?" she addressed the big black cat, who was double-checking James's work by sticking his nose into the box of books.

Hamlet raised his fuzzy face from the volumes and gave her a cool green look that said, *Your opinion, not mine.* Then, leaping off the counter, he flopped onto the floor and threw a hind leg over his shoulder as he commenced licking the base of his tail.

"Oops, guess Hammy didn't like the passages I read aloud to him, after all," Darla said with a chuckle at the cat's display of disdain. "But I even brought the book down here with me to read on my lunch break."

"Excellent. And once you have made your way through Hawthorne's oeuvre, I will be glad to recommend another nineteenth-century author to you."

Mildly alarmed at that last—an occasional dip into the classics was all well and good, but she wasn't prepared to turn her personal reading time into a mini college course—Darla simply nodded. At least James hadn't suggested she write a book report for him to grade!

James, however, was ready to change the subject. "How did Mary Ann hold up getting the estate sale put together?"

"Pretty well. We had to whip out the tissue box a few times, but overall she got through it fine. And I saw some pretty high-ticket items while I was there, so with luck she will make a nice percentage off it."

"I am pleased to hear that." Then, frowning a little, he added, "And should I presume Detective Reese has not phoned with any updates?"

Darla shook her head. "We're talking a total news blackout. Even Mary Ann hasn't heard anything. But I'm tempted to get hold of him and see if he can tell us *something*."

"Then here is your opportunity," James replied as the bells on the front door jingled. "It appears it will not be necessary to send the mountain to Muhammad."

Darla was just about to ask him what in the heck *that* meant, when she turned in the direction of the door and saw a grim-faced Reese stalking toward them.

Bad news, was her first thought. But before she could ask what had happened, he jerked a thumb toward the door and said, "Car's running. Hurry up and let's get going."

"Going? Where?'

Darla felt her stomach clench. Was she being brought in for more questioning about Mr. Plinski's death? Or maybe Reese needed her to identify a new suspect in a lineup. Whatever their destination, she had a feeling it wasn't going to end well for her.

And his answer proved her right.

"Today's Tuesday. Connie's got her alteration appointment over at the bridal place, remember? Jake bailed on us, so it's just you. I'll drop you broads off, but you'll have to hoof it back."

"But I didn't—"

"Hurry up. We're running late. Grab your stuff, and we'll meet you in the car."

Before Darla could finish her objection, Reese was already out the door again, bells jangling in protest at his hurried exit.

Darla turned a helpless look on James. "What the heck? I never said I'd go," she sputtered. "Maybe she assumed . . . I really don't want to . . . I mean, do I really have to suck it up and go?"

"Certainly not," James replied. "But rather than railing at cruel Fate, you can look at this as an opportunity to build a bit of goodwill with Detective Reese by way of his fiancée. And perhaps said goodwill may make him a bit more forthcoming regarding the whole Bernard situation."

"Maybe. But he can be pretty closemouthed when he wants to be. He'll probably talk about how revealing evidence is on a need-to-know basis, and that I don't really need to know."

Then, as her manager chuckled a bit at that, she went on, "Seriously, it's a beating doing anything with that woman. All that bragging and complaining can wear a person out . . . and I'm not talking about her being the tired one. If you'll remember, our first two outings weren't exactly a picnic, especially the second."

"Then perhaps your third excursion will be the lucky one," James reassured her. "And if I get too busy down here, Robert can always leave the coffee bar temporarily and lend a hand."

"You're supposed to tell me that you can't possibly spare me," Darla grumbled, even as she reached beneath the counter for her purse.

"Might as well take this with me, too," she added, pulling out her copy of *The Marble Faun* and sticking it in her bag. "At least I'll be able to get in some reading."

Grabbing her heavier coat off the rack and checking to make sure she had both scarf and gloves, she gave James a sour wave good-bye and headed out of the store.

Reese was waiting at the curb alongside his illegally parked sedan, looking like a presidential bodyguard ready to hustle her into the backseat of the vehicle. But before he opened the door, he stopped her with a hand to her arm.

"I really appreciate you coming along," he told her, sounding fractionally less impatient than before. "I know this whole situation with Mr. Plinski has been pretty tough on all of you, so it means a lot that you made the time to do this for Connie."

"Sure, I'm glad to," she responded, feeling a bit guilty for her small tirade to James a few moments earlier. In the scheme of things, what was an hour or so spent doing a favor for a friend? Or, rather, the fiancée of a friend? Still, she intended to collect on her part of the bargain she'd made with him . . . not that the detective actually knew anything about said bargain.

"Look, Reese," she said in a rush as he reached toward the car's door handle. "I haven't called or texted you since the other night with Jake, since I knew you were busy investigating Mr. Plinski's murder. But all of us are getting pretty nervous knowing that Mr. Plinski's murderer hasn't been caught yet. Can you tell me anything about what's going on?"

"No."

He opened the door and gestured her inside. Biting back her retort to that negative monosyllable, she climbed in and slid over so that she was behind the driver's seat.

As Reese closed the door after her, Connie spun around in her seat to look at her, her expression one of exaggerated relief.

"Oh, Darla, thank Gawd you can make it," she said with a pop of her gum for emphasis. "I was afraid maybe you'd forgotten after . . . well, you know. But I really need you there with me. I'm feeling real nervous now about going places alone, know what I mean?"

Darla felt a sudden surge of sympathy for her, since she'd dealt with similar anxiety after her own past encounter with violent death. While it was easy enough for someone to suggest that one simply get over it, she knew firsthand that the aftermath *could* be debilitating.

"I get it," Darla assured her. "It'll take some time, but that feeling will pass. And if it doesn't, well, I know Reese—er, Fi—will know someone you can talk to. But let's try to forget that for now and just concentrate on how great you're going to look in that dress."

By now, Reese had opened his door and slipped into the driver's seat. Connie flipped back around to face him, giving him a sly little pout.

"I *am* gonna look great in that dress," she told him. "Too bad you can't see it in person until I'm heading up the aisle to the altar."

"I'll take your word for it, Conn," he absently said as he signaled and pulled out into traffic. "You look good in anything, you know that."

The pout became a bit more genuine, but Connie apparently decided her fiancé had more important things on his mind than wedding dresses. Still, she did content herself with a quick aside—"Well, just wait 'til you see what I bought for our wedding night"—before settling in for the brief ride.

By the time they pulled up to Davina's Bridal a few short minutes later, Darla had decided to try breaking through the news blackout again. Since she was seated behind Reese, he opened her door first.

She scrambled out and let him shut the door again, then

said, "Look, I know this is an active investigation, you can't talk about it, blah, blah, blah . . . but, bottom line, this murder happened to all of us. Can't you tell me something about what's going on?"

"What's going on," Reese said as they walked around to Connie's side, "is that Mary Ann's boyfriend is still on my radar. I don't suppose you knew that Camden's wife died in an accident, and he just collected a nice little insurance settlement."

The merry widower!

Darla stared at Reese in alarm. Could Doug's theory have been right, after all? But then she remembered how Hodge had rushed down the stairs that night to protect Mary Ann against a seeming intruder. Surely that wasn't the work of a man plotting yet another murder. Still, it seemed that at least once a week she read a news story about a husband arranging an "accident" for his spouse, usually to collect on a convenient insurance policy.

"Are you saying you think Hodge had something to do with his wife's death?" she cautiously asked him.

Reese shrugged as he opened Connie's door for her. "Insurance company paid up, so I guess they didn't see any red flags. Is Mary Ann still seeing him, do you know?"

"Yeah, she's been seeing quite a bit of him."

She thought about adding, *and actually, so have Jake and I.* But she didn't want to embarrass either Hodge or Mary Ann, even indirectly, so she kept her mouth shut. Besides, if Reese still believed Hodge was guilty of murder, he'd be making sure that Mary Ann stayed far from the old man.

Connie, meanwhile, had climbed out of the sedan and was balancing in three-inch-high blue wedge ankle boots. Her designer purse was slung over one shoulder of her leopard-print jacket, and she cradled a fancy shopping bag in which Darla knew were her official heels to go with the wedding gown.

"We gotta go now," Connie told Reese. "Now, remember, you've got to pick us up when we're done."

"Text me when you're done, and if I can break free I'll swing by and get you girls. If not, just call for a car. Deal?"

"Deal," she echoed, leaning in to give him a loud smooch on the lips. Turning to Darla, she said, "We better hurry, before someone else tries to take our spot."

"Connie, go on in," Reese told her. "I need to talk to Darla a sec."

The other woman paused, and the look she turned on Darla was—if not exactly suspicious—questioning. Then, with a shrug, she said, "Fine, see you in there."

He waited until the shop door had closed after her before addressing Darla again.

"All right, I guess I owe you a little something," he conceded. "Let me see what I can tell you that's not going to come back and bite me. For starters, I did go through that whole security camera file you downloaded for me. Do you know that in the original two-hour window we looked at, we've got nineteen pedestrians caught on video? Twenty-four, if you count the ones who made the return trip. And that's not including you and Connie."

"That's a lot of people to eliminate from the list, I guess. Did anyone else have cameras filming the street?"

Reese shook his head as he leaned against his car door, muscular arms crossed over his broad chest, looking even more like a bodyguard.

"Nope. I checked the Plinskis' neighbor on the other side, but they don't have cameras, either. The guy across the street does, but the way his is angled, there's not much view past his sidewalk. But what I'm trying to get to is, when I ran through the whole twelve hours of video, I found something kind of interesting."

He paused a beat as Darla gave him an expectant look, and then finished, "I caught Mary Ann Plinski getting out of a hired car about seven that morning and heading toward her place."

"Wait, what?"

Darla stared at him, wondering what in the world could have caused the old woman to be traveling about the city at that time of the morning. And then it hit her. She scrambled a moment for the right words before finally blurting, "Are you trying to say you caught Mary Ann doing the walk of shame the same morning her brother was murdered?"

"Kind of looks like it," he replied, and to Darla's surprise he didn't look even faintly amused. "I haven't gotten the records from the car service back yet, but chances are she was picked up from Rodger Camden's place."

"Wow."

Though, of course, the revelation shouldn't have been that surprising, since she and Jake had already caught Mary Ann and Hodge in flagrante, as the old woman had put it. She added a silent *You go, girl!* And then it occurred to her that she probably owed Reese a bit of clarity on that last.

"Did Jake tell you that Hodge was at Mary Ann's Saturday night when we stopped by?"

"Yeah, she said it got interesting."

His dry tone told her that Jake had shared at least some of the gory details, sparing her having to tell him about their elderly friend's sex life. Then, since the conversation had started to get off track, she brought it back on line. "Maybe you can keep that part out of the official record. You know, so you don't embarrass her. But that's it? You didn't see any other suspicious people on the video?"

"I didn't say that."

With that small bombshell, he paused and glanced toward the door of Davina's. "You ought to get going. Connie will be waiting on you."

He straightened and started walking back around to the driver's side. Darla shot him an incredulous look. "Hold up. You can't just hint that there's something else going on and then drop the subject. Who's this other suspicious person?"

Reese halted near the front of his sedan and turned. Whipping off his sunglasses, he fixed her with a cool blue gaze that sent tingles through her . . . and not the good kind.

"Need-to-know basis, Red. This is still an active police investigation."

"I understand that. And, Reese, I really need to know."

She held his gaze for a few moments. Finally, he shook his head and strode back to her so they were standing eye to eye . . . or, rather, eye to chest.

"I'm going to tell you this only because I told you too much already," he said, lowering his voice even though there were no passersby to listen in. "What I'm about to say isn't for public consumption. That means no blabbing to Jake or to James or to Robert. Or to the butcher down the street, or to the guy at the newsstand. And, especially, you can't breathe a word to Mary Ann. Got it?"

"Got it," was her uneasy reply. Maybe she *didn't* want to know . . . especially not if she couldn't talk about it with someone. *Too late now.*

"You already know this part. Mary Ann's official statement was that she left her place around nine the morning her brother was murdered to talk with the estate executor in Queens."

Darla nodded.

"Well, I did the math on the trip," he continued. "If she

left around nine, with the traffic that morning she'd have had about a forty-five-minute trip. Up and back, that's an hour and a half. You made the same trip yesterday. Am I right?"

"Pretty close," she conceded.

Trying to follow what she assumed was Reese's logic, she did the math herself. Since Mary Ann had been back at Bygone Days a little after eleven, that would have left the old woman a thirty-minute window to discuss the whole estate sale shebang with the executor.

Seemingly reading her thoughts, the detective said, "A half-hour meeting is pretty short for a project like that."

"But it's not like this is her first rodeo—her first time handling an estate sale." She hurriedly translated from the Texanism to Standard English when he gave her a questioning look. "If they'd already done a lot of the work over the phone and by email, maybe that's all she needed with the guy."

"Maybe. But it kinda bugged me that she was on such a tight schedule, on that day of all days. Perfect timing, so to speak."

Darla felt her stomach clench as she realized in a flash just what he was implying. But she was going to make him say it out loud.

"What are you getting at? Mary Ann got home early in the morning after a night out, took a shower and got changed, and left again at nine, while Mr. Plinski was still alive. I still don't see what's so suspicious."

"Darla, I'm a cop. I'm supposed to be suspicious, even when we're talking about a seventy-five-year-old, really nice lady who I admire a lot. So I got hold of the executor to make sure that she really did meet him. And the guy confirmed she was there."

Darla heaved a sigh. *She'd been there. Who cared about the timetable?*

But relief had barely flashed through her when he added, "The problem is, she was there on Thursday morning, not Friday morning.

"Darla, Mary Ann lied about where she was the morning of her brother's murder."

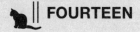 **FOURTEEN**

"HEY, DARLA," CONNIE CALLED FROM THE DOOR OF THE bridal shop, "you coming in, or you gonna stand there yakking with my fiancé all day? Hurry, they're bringing out the dress."

Darla, meanwhile, gave Reese a despairing shake of her head.

"I can't believe Mary Ann, of all people, lied. I know there has to be a good reason she did that, and I know it had nothing to do with Mr. Plinski. But if she didn't go meet the executor in Queens, where was she that morning?"

"That's what I'm going to find out."

He put his hands on her shoulders, and for a fleeting moment she thought he would pull her in for a hug. Instead, he spun her about and gave her a gentle shove forward.

"Go help Connie. I'll try to stop by the bookstore later today so we can talk again. Remember," he added as she stumbled toward the door where Connie waited, "not a word to anyone."

Connie shot her a suspicious look as Reese got into his car and pulled out into traffic. "I heard that. What did he mean, not a word to anyone?" Her suspicious squint deepened. "Is something going on between you two?"

"Of course not," Darla replied, managing a smile and a slight laugh. Then, thinking quickly, she lowered her voice and said, "Don't tell him I told you, but he's planning a little something special for the engagement party on Saturday, and he was getting my opinion on it."

"O-o-o-oh."

Her squint turned into a wide-eyed smile. "But what— oh, never mind, it's more fun if it's a surprise. I promise, I won't say anything. And sorry for thinking anything bad about you. Like I said, it's just nerves."

"No need to apologize . . . and I'm totally on board with the nerves thing. Come on, let's get this dress squared away."

They went inside the bridal shop to be greeted by an unctuous Daniel, dressed in his same uniform of black tuxedo pants and pleated white shirt. Taking Connie by one arm and holding the other out to Darla, he escorted them from the front desk and out onto the showroom floor.

They halted at the same mirrored spot where they'd gathered the first time while Connie did her try-ons.

The Gown, as Darla found herself thinking about it, was displayed on the platform before the trifold mirror, hanging from a cute vintage-looking mannequin made of white wire. Connie sighed audibly as she halted before it.

"It's so gorgeous. Daniel, you're such a genius, picking out the perfect gown for me."

"You are too kind, my dear," he replied with a grin and a stagey little bow that sent a faint wafting of body spray their way. "Of course, it helps when the bride-to-be is drop-dead gorgeous herself."

"Oh, Daniel."

She giggled, smacked her gum, and gave him a playful little "stop that" flick of her hand before getting down to business. "Okay, so what are we gonna do to make this dress even more perfect?"

"We'll need to take it in a couple of places here, and here"—he hopped onto the platform and pinched a bit of the gown's fabric—"and maybe let it out just a tad here so your derriere is perfectly highlighted. And I thought we could make a slight alteration to the neckline. Oh, you did remember to bring your wedding shoes with you, didn't you? Good."

While he and Connie discussed nips and tucks of the fabric variety, Darla slipped to one side and took her familiar seat on the wicker settee. Still reeling from Reese's revelation about Mary Ann, she shut her eyes. Surely once she was questioned by the detective, the old woman would confess some logical if possibly embarrassing reason to explain the deliberate deception.

But what if there was no logical explanation except one . . . an explanation that Darla couldn't even begin to entertain?

Biting back a groan, she reached into her bag and pulled out her copy of *The Marble Faun* as a distraction. But as she flipped over to the page where her bookmark lay, it occurred to her that maybe this wasn't the best of stories to be reading, under the circumstances.

For, rather than being simply an overblown travelogue of mid-nineteenth-century Italy, the book had turned out to be a treatise on murder and guilt coupled with increasingly silly references to the male ingénue character possibly having pointed little faun ears. Still, there was something strangely compelling about the morality tale, so that despite herself she had kept on reading the night before. She had reached the midway point where one of the story's unsavory characters had met a poetic death off a towering precipice. And said murder had been witnessed not only by the killer and his morally responsible accomplice but by an innocent bystander.

Who knows, maybe Hawthorne does have some decent advice for situations like mine, she thought as she resumed reading.

Today, however, the florid tale couldn't hold her attention. She found herself glancing up every few paragraphs to see what Connie and Daniel were doing. Finally, with a flourish, the bridal shop owner stepped back off the platform and exclaimed, "*Fini!* What do you think?"

He and Connie circled around the platform wearing twin expressions of concentration as they pointed and muttered. For her part, Darla couldn't tell much difference, other than the fact that the neckline appeared a bit more rounded off than before. But the changes apparently satisfied the other two, for Daniel clapped his hands.

"Very well, let's try the gown on you and see how it fits."

With much rustling of fabric, he and his assistant carefully removed the gown from the dress form. Then, with Connie trailing after them, the trio set off for the changing room. Darla sighed and opened her book again. The second time proved a bit more productive, so she was firmly back into the story when a voice from above her said, "Not much fun being the one left sitting around, is it?"

Startled, Darla glanced up to see Daniel's half brother, Vinnie, looming above her. In one well-manicured hand he held a napkin-wrapped, open champagne bottle and, in the other, a champagne glass.

"Looks like they forgot to give you the old Davina's treatment," he said as he poured out the sparkling wine and then handed her the flute. "I can get you some petits fours or some cheese puff things, too, if you want."

"Just champagne is fine."

She warily took the glass, recalling as she did so his previous tirades there in the store . . . the one he'd pulled in front of her and the one she'd witnessed through the shop window afterward. The last thing she wanted was to be alone with the guy if he went off for some reason again. And he did appear on edge, features drawn and eyes ringed with purplish circles. Must have been a trying week in the bridal biz . . . but probably nothing compared to her past few days!

Without actually meaning to, she finished off the champagne in a single long swallow. "Wow," she said as she lowered the glass, "guess I needed that more than I thought."

"I know how that goes," he answered, refilling her flute and then settling on the same wicker love seat where Jake had sat the last time. Raising the half-full bottle, he added, "Believe me, if it weren't working hours, I'd be drinking, too."

Though something about his haggard demeanor made her think he'd been doing plenty of imbibing after hours to make up for it. Just as she began feeling slightly uncomfortable with the unexpected familiarity, he frowned at her. "Do I know you?"

"I was in here last week with my friend Jake, while Connie was trying on dresses."

"No, that's not it. Do you live somewhere here in the neighborhood?"

"Actually, I'm the owner of Pettistone's Fine Books. The bookstore is only a few blocks from here."

Dismissing an uncomfortable feeling—he likely was simply trolling for a friendly ear—she put down her glass on the side table and dug into her oversized purse. Pulling out a business card, she explained, "We sell new books, and collectible and rare volumes, and book-related gifts. You should stop by sometime."

"Sure."

He studied the business card, lips pursed, and the creepy feeling resurfaced. She'd begun to wonder if she was going to have to request some cheese puff things to get rid of him, when he stood and tucked the card into his pocket.

"Well, I'll leave you to it. Stock to order, brides to make cry . . ."

"Books to read," Darla cheerfully finished for him, raising the book from her lap by way of illustration and then proceeding to do just that.

She was halfway through the next page when she realized the man was still standing there. Frowning a little, she looked up from her reading to find his intent gaze fixed on her . . . or, rather on the book she held.

"I'm sorry," she said, "was there something else?"

Vinnie jerked his hollow-eyed gaze up to meet hers and took a step back, as if she'd startled him. "Oh, I didn't mean to be rude. I was curious about that book you're reading. It looks pretty vintage. Where did you find it?"

"At my store. It came in with some other books we bought at an estate sale." When he made no reply to that, she tried again. "So, do you like old books?"

"Some of them," he said with a shrug. "I suppose this one just struck my fancy. Would you mind if I took a closer look at it?"

For some reason, her first impulse was to clutch the book to her chest and invoke *The Hobbit* with a Gollum-like hissing of *My precious!* But since he seemed sincere in his request—and because she didn't want to scare off a potential rare-book customer—she closed it and handed it over.

He set down the champagne bottle with a clatter and reached for the book. Gently, he opened its front cover, and she saw him nod.

"The endpapers are lovely, aren't they?" she agreed. "And the title page is simply gorgeous. Of course, it's not that valuable for all that it's pretty old. But it makes for a nice book to display on the shelf."

While she was speaking, he was leafing through the pages. *Sorry, I already looked through it for money and clipped recipes*, she thought with an inner chuckle. Then he closed the book with a sharp clap that made her jump and said, "I know someone who'd really like this as a gift. How much would it be?"

"Actually, that's my personal copy, so—"

"But would you sell it to me? I can give you a couple of hundred bucks for it."

She hesitated as the creepy feeling returned, full-blown. James had shared many tales of his more eccentric book-collecting customers, but this was the first time she'd encountered one herself. Though Vinnie the bridal shop owner was obviously no true collector, since he had no clue of this book's value. Besides which, she had grown rather attached to the charming little volume and didn't particularly care to sell it, even for a nice profit.

"We have an 1871 edition at the store that's much more valuable than my copy," she offered by way of compromise. "Volumes one and two in a nice slipcase. You could get it for that same price."

He shook his head. "I already . . . I mean, I like this version. Are you sure you won't sell it?" He reached into his pocket. "I can give you the money now. Like they say, cash in hand."

Cash in hand?

Wasn't that what James had said his *Marble Faun* buyer—the one who'd stomped out in a fury over the wrong volume—had said? She gave Vinnie another swift, covert look. Bundle him in a full-length coat and pull a ski cap down over his forehead and ears, and he could quite possibly be BookBuyer75.

But if he was, why wouldn't he simply admit that he'd been at their store searching out a copy of that same book a few days earlier? And why was he set on this exact volume?

"Tell you what," Darla said with a bright smile. "Let me think about it the rest of the day, and if I decide to sell it for two hundred dollars, I'll get in touch with you. Can you give me your number?"

He nodded and pulled a slightly crumpled business card from his pocket, which he handed to her.

"Thank you," she told him as she took it, and then she put out her other hand.

For an instant, she thought that *he* was going to do the "my precious" routine himself, for the book was still clutched to his pleated shirtfront. But after the merest hint of hesitation, he handed the volume back to her and smiled.

"I hope you do call me. I know my friend would really like the book. But even if you don't, maybe I'll stop by your store anyhow." He looked again at the business card she'd given him. "I think I know where this is. You're right next to the antiques store where—"

He broke off, expression embarrassed, and Darla knew without asking what he was going to say. She nodded. "Yes, unfortunately, that's us."

"Say, do you rent out any space in your building?"

At her quizzical look at this seeming non sequitur, he added, "I'm asking for that same friend. He's going to need some local square footage, and your place looked pretty nice from the outside. Or maybe you're like some of the other retailers and live over your own shop?"

"The top-floor apartment is mine," she told him, not exactly comfortable with divulging her living arrangements but wanting to make certain he knew that there weren't any "For Rent" signs hanging in her windows. "And my friend Jake leases the garden apartment. So, sorry, no room at the inn."

"That's okay. I'll tell him to keep looking." Picking up the half-empty champagne bottle again, Vinnie turned and started toward the front desk, leaving her blessedly alone with Mr. Hawthorne's work.

Really, really strange, she thought as she tucked the business card into her book. She'd have to tell James all about this odd encounter. Maybe he could figure out a reason why the man seemed so fixated on acquiring that particular volume.

But she'd barely had time for a sip from her refilled glass when Daniel and Connie—the latter in a flurry of white satin—came marching back in.

"What do you think, Darla?" the woman asked in excitement as, with Daniel's help, she scrambled onto the platform.

Darla stood to take a better look while the bridal shop owner did the usual rearranging and fluffing of the gown. Even though she'd seen Daniel's pinning and tucking routine earlier, now that Connie was wearing the dress, she couldn't remember what he'd fixed. But she could see a subtle if definite difference in the way the gown now hung, as if it had been custom-made for Connie.

"It's perfect," she told the other woman as Daniel stepped

aside to let Connie see the full effect. "Really, it's fabulous. Here, let me get a picture."

She pulled out her smartphone and took a few quick shots while Connie posed and preened.

"Just don't send any of those to Fi," the woman warned, smile bright as the shiny white satin of the dress. "Remember how he got all superstitious about it last time?"

"I won't," Darla promised. "I'll send all the pictures to you."

Daniel, meanwhile, stood with hands clasped and looking almost as radiant as the bride-to-be.

"Truly stunning," he said, and Darla suspected he meant his modifications to the dress as much as Connie. "I don't think we need to make another adjustment. Let's get that off you now—which is what your new husband will be saying when he sees it—and we'll get it queued up so the alterations can be finished by next week. We'll need one last fitting after that, and then the next time you wear the dress, you'll be saying *I do.*"

"Oooh, I can't wait!" she squealed.

Daniel nodded and then gestured to Liz, who was lurking near the dressing room, to lend a hand. As the two headed toward the back, Daniel turned to Darla. "Weddings make everything nicer, don't you think?"

"Well, they make a great excuse for a party," she agreed.

He smiled a little at that, and then his cheery expression faded. "I hate to bring up something unpleasant, but I read all the news accounts of the recent murder here in our very own neighborhood. That happened near your bookstore, didn't it?"

Darla sighed and nodded. "The victim was my next-door neighbor. Mr. Plinski was a truly lovely old gentleman. We're all horrified by what happened."

"As were my brother and me." The bridal shop owner

shook his head. "You don't expect something like this in a pleasant community like ours. Do you know, is there any hope of solving the case?"

"I hope so. Unfortunately, I believe the police are looking at it as a random crime."

Although one cop seems to think it was an inside job, she mentally qualified.

Daniel's frown deepened.

"Really? I suppose I always thought of guns and knives as the weapons of choice in a random murder, not silly embroidered pillows," he observed. "But I think we should be relieved that's what it is turning out to be. Because if it was random, what are the chances of it happening again?"

"Not very good, I hope," she said, and took a large swig of her bubbly. Maybe she should have asked Vinnie to leave the half-empty champagne bottle behind.

Sadly shaking his head, Daniel left her to attend to another customer who had just walked in. Darla contemplated her book again, then stuffed it back inside her purse. In a contest between book and champagne, the latter was going to win this round.

By the time Darla had sipped her way through the second glass, Connie had changed back into her street clothes and blue heels. As before, she had her leopard-print coat over one arm, and purse and shoes over the other.

"I texted Fi," she said with a pout, "and he said he's still tied up. But he said if we want to walk, he can meet us over at the deli by your bookstore as soon as he's done, and he'll buy us a late lunch."

"Might as well. By the time a car shows up, we'd almost be there, anyhow." And besides, she added to herself, the crisp air would help blow the champagne cobwebs from her brain.

Once Connie had made arrangements for her final fitting,

the two headed out into the chilly afternoon. As they started down the sidewalk, Darla gave the other woman an admiring look. "I don't see how you do it, hiking for miles in shoes like that. Don't your feet kill you wearing them?"

"No, never. Of course, I've been wearing heels like this since I was twelve."

She grimaced a little, and added, "The only problem is, I can't wear flats like yours anymore, and it hurts when I go barefoot. The doctor says I have a shortened Achilles tendon. Fi says I'm like the girl in the movie who can't run when she's being chased. He laughs and says I'd better hope I'm never chased by zombies, because I'll end up eaten."

And then, quite unexpectedly, she burst into tears.

"Connie, what's wrong?"

Connie didn't answer. Instead, while Darla stood helplessly by, the other woman began pawing through her purse. By the time she dragged out a handful of tissues, the volume of her bawling had reached epic proportions, so that a few passersby stared at her in alarm.

More than a little concerned now herself, Darla took Connie by the arm. Vinnie and his traveling bottle of champagne would have come in handy right about then, she told herself. But she spied the second best thing . . . a narrow concrete bench stationed just outside a nearby trendy children's boutique. Darla steered the weeping woman in that direction, plopping her down onto the cold, hard seat and then joining her there.

With luck, she told herself, her hindquarters wouldn't freeze before the teary storm subsided.

A few moments later, when it seemed the woman was beginning to regain her composure, she gently said, "Connie, you know Reese was kidding with you. You know he'd never let anything happen to you."

"Yeah, yeah, I know," she half said, half wailed through the flurry of tissues she held to her face.

"Then what are you so upset about?"

Connie snuffled a minute longer into the tissues, which by now had pretty well dissolved into a soggy wad. When she finally raised her face again, her mascara had run half-way down her cheeks, so that she looked like one of Robert's goth friends after a particularly rowdy night.

Shaking her head, Darla dug into her own bag and found some clean fast-food napkins and a packaged wet wipe. She used the latter to clean the worst of the mascara streaks off Connie's cheeks and then handed her the paper napkins.

"All right, now take a couple of deep breaths, and maybe you can tell me what's really wrong."

Connie gave a final snuffle and did the breathing thing, and then turned to Darla with a watery smile. "Oh, Darla, you're so nice to me, and you're not even my friend. I mean, you're my friend, but a different kind of friend. Not like the girls I grew up with."

"Thanks . . . I think," was Darla's wry reply, though she smiled, too. "Now, what's wrong? Are you still upset about what happened to Mr. Plinski?"

"No. I mean, of course I'm upset, but that's not what's wrong." She twisted the paper napkins into a tortured knot, then said, "If I tell you something, will you swear you won't tell anyone else?"

"I swear."

Connie pursed her red-lipsticked lips as if still debating whether to confess. Then, finally, she blurted, "I love Fi. I really do. But I kind of think I don't want to get married to him anymore."

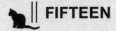 **FIFTEEN**

"YOU DON'T WANT TO MARRY REESE?" DARLA ASKED IN confusion. "Why in the world not?"

Connie shook her head. "It's not that I don't want to get married to him, but I'm thinking maybe it's not such a good idea. I mean, he's always busy, or having to leave places early, or get there late. It's like I can't depend on him."

"But he's a cop," Darla reminded her. "Being busy, or early, or late all comes with the job. You knew that when you started dating him, didn't you?"

"Yeah."

"Then, if you love him, you put on your big-girl panties and deal with it, right? Forget the times you're disappointed and concentrate on all the positive things about being the future Mrs. Fiorello Reese."

Connie gave a small smile at that last. Then the flicker of amusement faded, and she fell silent again as she began tearing the paper napkins into strips.

Finally in a small voice, she said, "I can do that. And I understand that he's a cop. I got a couple of cousins and an uncle who are all cops. I guess I really didn't think about it before, but when I saw that dead guy in the store the other day, I got scared. I mean, what if someone murdered Fi. I-I wouldn't know what to do."

Darla caught a breath. Of course, that would be something she would worry about. Anybody who read the papers or watched the news would know that an officer dying in the line of duty was always a possibility—seemingly more so these past months. But she'd looked up the statistics once herself, and found to her surprise that being a cop was far from the most dangerous job there was.

She told Connie as much, adding, "And even if it were the riskiest job on the list, that's not a good reason not to marry him. He could be a nine-to-five guy working a nice office job and still get T-boned by a semi on his way home from work one day. You never know what life is going to hand you, and nobody gets any guarantees."

Connie thought about that for a moment and then slowly nodded.

"You know, you're right. He could be a construction guy and fall off a building, or a longshoreman and get squished by one of those giant cargo containers. Or a high school principal and get shanked by some punk kid. Or—"

"I get the picture." Darla dryly cut her short. "So, do you think you can put aside your fear and go ahead with the wedding? Because, if not, I've got a party to cancel on Saturday."

Connie laughed outright at that. "Darla, you are so funny. Don't worry, you don't need to cancel the party. If I did, Ma would kill me, anyhow, because that would be two dresses down the tubes."

"Well, I'm glad that's settled," Darla said as she stood and gingerly rubbed her half-frozen rear end. "Now, let's get to the deli before I turn into a complete icicle."

But, as it turned out, neither was in any danger of succumbing to the weather. They had walked but another block when they heard the sharp blat of a car horn, and Reese pulled up alongside them.

"Change of plans," he called through the open window. "Hop on in."

"I thought there was a law against nonemergency honking in this town," Darla said with a sly smile as she slid into the backseat.

Reese blandly met her gaze in the rearview mirror. "Yeah, well, go tell a cop." To Connie, he said, "Sorry, babe. I gotta drop Darla off at her place and take you to your mom's. So it's a rain check on lunch."

Connie opened her mouth to protest; but then, apparently thinking better of it, she clamped her lips shut again.

Darla gave her a mental nod of approval. Aloud, she lightly said, "Anything we need to know?"

Reese shot her another look in the mirror, but all he said was, "Active police investigation. You know the drill."

Right. Need-to-know basis.

Trying to be a good example to Connie, Darla bit her lip for the couple of minutes that it took to reach her bookstore. Once they pulled up in front of her stoop, however, she raised a bent little finger and said, "Reese, before I get out of the car, I want your pinky swear that you're going to be at the engagement party on Saturday . . . no ifs, ands, or buts."

"Pinky swear? Seriously?" He turned in his seat and looked at her from over the top of his mirrored sunglasses. "That kind of stuff's for teenage girls."

Connie snorted and gave her gum a smack. "Yeah, well, you could do like they do in the movies. You know, slice your palms with a hunting knife and then slap them together in a big old macho handshake. Or spit in your hands and shake. Or—"

"How about I just tell Darla that I've got the day off and I'll be there . . . no pinkies or spit or blood necessary?"

"Works for me," Darla told him. To Connie, she said, "I'll email you the pictures."

She hopped out and hurried up the steps into the bookstore, only to be greeted by what sounded like some DEF-CON 1 alert.

"What in the world? James! Robert! What's going on?" she demanded, rushing toward the back of the store where the piercing sound seemed to be originating, along with a definitely chilly breeze.

Sure enough, the door to her courtyard was open, and both James and Robert stood there peering out. At her approach, they turned, and Robert exclaimed in an excited voice, "We got her, Ms. P.! We captured the mystery cat!"

"What did you do, catch her in a leg snare?" Darla facetiously asked as she peered out into the courtyard as well.

Sylvie—Robert's friend from the pet rescue group—was crouched over a large wire cage from which the high-pitched keening originated. Managing to hear Darla's question despite the literal caterwauling, Sylvie stood and waved.

Slim and pert, with shoulder-length black hair currently topped by a bulky multihued ski cap, the young woman was a part-time college student who worked with her mother's animal rescue group when she wasn't busy with her studies. Sylvie had been by the bookstore several times, and not only on animal rescue missions.

Darla smiled to herself. As far as she knew, Sylvie and

Robert were just good friends, having bonded over their mutual love of animals. But Darla had noticed the way her young barista watched the girl when the pair were together, and she suspected that there might be a budding romance . . . at least on Robert's part.

"Hi, Ms. Pettistone," the girl called as Darla waved back. "This was an easy one. We just put an open can of some really stinky cat food in the trap, and she ran right in."

By now, the high-pitched cries had begun to abate somewhat, so Darla went over to take a look at the no-longer-fugitive feline.

"Yep, that's her," she confirmed as she bent over the cage. A pair of emerald green eyes the same shade as Hamlet's stared back at her. "Robert says you'll take her to the vet to have her scanned for a chip and checked out to see if she's healthy?"

"Right. I didn't think we'd catch her this fast, so I need to call my mom and tell her to head on back to get us."

"Well, in the meantime, we can wrap the cage with some blankets to keep her snug in there, and Robert can whip you up a nice hot latte or whatever you want while you're waiting. Robert," she called back to the youth, "there are a couple of moving blankets up in the storeroom if you want to get them for Sylvie."

"Sure, Ms. P."

While Robert hurried to comply, Darla left the girl in charge of the captured kitty and followed James back inside, closing the door after her.

"So I thought *I* was going to have all the excitement," she told her manager with a smile. "I wonder what Hamlet thinks of all this."

"Hamlet has made himself scarce throughout the proceedings," James replied. "And I believe that his strategy was the correct one. My ears are still ringing from our captive's protests."

"Well, it's definitely all for the best. The cat will end up in a safe, loving home and Hamlet won't have to worry about a usurper anymore."

"So how did your mission work out?" James asked as they reached the front counter. "Were you able to learn anything from Detective Reese about Bernard's case?"

Darla set her bag near the register and shrugged out of her coat.

"He basically did the old need-to-know routine, like I predicted, said it was still an active investigation." She hesitated, choosing her words carefully, and then added, "He learned something rather disturbing about one of the witnesses, but that's all I can say since he swore me to silence."

James nodded. "Understood. For all that, I think we must take comfort in the fact that Detective Reese is good at his job. I have every confidence that he will unravel this terrible crime and bring our friend justice. And Ms. Capello's dress adventures went well?"

Darla snorted. "The dress fitting part went fine. But something pretty strange happened at the bridal shop that might interest you. I think I know who BookBuyer75 is."

She hurriedly hung up her coat, smiling as she saw Robert clomping down the stairs with moving blankets tucked under his arm. While he dashed past her, she returned to the register and pulled her copy of *The Marble Faun* out of her purse, sticking the latter beneath the counter and the former atop it.

"While I was waiting for Connie during the fitting, one of the shop's owners sat down with me. His name is Vinnie, and he and his half brother, Daniel, own the place. He saw what I was reading and wanted a closer look at the book. Then he offered to buy it for two hundred dollars."

"Interesting." With a gesture at the volume, he added, "And, obviously, since it is still here with us, you did not accept the offer."

"Well, like I told you, I've gotten pretty fond of it," she countered with a wry smile. "Anyhow, I mentioned the 1871 set he could have for that same price, but he wasn't going for it. I think he started to say he'd already seen it, but he caught himself in time. He claimed he wanted this particular edition as a gift for a friend," she ended, giving that last word air quotes.

"But you only saw my buyer from a distance. Are you are sure this Vinnie person is he?"

She nodded.

"Pretty sure. He even used the same phrase you said he told you—*cash in hand*. Besides, it would be too much of a coincidence for him to be homing in on the exact same book. And he did say he thought he knew me, though he swore he'd never been to our store before. So we exchanged cards, and I told him that if I changed my mind about selling, I'd give him a call."

Then she frowned. "And that wasn't the only odd thing. He started asking about real estate and wanted to know if I had space to lease in the building and did I live here. He said he had a friend who was starting up a business and needed a place."

"Probably the same friend whom he wished to gift with a copy of *The Marble Faun*," James absently replied as he bent over the computer keyboard and started punching keys.

Then, after a few mouse clicks, he said, "Aha. I have found the website for Davina's Bridal, where the owners have thoughtfully posted their pictures on the 'About Us' page. And this"—he pointed to an untitled headshot that showed a slightly beefier, happier version of Vinnie—"appears to be the gentleman with whom I recently dealt. Although the person in the second photograph does look surprisingly like him."

"That would be his half brother, Daniel, the guy who sold Connie her dress," Darla confirmed as she looked over James's shoulder. "So at least that mystery is solved. But I have to say, I'm dying to know why he wants this book so badly."

While they were staring at the computer screen, Hamlet had returned from wherever he'd taken refuge during the "mystery cat" incident. Now, he leaped up onto the counter. But whether by design or accident, the brawny feline slid right into the Hawthorne volume and sent it flying off the countertop onto the floor behind the register.

"Hamlet," she scolded him, "careful! That's my book."

As she bent to retrieve it, she saw that the impact had jostled loose Vinnie's business card from its pages, so that the small rectangle of white cardboard fluttered to the ground almost at James's feet. The store manager picked it up.

"Darla," he said in a considering voice as she set her book back on the counter, "did you happen to look closely at this card?"

"No, I just stuck it in the book. Why?"

James moved over to where the volume once again lay on the countertop. Fortunately, since the area behind the counter was carpeted, the old book had suffered no damage. He gently flipped open its front cover and laid the business card atop the pasted-down endpaper. "Do you notice anything interesting?"

"You're kidding," Darla gasped as she took a look. He'd

laid the card just below the faintly lettered name of the previous owner, one V. Modello. The printed name on the business card underneath read, in embossed black script, *Vincent Modello.*

"I had no clue what his last name was. So it was Vinnie's book all along?"

James shrugged. "Perhaps, though I would say it was more likely that it belonged to a parent or grandparent with the same first initial as he. And chances are he's been checking with all the used-book dealers and online auction houses looking for this particular volume, perhaps for some time now."

"But why be so mysterious about it? If I were Vinnie and I'd seen me with the book, I would have told me, *Hey, this belonged to my dearly departed relative, do you mind if I buy it off you?* And of course, I would have said yes to that."

"An interesting point. I rather think your first instinct was correct. I suggest that you hold on to the book for a while, and I shall do some more research on this edition."

"Right. And if he calls, I'll let it go to voice mail. Who knows, maybe this particular *Faun* is worth a lot more than two hundred dollars!"

SEVERAL HOURS LATER, WITH THE BOOKSTORE LONG SINCE CLOSED AND she and Hamlet well-fed, Darla settled on the couch with her copy of *The Marble Faun.*

"We're going to solve this mystery," she told the cat, who was lounging on the sofa back. "Let's go through the pages again first, in case we missed something stuck in them. Or maybe there's an underlined paragraph that will give us a clue."

For the next several minutes, she paged through the old

volume one leaf at a time looking for something out of the ordinary. Once, she was certain she'd found a secret code in pencil on one page, and obviously written by the same person who'd inscribed his or her name on the endpaper. But a quick online search revealed that the letters "akshard hamdelhi" faintly lettered beneath the phrase "Carrara quarries" referred to Akshardham, a Hindu temple in New Delhi built in the twenty-first century.

"Someone liked either temples or marble," she muttered to Hamlet, "but unless this is a clue to a valuable marble sculpture from India, I think it's a dead end."

She flipped through a few more pages, and then her cell phone abruptly rang. Leaving the book on the sofa, she rushed over to her desk, where the phone was charging, and checked the caller ID.

Jake.

"Hi, what's up?" she asked as she hit the green button.

"Just being a nosy neighbor," the PI replied. "Flip off your living room light and go take a look out your front window."

"What? Why?"

Not waiting for Jake's answer, she hurriedly shut the light off and then eased her way over to the window in question. Then, keeping to one side like she was a cowboy trying to avoid a shootout, she flipped the curtain a little and squinted through the darkness to the street below.

"See anything?" came Jake's voice in her ear.

Darla squinted a moment longer. "Not from here. The sidewalk looks empty. Why, what did *you* see?"

"Well, I snuck out for a quick smoke—don't say anything, it's only the second cigarette this week—when I noticed some guy had beat me to it. He was leaning against that fancy metal trash can puffing away and looking up at your place."

Smoking next to the trash can. Just like the night before Bernard's murder!

Darla shivered. "Did you get a good enough look at him to identify him?"

"No. Since I was walking up my steps, I saw him before he saw me, but I was looking through the wrought iron, and he was pretty well bundled up. I couldn't call from where I was standing, because he'd hear me, so I went back inside again to call you. Maybe he heard my door close, and it scared him off. It's probably not anything, but I thought I should let you know."

Darla took a steadying breath.

"Actually, it might be something," she replied. "I saw something—someone—doing the same thing out there the night before Mr. Plinski's murder. I didn't tell you or Reese, because it didn't seem like anything, but now I'm not so sure. If you want to come up, I—Hamlet, no!"

She had turned from the window in time to see the cat pounce on her book, kicking open the front cover as he did so with his big back feet. And then, to Darla's horror, he began clawing at the pretty vine-and-leaf-design endpapers.

"No! Hamlet, stop!" she shrieked again. And then, "Jake, I'll call you back."

Not waiting for her friend's reply, she ended the call and rushed over to the sofa. By that point, Hamlet had seemingly exorcised whatever wild hair had gotten hold of him and was now sitting placidly on the sofa's arm. Shooting him an outraged look, Darla carefully picked up the abused book to examine it for actual damage.

To her surprise, it seemed that the book had suffered no

major harm after all, except for the spot where one corner of the glued endpaper had come up.

"Hamlet, whatever possessed you to do that?" she demanded as she examined the endpaper more closely. "You know better than to tear up a book. You've always been so good around the stock, and—oh!"

She looked up from the book to the cat, who was watching her with interest. "You weren't trying to rip it up, were you?" she slowly asked. "You were trying to show me something."

With that, she carried the book over to her desk and switched on her task light. Sure enough, beneath the lifted edge of the endpaper she spied what looked like a second bit of paper. Hadn't James said something about the volume's endpapers not being original when he'd first estimated its value?

Frowning, she reached into her desk drawer for the flat, almost knife-sharp letter opener she had there. Then, carefully, she slipped the opener's blade under the loose section of paper and began to slowly work the glued edge.

It was a tedious process as she took care not to damage either the book or the endpaper. From what little she knew of book repair—mostly gleaned from conversations with James—whatever glue had been used did not seem to be any of the traditional bookbinder's animal-based glue. Definitely an amateur job, even if quite neatly done. After about fifteen minutes, she'd slit open an entire edge, so that the paper beneath was clearly visible.

"Keep your paws crossed, Hammy," she called back to the cat, who'd decided his part was done and was holding down the sofa once again.

She tilted the book so that the hidden paper slid a bit toward her. Then, using an old pair of flat-edged tweezers she had stashed in the desk, she caught one edge of the paper. Holding her breath, she gently tugged until a folded sheet of paper slightly larger than traditional letter size slid out. Carefully, she opened the page and gently smoothed its crease so she could read it.

Darla read the page twice, just to be sure. Then, reaching for her cell phone, she dialed Jake. "Hey," she said when her friend answered, "Hamlet found something kind of interesting hidden in my book. Can you come up for a minute and give me your opinion?"

Then, hanging up on Jake, she sent a text message to James.

I think I know why Vinnie wanted my book.

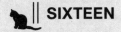 **SIXTEEN**

"ARE WE CERTAIN THAT THIS IS A LEGAL DOCUMENT?" JAMES asked the next morning in the bookstore once he'd deliberated over the paper that Darla—or, rather, Hamlet—had discovered secreted in Darla's 1912 edition of *The Marble Faun.*

"Jake was pretty sure it was," Darla replied, "though she said there'd probably be a big peeing contest between attorneys before it would be accepted, let alone enforced after all this time. But I have to admit, I'd never heard of a secret trust before now."

James studied the page again.

"I am no expert in that field, either," he conceded, "but my understanding is that it is a somewhat antiquated version of a will. The testator—the individual originating the trust—arranges that his bequest will be transferred to a trustee upon his death, with the understanding that said trustee will then transfer the money or property to the rightful beneficiary.

But as this document is meant to be secret, it is not mentioned in the testator's actual will. And thus, the beneficiary will usually have no idea that he is due that settlement."

Darla frowned. "Let me get this straight. Since it's a secret, if the trustee decides to keep the bequest for himself, there's a good chance the beneficiary wouldn't ever find out about it?"

"Nor would anyone else. It is a form discouraged by most attorneys these days, but you can see that the notary date is almost twenty-five years ago. I believe these trusts were most commonly used in the case of mistresses or illegitimate children."

He handed the paper back to Darla, who refolded it and tucked it safely beneath the book cover again.

Fortifying herself with a long sip of latte, courtesy of Robert, she said, "So, it looks like Vinnie was due a nice chunk of change from his grandfather—the original Vincent Modello—that he got cheated out of. But, somehow, Vinnie knew the proof was in this book. No wonder he was so eager to find it."

"Well, I am certainly relieved to know that my appraisal skills were not entirely off in this matter. I suppose we should contact Mr. Modello and let him know we have the document he has been searching for."

A customer stepped up to the counter before Darla could reply. James graciously did the ringing up, giving Darla a chance to take another sip of latte and gather her thoughts.

Of all the reasons she'd thought Vinnie might have coveted the book, a hidden secret trust had not been one of them! On the other hand, while Darla was helping with the estate sale prep, hadn't Mary Ann emphasized that people tended to hide money and documents in old books?

Estate sales. Documents in old books.

Abruptly, a couple of mental puzzle pieces snapped together. She should call Mary Ann, and—

"Hey, Ms. P.," Robert called, rushing down the steps from the coffee bar and breaking her train of thought. "I just heard from Sylvie. There's good news and bad news about the mystery cat."

Momentarily distracted, she asked, "So what's the scoop?"

"It turns out the cat was, you know, chipped, and she's healthy as Hamlet. And Sylvie's mom even got hold of her owners."

"That sounds like great news. So, what's the bad?"

"The owners don't want her anymore."

Darla stared at him, appalled. "But she's a beautiful girl, and I'm sure when she's not afraid she's friendly as can be. Why in the world wouldn't they want her back?"

Robert rolled his kohled eyes in disgust. "Sylvie said they told her mom that their kids were allergic. That's why when the cat ran away"—he gave those last two words finger quotes—"they didn't go looking for her or put up any signs."

"Right. And what that really means is they got tired of the cat and so they dumped her out on the street." Darla shook her head. "I swear, it makes you embarrassed to be a human sometimes. So, what happens with the cat now? Can she be adopted?"

"The owners have to sign surrender papers or something, and then I think it has to go through, like, the animal control people. But they're going to let Sylvie foster her in the meantime."

He turned to head back up to the coffee bar, only to halt again. "Oh, yeah, I forgot to tell you, Ms. P.," he said as he glanced back at her. "Guess what her name is?"

When Darla shook her head, he grinned and said, "Ophelia."

She smiled at that as she took another sip of latte, while phrases like *meant to be* and *Fate* came to mind. To be sure, Hamlet would never stand for another cat in his domain. But maybe Jake or Mary Ann would be interested in a furry little friend.

Mary Ann.

At the thought of her elderly friend, Darla hopped back on that lost thought train. Talk about *meant to be* and *Fate*. Surely it had to be more than coincidence that the very book Vinnie was looking for just happened to show up in a box that came from the Plinskis' store. What had James told her originally? Some of the books were leftover stock they were trying to move, and some had come from their most recent estate sale.

An estate sale that had taken place only a couple of weeks before Mr. Plinski's murder.

And there was one other thing, she realized, abruptly putting down the latte cup as a new thought hit her. *That* was what had bothered her when Reese had talked about Mary Ann's strange behavior that morning. Mary Ann had told her the day before the murder that she would be speaking to the executor of her upcoming estate that next day. She'd already set the excuse for being gone a portion of that day, likely to hide something else—another visit to Hodge, perhaps?

"James." She called to her manager, who was straightening the history section. "I've got to run over to Jake's apartment for a minute. Can you cover things here?"

"Of course," he replied. Then, noticing that she'd tucked her copy of *The Marble Faun* under one arm, he asked, "Would this have anything to do with Mr. Modello?"

"I think so," she said. "I'll let you know."

Brain on fire—or so it felt!—Darla rushed out of the store, for once welcoming the resulting blast of cold air.

Hopefully, the PI was "In," to borrow a certain running gag from Charles Schulz. She wanted to run her theories by Jake first before calling Reese.

To her relief, she found Jake at her desk when she walked inside, though Jake was embroiled in what seemed to be a heated phone conversation with someone. Spying Darla, she gestured for her to take a chair. The conversation continued another minute, until Jake finally growled into the cell phone, "I'll call you back tomorrow, and you'd better have that answer."

Then, hanging up, she gave Darla a wry look.

"I sure miss the good old days of landlines where you could slam down a receiver when you were ticked at someone. Pressing the 'End' button just doesn't have the same effect."

"I know what you mean. I still have one of Great-Aunt Dee's Princess phones hanging in my kitchen, and that sucker weighs a ton. Maybe Mary Ann has a refurbished model you could buy. Speaking of which . . ."

She set down *The Marble Faun* on the desk across from Jake and pulled out the copy of the secret trust. "I showed this to James, and we're all pretty much in agreement what it is. Obviously, Vinnie knew the document existed; he just had to find the book where his grandfather had hidden a copy. James said we should call Vinnie and let him know we found it, but I'm not so sure."

"What do you mean, kid? It's not worth anything to anyone but him . . . if that."

"Maybe. But before I give it to him, there's something we should check out. James isn't sure if this was one of the books that came from existing stock the Plinskis had, or if it was one of the estate sale books, since he bought everything as a lot. The only way to put this to bed is to find out the name of the dead guy whose estate the Plinskis were selling."

Jake frowned as she considered Darla's words; then, abruptly, her dark eyes widened.

"Hold it. Remember that day at the bridal shop, when Connie thought she'd seen a dead body, and Vinnie went bonkers? Daniel told us that his half brother was under stress because he'd recently lost his father. If the Plinskis were the ones who'd held his father's estate sale, and Vinnie knew it, then maybe he didn't stumble across it—and you—by accident."

"And maybe he paid a visit to Bygone Days trying to find out where his book had gone," Darla finished for her.

They stared at each other for a moment. Then Jake shook her curly head.

"It fits, but it's almost too perfect. How would he even know the copy of the trust was hidden in the book? Isn't that the whole thing about them, that they're secret?"

Darla shrugged. "In the old movies, there's always a deathbed confession, or else the under parlor maid overheard something, or an anonymous letter shows up in the mail telling exactly where to find the hidden document."

"Right." Jake pursed her lips, but Darla doubted she was considering anonymous letters and under parlor maids. Then, her words slightly bitter, she said, "Before we go off half-cocked, we need to see Mary Ann and get that estate sale name. If it matches, we dump all this on Reese. If it doesn't, I say give Vinnie his birthright, or whatever it is, and let's move on from all this the best we can."

With that, she shoved back her chair and reached for her keys. Grabbing the book, Darla followed her out of the apartment. Jake paused to lock the place, so Darla was a few steps ahead of her. And so she was the first to notice that Reese's car was parked in front of the antiques store.

Darla felt her stomach clench. No doubt the detective was there to question the elderly woman about the discrepancy in her official statement. But maybe that would become a nonissue if it turned out Vinnie's grandfather's estate had been Estate1507.

"What's he doing there?" Jake asked as she came up behind her.

Remembering she'd been sworn to secrecy, Darla replied as honestly as she could, "I'm not sure. I think he had more questions for her."

She and Jake entered the antiques store cautiously, the bells barely jingling behind them. For the moment, it seemed there were no customers within. Darla could hear Reese's voice, though she couldn't quite make out the words. And then came a sudden, single sharp word from Mary Ann.

"No!"

"Oh, boy," Darla murmured, glancing over at her friend. "We'd better see what's going on before Mary Ann gets hustled out of here in handcuffs."

Jake nodded and gestured her forward. "Hey, Reese, it's me and Darla. Anything wrong? We stopped in to visit with Mary Ann a minute."

"Might as well join the party," they heard Reese clip out before they rounded the aisle and saw him.

He was standing on one side of the main counter, while Mary Ann stood at the other. And then Darla gasped as she saw that the old woman had a heavy silver chain wrapped and padlocked around her thin waist. The end of that chain was, in turn, wrapped and padlocked around her old-fashioned boat anchor of a cash register, effectively holding her prisoner.

"What the—? Reese, how could you?" she and Jake chorused as they rushed over to the old woman.

Setting down her book on the counter, Darla quickly hefted the chain, which was surprisingly heavy. "Where's the key to this thing?" she demanded of Reese.

Jake, meanwhile, was tugging on one of the padlocks. "I know interrogation techniques have changed since I was on the force," she said with a disbelieving look at him, "but was this really necessary?"

"Wait. You think *I* did this to her?"

Reese gave his head a disgusted shake and sank into the chair beside him.

"I came in to question Mary Ann about Mr. Plinski's case," he said, his attitude that of a man doing his best to hold his temper. "She had a few discrepancies in her original account, and I told her we needed to resolve it. She said she felt faint and asked me to bring her a shorter chair. When I came back with it"—he indicated the ladder-back chair he sat on—"she was chained up like one of those crazy tree-hugging protesters."

"Girls, thank you for your support," Mary Ann broke in, her tone dignified, "but Detective Reese is correct. This is my own doing."

To Reese, she said, "I do apologize for my rude behavior, but I'm afraid this was necessary. I just couldn't risk your trying to take me downtown, as I believe you police officers say."

"I wasn't going to take you anywhere," he replied, obviously striving to be reasonable. "All I want is to know where you really were the morning your brother was murdered."

"Detective, I told you—"

"Mary Ann, what you told me wasn't the truth." He cut her short. "I talked to the executor for your next estate sale. He said you were there with him on Thursday, not Friday. If you can't tell me the truth about where you were, I can't eliminate you from my suspect list."

"And I told you, Detective, that I am sticking to my story. So I suppose I must remain on your list."

"Fine." Reese got to his feet and shoved back on the mirrored sunglasses he'd tucked into his shirtfront. "Let me know when you're ready to tell me the truth."

Not bothering with a good-bye, he grabbed his overcoat from the counter and stalked off down the aisle. A moment later, they heard the bells on the front door jangle after him. Then Jake said, "First things first. Mary Ann, tell me where the keys to these locks are, and we'll get you out of this contraption."

"Oh, no need for that, my dear," the old woman said.

As the two of them watched in surprise, she gave the lock at her waist a twist. It promptly gave way, so that the chain slipped down her hips and clattered to the ground. She did the same with the register lock and then smiled at them both.

"It's a magician's trick. Brother bought it at a sale once. I thought it was a foolish thing, but he got such a kick out of it. And I suppose it did come in handy, at that."

She gave a small, hiccupping sob; then, quickly regaining her composure, she asked, "You girls said you wanted to talk to me?"

"Please, sit down, Mary Ann," Darla urged, sliding over the chair Reese had just vacated, while Jake gathered the length of chain into a roll. "There's something we need to know about a book Mr. Plinski sold to James."

She reached for her volume of *The Marble Faun* and handed it to the old woman. "Do you recognize this? From what James said, it was either old stock you were trying to clear out, or else it came from the estate sale about two weeks ago."

"It does look familiar . . . but then, I do tend to remember any works of Mr. Hawthorne that pass through our hands. Let me see. Yes, I do believe it was from the estate sale."

Taking back the book, Darla persisted, "The number on

the box James brought back was Estate1507. Can you look up the name of the person whose estate you were selling?"

"Well, let me see. Of course, I remember the executor . . . no need to look up that name. He was a charming gentleman named Mr. Lawson."

"And the gentleman whose estate it was?"

"Oh, dear, let me try to remember. Montello . . . no, Madera . . . no," she finished triumphantly, "Modello. It was definitely Modello. But why do you ask?"

Darla and Jake exchanged glances, and she was pretty sure the PI was thinking the same thing as she was. Given that the dead man was Vinnie's father, the Mr. Lawson in question could only be Vinnie's half brother, Daniel. But why would the deceased man choose his stepson over his son to be his executor?

"I ended up buying this edition for myself," Darla replied in answer to Mary Ann's question, "and I found a rather important document glued under the front endpapers. I just wanted to be certain I returned it to the right person."

"That's very good of you. I know that Brother and I have done the same thing on more than one occasion." Then, her tone expectant, she asked, "Was there anything more?"

"Not for now," Jake told her, smiling. "So, promise us you'll stay out of chains, and we'll get out of your hair."

Once out on the stoop of the antiques store again, Darla paused there despite the cold.

"That's it, then, isn't it?" she excitedly asked Jake. "Vinnie somehow found out that the secret trust existed, and that it was hidden in the book. He must have killed Mr. Plinski while he was trying to find out where the book had gone after the sale. Motive and opportunity, both. We have to get hold of Reese again and show him this trust document so he can arrest Vinnie."

"Jumping the gun, kid," Jake warned her. "Right now, that trust is about as secure a piece of evidence as that trick chain and padlock of Mary Ann's."

When Darla would have protested, Jake added, "Remember that Vinnie saw the book right there in your dainty little hands yesterday, and all he did was offer to buy it from you. If he'd really kill for it, he would have figured out a way to take it from you right then. You know, spill some champagne on it and rush it to the back to clean it up, and pry the document out without your ever knowing."

"I guess. I did tell him I'd consider selling it to him, so maybe we can coordinate it with Reese somehow."

Jake nodded. "We'll tell Reese what we know and give him the paper. He can take it from there and build a case, if there's a case to be built. But in the meantime, maybe you should let me hold the book for safekeeping."

Nodding, Darla handed over the volume to her friend. "Here you go, but make sure Reese knows I want it back. After all, I paid twenty bucks for it," she said, trying for a light tone despite the fact that the situation surrounding the book had suddenly become all-too-serious.

The PI gave her an encouraging look as she tucked the book under her arm. "I still don't think Vinnie is our guy, but you can't be too careful. Now, you go sell some books. I'll call Reese and see if he can meet us later to talk. And just in case someone comes poking around my place looking for it, I think I'll scan that trust and send it off to Reese once I get back to the apartment."

But by the time Jake stopped by later with an update, it was midafternoon, and all indications were that Reese would be unavailable until morning.

"Hang tight, kid," Jake told her. "He's got that scan I sent him, so we've done as much as we can for the moment. And since there's no spotlight on him, I don't think our friend Vinnie will be going anywhere, or trying anything, in the next twenty-four hours. But, just in case, it might not hurt if you camped out at my place tonight along with your book."

Darla considered that a moment, then shook her head. "I've got Hamlet and my alarm system, and I'm not going to answer the door after hours, so I should be fine. Besides, you're just a phone call away, right?"

"I am tonight," the PI confirmed with a faint smile. "But if you change your mind, let me know."

The remainder of the afternoon passed without incident. Since it was Wednesday, James had worked his usual half day, so it was only her and Robert—and, of course, Hamlet—when they began getting ready to close at a few minutes to six.

"Go ahead and make the final rounds upstairs," she told the youth, "and I'll take care of things down here."

By the time she'd checked for stragglers—none—and picked up any wayward books—only a copy of *The Brothers Karamazov* that had ended up in the cooking section—Robert was there waiting for her, his usual backpack slung over his shoulder. He gave the lounging Hamlet a final scratch under the chin and asked, "Can I go? I need to walk Roma real quick, and then I'm going to meet Sylvie at the Ice Cream Shop."

Which wasn't, Darla knew, a literal ice cream parlor but was instead an ironically named goth hangout that had just opened a few streets over near the e-cigarette store.

"Go ahead and go," she told him with a smile. "I need to finish filling out this order form and then I'll lock the door behind you."

He gave her a cheerful wave and then rushed out, the bells clanging enthusiastically after him. *Pretty bad when your teenage clerk has twice the social life that you do.* But the last jingle had barely faded when the bells rang again.

"What did you forget this time?" she wryly asked, not bothering to look up from the computer when she heard the door fly open once more. Despite the backpack that should have kept all his stuff safely stowed, the youth had a habit of forgetting a random book or bag of chips when he left each day.

"I know what *you* forgot," replied a voice that, while vaguely familiar, was not Robert's.

She jerked her gaze upward to see Vinnie Modello headed toward her, ski cap pulled low on his forehead and bundled in a heavy coat. *Definitely BookBuyer75*, she thought, taking an involuntary step back.

"I've been waiting for your call all day," he told her, sounding accusatory. "Why didn't you phone me about selling me that copy of *The Marble Faun*?"

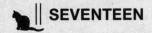 || **SEVENTEEN**

"VINNIE—MR. MODELLO—I'M AFRAID WE'RE CLOSED FOR the evening. You'll have to come back tomorrow," Darla said in as firm a voice as she could muster, even as she could have kicked herself for not immediately locking the door after Robert.

Vinnie apparently realized he'd come on too strong, for he raised his well-manicured hands in a "hey, take it easy" gesture.

"Sorry, let's try this again," he replied. "I'm not trying to be a jerk or anything. It's just that I really want that book. I'm willing to pay a fair price for it . . . more than fair, if that's what it takes. Can't we talk about this?"

Darla hesitated. After talking with Jake, she wasn't sure any longer that Vinnie had anything to do with Mr. Plinski's death. On the other hand, the man was being scarily persistent in his pursuit of the book. If he'd only admit what he wanted, she'd feel more comfortable.

She glanced over to Hamlet for moral support. The store mascot still was on the counter, but he'd roused himself and was now seated neatly at attention. Sleek and unmoving, he resembled one of those tomb-guarding Egyptian cat statues as he fixed the bridal shop owner with an unblinking green gaze.

She gave the big cat a puzzled look. Usually when danger threatened, Hamlet became a yowling, bristling, feline ninja warrior with razor-sharp claws that he was not afraid to wield. But he didn't seem overly distressed by the current situation. Maybe the canny cat had decided that Vinnie didn't pose the sort of threat that warranted feline ninja warrior skills.

Even so, she kept her guard up as she took a seat on the register stool, so that the counter remained between them.

"Agreed, let's start again. If I didn't already own the book myself, you could buy it outright from the store. But since it's mine, I'd really like to know first what's so important about it that you're basically stalking it all around town."

He shoved his hands into his coat pockets and shifted nervously on his feet. Would he admit to being on an inheritance treasure hunt of sorts, she wondered? Or was he trying to think up some logical-sounding lie that would induce her to part with the book?

But before he could speak, the front door bells abruptly jangled again.

"Ms. P.?" Robert called, rushing in from outside. "I, like, forgot my cell, and—"

He broke off abruptly at the sight of Vinnie standing there at the counter. Expression wary, he asked, "Everything okay? The front door wasn't locked like it was supposed to be."

Unasked, she knew, was the question, *Is this guy supposed to be here?*

"Robert, this is Mr. Vincent Modello from Davina's Bridal Shop. You know, the place where Connie bought her wedding dress. He was in here the other day talking to James about a book, and now he's come back for more discussion."

Which actually meant, *Now everyone knows who he is and how to find him, which means he'd be an idiot to try anything crazy.*

Robert slowly nodded as he went around the counter to retrieve his cell phone from the shelf beneath it. Vinnie, meanwhile, smiled a little, obviously having no problem understanding the subtext. He reached into his coat pocket and pulled out a business card.

"Here you go," he said, handing it across the counter to Robert. "Name, address, phone number. No secrets."

"Sure . . . like, okay," Robert answered as he took the card and stuck it in his coat pocket. With a questioning look at Darla, he asked, "Should I, you know, stick around a minute?"

"I'm sure Mr. Modello wouldn't mind," Darla said, smiling, though her voice was firm. Even though Hamlet hadn't raised any alarm, no way was she going to hang out with Vinnie all by herself. "He was just about to tell me why he was so interested in my particular copy of *The Marble Faun.*"

Vinnie nodded, though his smile hardened just a bit.

"The more, the merrier," he replied. "Like I said, no secrets. So, here's the short version of my story. There's a name written inside the front cover of your book. It says *V. Modello.* That was my grandfather, the first Vincent Modello. He got a grant to study overseas in Italy for a semester when he was in college, and he told me that book was better than any tour guide. When I was a kid, I'd stay with him over summer vacation, and Grandpop would read chapters of it to me each night."

He smirked a little. "It's not exactly a kid's book, know

what I mean? But I guess I found all the descriptions of the temples and sculptures fascinating. That book came to mean a lot to me, mostly because it meant a lot to him."

The smirk faded.

"He'd always promised he'd give the book to me one day," the man explained, "but it vanished when he died approximately twenty years ago. I figured my grandmother maybe donated it to the church sale or something. I figured it was gone for good. But after my father died, it showed up on a list of books that were supposed to go in the estate sale. It got sold before I could lay hands on it, so I've spent the past few weeks trying to track it down. It turned into kind of an obsession, I guess."

Darla nodded, giving him a considering look. "I'm curious about one thing, Mr. Modello. You say this book means a lot to you, but what you originally came to the store to buy was a two-volume set, not a single book like my copy. Why did you commit to that auction listing, when it clearly was something different?"

Vinnie shot her an irritated look, obviously not expecting this question.

"I don't know, I was confused. It'd been, what, twenty, twenty-five years since I'd seen the book. I figured it had to be the same one, since your place was next to the antiques store. I was taking a chance the listing was wrong, but I knew the minute I saw it I'd made a mistake. I'd just about decided I'd never see it again, and then there you were in my shop with the book in your lap. It was like Grandpop reaching out a hand to me and saying, *Here it is, Vinnie.*"

He choked a little on those last words and then, to Darla's astonishment, broke down into harsh, dry sobs that seemed ripped from his chest. She exchanged glances with Robert, who seemed equally stunned. And then, to her surprise, the youth rushed around the counter to the anguished man.

"Hey, it's okay," he said, giving Vinnie a consoling thump on the shoulder while Darla pulled a box of tissues from beneath the counter and left it within reach of the man. "I, like, just lost a friend who was like a grandpa to me. It's pretty tough."

Vinnie quickly regained his composure, swiping at his face with a handful of tissues.

"Sorry," was his gruff response, not glancing at Darla or Robert. "I've been under a lot of stress the past few weeks since my father's death, what with my brother, and the will, and all."

Will? Maybe that would shed some light onto the issue of the secret trust. At the very least, Vinnie might say something that would be helpful to Reese. Her tone sympathetic, she told him, "I've heard it can get pretty tense, trying to settle an estate. Did you and Daniel clash a lot over things?"

The bridal shop owner snorted. "There wasn't much to settle, nothing to clash about. My little brother got it all."

"Daniel got everything?" she echoed. Then, recalling her earlier conversation with Mary Ann about the Modello estate's executor, she said, "I don't understand. I know you two are half brothers, but why would your father leave all his assets to someone else's son, and not you?"

"We both have the same father . . . it's our mothers who are different."

Darla gave him a puzzled look. "But you two have different last names."

"Yeah, well, that's Danny's thing," Vinnie said with a smirk. "Lawson's actually his middle name. He decided halfway through college that he wanted to be an actor, instead. Our father agreed to finance him on the condition that he use a stage name. He wasn't half bad. He actually landed a couple of off-off-Broadway parts, but he decided if he couldn't be an A-list actor by the time he was twenty-one, then he wasn't going to waste his time auditioning. But he kept the stage name to impress people."

So where in the heck did owning a bridal shop come into it, Darla wondered. But that was a question for later. What interested her now was the will . . . and, by extension, the secret trust. For, the more he revealed of his story, the more it seemed Vinnie might have had no idea that the trust existed.

"That's still pretty awful, the fact your father didn't leave you anything," she said. "Talk about driving a wedge between you and your brother."

So saying, she reached over to give Hamlet's fur a fluff. He was still in Egyptian cat mode, but at her touch he hunkered down with paws neatly curled to his chest. Apparently, this human's youthful history was starting to bore the big feline.

Vinnie, however, seemed oddly recharged by having an audience. Which made sense, since he couldn't let out all that childhood angst on unsuspecting brides-to-be . . . not if he wanted to keep customers.

Increasingly warming to the subject of himself, he replied, "It wasn't a big surprise, since my father never had much use for me. I was a big disappointment to him, I guess. I had asthma when I was a kid, so I was sick a lot, and it didn't help that my father smoked like a chimney. I didn't play sports, and I was always behind in school. Who wants a kid like that?"

Darla shook her head, feeling a rush of sympathy for the man despite herself. Getting kicked to the curb when one was a kid had to leave scars.

"My mother took off when I was eight," Vinnie explained, not noticing or else not caring that his tale had stirred a bit of concern on her part. "And bottom line was that my father really didn't want me around after that. I guess I reminded him too much of her. He found himself a new wife a few months later, and then along came Danny, the golden child. That's why I liked spending summers with Grandpop so much. He saw something in me that my father didn't." Vinnie gave a humorless smile. "I guess you guys are getting the long story now. Serves you right for asking."

"No, uh, that's okay." Robert replied for them both, and Darla realized the youth felt some solidarity with Vinnie, given his own rocky relationship with his parents. "I've got a new half brother who's going to be born soon, and he'll probably get everything my dad has someday. I don't care. I mean, you can't get mad at a baby."

The man shook his head. "I never was mad at him. Sure, we had our disagreements over the years, but Danny's a good guy," he insisted. "He even wrote me a check after the will was settled. He didn't have to do that."

And yet Darla had seen Vinnie and Daniel arguing that day through the bridal shop window, and it hadn't looked like a simple disagreement. But maybe she was giving that one incident too much weight. Still, something else occurred to her that seemed to not quite mesh with his story.

"About Daniel," she began, trying to word her observation as delicately as possible, "I'm surprised your father favored him over you, especially since you were the older one. Also, well, many people of your father's generation—men, especially—wouldn't be so accepting of a gay son, unless maybe he didn't know?"

Vinnie laughed outright at that.

"Danny's not gay. It's an act he puts on for the bridal shop customers. He says they spend more money when they can treat him like a girlfriend. And it works, believe me. I keep the books." He sneered a little. "Of course, every so often he lets a really cute bridesmaid turn him straight, at least for a night."

Darla raised her brows at that. Bad enough that Daniel put on the gay act as a calculated business tactic. Pulling a trick like that to lure an unsuspecting woman to bed was pretty darned low, in her book. Apparently, the man had honed his craft quite well during his time on off-off-Broadway.

Then she shook her head. While she wasn't one hundred percent convinced of Vinnie's honesty, if his story was even partially on the level, she'd feel like a jerk holding on to the book. But she wasn't ready to turn it over to the man yet . . . not until she had that conversation with Reese in the morning. After all, it could be that Vinnie was as much the actor as his brother.

"Look, Mr. Modello," she told him, "you seem to have a pretty good claim to that copy of *The Marble Faun*. For that reason, I'm willing to sell it at our standard markup . . . say, thirty-five dollars."

Then as his expression grew suddenly hopeful, she added, "But the book's not here. I left it with a friend. The soonest would be tomorrow afternoon before it's back here at the store to sell. Is that acceptable?"

She hesitated, reminding herself that she couldn't quite yet dismiss him as a suspect in Mr. Plinski's murder. His reaction to her offer would tell her whether he was on the up-and-up. If he insisted on laying hands on the book now— maybe even threatened her—she'd have to find a way to signal Robert to make a run for it and call Reese. But if he agreed to her suggestion, that likely meant he was being truthful about his interest in the volume. To her relief, Vinnie nodded.

"Yeah. So long as I know the book is safe, I'm willing to wait."

"Good. How about three o'clock tomorrow, here at the store?"

"Right."

With a nod in Robert's direction, he turned and headed out into the night. Darla waited until the door had closed after him and then rushed to lock it. Then she turned to her clerk.

"Wow."

"That, was like, intense," Robert agreed with a disbelieving shake of his head as she walked back to the register. "I mean, I get him and all, but that was kind of, well, public."

"I suppose if you keep it all bottled up inside, it has to come out sometime." Although, once again, she couldn't help but wonder if Vinnie had the same acting chops as his half brother, and this had been a performance for their benefit.

Swiftly, she told Robert what she knew of Vinnie's *Marble Faun* search. She told him, too, how she—or, rather, Hamlet—had discovered a legal document that seemingly entitled Vinnie to a large bequest from his grandfather. A bequest that had likely been appropriated by his father.

"Jake and James and I discussed it," she finished, "and we decided Detective Reese needed to know about the secret trust document before we gave it to Vinnie. The fact that the book got into our hands via the Plinskis concerns me."

Robert wrinkled his brow for a moment, considering, and then abruptly gave Darla a horrified look.

"No way! You don't think this crying dude murdered Mr. P. while he was tracking down that stupid book, do you?"

"I thought that, at first, but now I'm pretty sure he didn't. I truly think he doesn't know that the document was hidden in the book. I think all he wanted was the book, period . . . and that wouldn't be enough reason to murder an old man."

"Yeah," Robert persisted, his jaw set, "but maybe he wasn't trying to kill him. Just, you know, scare him into telling where the book was."

"Maybe," she repeated, trying for Robert's sake to keep her tone steady. "Or maybe this whole *Marble Faun* thing came out of left field and doesn't have anything to do with Mr. Plinski's murder at all. From what he's said, Detective Reese still has a few different suspects he's looking at."

Like the random street thug.

Or else Hodge.

Or else Mary Ann.

Darla winced a little at that last name. She knew in her heart that the old woman could never have hurt her brother. Still, she couldn't dismiss the fact that Mary Ann certainly gave off the most suspicious vibe of anyone, what with her lies and mysterious travels. Putting Vinnie on the list at least spread the perceived guilt around a little more.

Robert, meanwhile, was glaring at the business card he held, the previous solidarity with the bridal shop owner apparently evaporated.

"Yeah, well, crying dude better not have had anything to do with Mr. P.," he muttered. Tossing the card onto the counter, he added, "You want me to, you know, stick around? I mean, in case he comes back?"

Darla shook her head.

"Hamlet didn't seem overly upset about the guy, so that kind of makes me think Vinnie might be telling the truth about all this. Don't worry, I'm going to go straight to my apartment and send Reese a message about what just went down. Go ahead and meet Sylvie like you planned. She'll worry if you're late."

"You think?"

With those hopeful words, the youth hefted his backpack onto his shoulder, gave Hamlet a final pat, and headed off.

This time, Darla locked the door immediately after him and then turned to her mascot. "What do you say, Hammy? How about we call out for supper tonight?"

Hamlet gave an approving *meow-rumph* to that, knowing that takeout usually resulted in a little treat for him to go with his kibble. Gathering her belongings from beneath the counter, she hit the lights, set the alarm, and followed Hamlet upstairs to the apartment.

She took care of him first—fresh water in his cut-glass dish, and the appropriate amount of kibble in his pottery bowl. Then Darla placed her order with a home-style soup and sandwich place. Having been assured that the delivery person would be there in about forty-five minutes, she picked up her cell again and dialed Reese.

"You couldn't have sent a text?" He answered the call on the first ring, the words accompanied by a great deal of chewing. "Me and Connie finally got a night out for dinner. She's in the little girls' room right now, but if she comes back out and sees me on the phone, she's gonna blow her top."

"Sorry, I was going to text you, but this is important. I really needed to make sure you were going to be by in the morning. I know Jake already sent you the scan of the secret trust so you could check it out, but I just had a visit from Vincent Modello."

"The guy got you at gunpoint right now? No? Okay, then I'll see you in the a.m."

Then, before Darla could sputter back that he was being a jerk—this, after all she'd done for Connie!—his manner softened.

"Sorry, Red, I'm being a jerk," he confirmed. "So tell me what went down. Did he threaten you?"

"No, actually, he cried. And Hamlet didn't seem too worried, so I think he's relatively harmless. And since I gave the book to Jake to hold, I had a good reason to put him off. I told him to come by tomorrow at three and I'd sell him back the book. I really think he doesn't have any idea about the trust."

"Three o'clock. Not much time," he mumbled through another bite. "I sent that copy of the trust to a broad I know who works at a law firm. If she thinks it's legit, she'll contact the law firm that wrote it . . . assuming they're still around."

Then he muttered an oath. "Gotta go. Connie's headed back this way. Keep your doors locked and make that big cat of yours stand guard tonight. I'll see you tomorrow morning, nine sharp at your store. Don't call back unless someone's dead."

"Nope, no dead bodies here . . . yet," was her sarcastic retort, though the call had already ended. Looking over at Hamlet, who had strolled in from the kitchen, she said, "I swear if I ever get murdered, I'm going to haunt Reese until the end of time. If you've used up all your nine lives by then, want to give me a hand with that?"

Hamlet paused in midstep to give her a slow, emerald blink which she took as a *yes*.

Buoyed by the cat's support, she flipped on the television while she waited for her supper to show up. Then her cell phone chimed, indicating an incoming message.

Had msg from Reese u talked 2 him. Thought u might like some light reading before bed, the text from Jake read. Do the math. $$$$.

The attachment was the scan of the trust. Curious, Darla forwarded the message to her email and booted up her computer so she could take a second look.

Reading the document was like wading through a few paragraphs of Hawthorne, though at least on the computer she was able to blow up the font to a more comfortable size. Thus, by the time her downstairs front door buzzed, announcing the delivery driver's arrival, she'd come to a shocking realization that she had missed when she initially perused the document.

The dollar amount of the bequest being held in trust for one Vincent L. Modello III was not the comfortable but modest figure that she'd originally thought.

Instead, totaling up cash and stock, as well as property, the amount that had been left to him came to well over one million dollars.

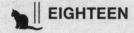 || EIGHTEEN

"IT LOOKS LEGIT TO ME," REESE SAID THE NEXT MORNING as he squinted at the actual copy of the trust, Darla having picked up the book and document from Jake thirty minutes earlier. "I probably won't hear back from my legal source until later today, but I'm pretty sure she'll say the same thing. So, what are you going to do with it?"

It was a little after nine the next morning. Reese had pulled up on the dot, as promised, foam cup from a competing coffee shop clutched in one hand. He and Hamlet had exchanged their usual distrustful looks as the detective settled against the counter to chat with Darla. Hamlet had situated himself a short distance away, still on the countertop, though out of paws' reach . . . but not so far from them that he couldn't pounce into action, if need be.

"That's the original reason why I asked you to come over," Darla replied, impatiently flipping her single red braid so that it rested neatly over her right shoulder. "I thought

Vinnie should know about the trust, but I wanted your blessing before I handed over anything that could be considered evidence. But now I'm starting to wonder again if he didn't know about it after all. I'd think that a million bucks would be pretty good motivation for murder."

Reese snorted. "Red, I've seen one guy kill another guy over a ten-spot. Motivation doesn't always make sense."

Darla shook her head and mentally threw her hands up. The whole situation was getting more complicated by the minute. With a sigh, she added, "Maybe he guessed there was something up about the book, since he said his grandfather specifically wanted him to have it, or maybe he didn't. But trust or no trust, I'm pretty sure he does want the book for sentimental reasons."

"Wouldn't it be easier if he just bought himself a new copy?"

"What didn't you understand about the words *sentimental reasons*?" She pointed to her edition, which was sitting on the counter. "This book actually belonged to his grandfather. It's not the same thing if it's a random copy he buys off Amazon, or something."

Then, as Reese still looked skeptical, she asked, "So what do you think? Is it possible Vinnie had anything to do with Mr. Plinski's murder?"

"Anything's possible. And just so you know you're getting your tax dollars' worth out of me, I already did a little checking on the guy. As far as I can tell, he's an upstanding citizen, no criminal record, has been working at that bridal shop for almost three years."

"Working?" Darla echoed with a frown. "I thought he was part owner."

"Not from what I found. The records show that Davina's Bridal is jointly owned by one Daniel Lawson Modello, aka

Daniel Lawson, and one Davina Lawson . . . aka Daniel Lawson's mother."

So much for the "Da"—and the "Vin"!—in Davina.

Darla's frown deepened. Yet hadn't both Vinnie and Daniel indicated that Vinnie was a partner, and not simply an employee? Perhaps that was another example of Daniel's kindness to his brother, letting him save face by being referred to as an owner.

Reese, had set the trust paperwork aside. Gesturing at the book, he said, "Now show me exactly where you found the document."

She reached for the copy of *The Marble Faun* and flipped open the front cover. "It was here," she replied, indicating the unglued front end paper. Then, by way of demonstration, she folded the document again along its original creases and carefully slipped it back where she had discovered it.

"Hamlet was the one who figured it out," she told the detective with a proud glance over at her cat. "He clawed away the page just enough so I could see that something was underneath. When James was initially appraising the book, he said he didn't think these were the original endpapers, and he was right."

She slid the book closer to Reese.

"And, look, you can tell where something was cut out," she explained, showing him what she'd discovered with further examination the night before. The narrowest ribbon of a raw edge stuck up behind the loose endpaper where someone had sliced away a page.

"If you peeled off the glued paper all the way, you'd see the original paper they used when the book was bound. Someone obviously wanted the trust document hidden, but put someplace it could be easily retrieved if need be," she smugly finished.

Reese gave her a nod.

"Not bad for an amateur, though Hamlet probably thought the book smelled like mice, which is the only reason he was clawing around on it. So what time did you say Modello was coming back?"

"Three o'clock."

"Well, I might just have to stop by around then. You know how we cops are about our coffee. I'll probably be looking for a refill," he said, and lifted his foam cup by way of example.

Darla suppressed a smile.

"Right. Oh, and speaking about how cops are, I had to make up a lie to Connie the day you dropped us off at Davina's. She got a little suspicious over how long we talked, so I had to deflect her somehow. The only thing I could think to tell her was that you were planning a surprise for her at the engagement party. So you'd better start planning something good."

Reese heaved a sigh. "Great. Now I've gotta think up something clever. What, you think maybe a male stripper?"

"That would be a *no*," Darla shot back with a roll of her eyes, trying to decide if he was making a bad joke or if he truly was that clueless. "It should be meaningful. And you get bonus points if you make her cry a little."

"Thanks for the pressure. The only thing I can think of offhand that would make her cry is if I had to leave halfway through, and then she'd probably throw the ring back at me. It woulda been easier if you'd told her you and I were seeing each other on the side," he finished with a mournful shake of his head.

Then, at the stunned look Darla shot him—*why had that, of all things, occurred to him to as an excuse!*—he held up both hands.

"Wait, it was a joke. You know I'd never cheat on her. Especially not with you." Then, apparently realizing how *that* sounded, he stumbled on. "I mean, not that I wouldn't want to—I mean, if that was something I'd do—but we're friends, and it would be pretty awkward . . ."

"You mean, awkward like this?" Darla asked with a wry smile as he helplessly trailed off. "Don't worry, I get what you mean.

"And I've got an idea for you for that engagement party surprise," she added as a solution occurred to her. "Robert's friend Pinky is going to be our substitute barista tomorrow and Saturday while Robert is helping with Mary Ann's estate sale. Maybe you can hire him to show up at the restaurant dressed up in a tux and singing something romantic just for Connie. You know he has that beautiful tenor voice. She'd love it."

"Yeah? Good thinking," he said with an approving nod. "Give me his number, and I'm on it."

She texted him the number in question and then asked, "I guess that's it for now? I mean, about Vinnie and the book?"

He nodded again. "I'll get here a little before three and hang out in the bookshelves while you and him talk. Give him the book and the paperwork, everything you need to finalize the deal. If it all goes down smooth, I'll just follow him outside and have a little chat with him. If things go south for some reason, I'll be here to handle it. Either way, at least we'll put this to bed so I can concentrate on finding Mr. Plinski's killer."

"What about Mary Ann?" she ventured, needing to know for her own sake where that stood. "I haven't been by to check on her yet today. Did you ever get to talk with her again after . . . well, you know, yesterday?"

He gave a rueful chuckle.

"You mean after Mary Ann did her best chain gang imitation? Yeah, she gave me a call, and she apologized for being—and I quote—a stubborn old biddy. And then she explained about where she'd been that morning, and why the lies."

Darla had been smiling after the "biddy" quote, but at his next words, she gasped.

"She told you? Where was she? Did it have anything to do with Mr. Plinski?"

"Let's just say she had a legitimate excuse that I was able to verify, and it puts her in the clear. So she's off the suspect list."

"But where was she?" Darla persisted. "If she's in the clear, why can't you tell me why she lied?"

"Because she asked me not to."

With that, he plucked the sunglasses from atop his head and shoved them back into place. "I'll see you a little before three," he told her, and took off via the front door.

"Well, at least he didn't say, *Ah'll be back*," she muttered to Hamlet, who had watched the detective leave with a look of feline satisfaction. "But what in the world did Mary Ann tell him about that morning?"

Hamlet had no response, preferring to wander up to the lounge where Robert was getting set up for the morning coffee rush . . . no doubt hoping to score a bit of leftover foam. As for Darla, with Vinnie temporarily put to the side, she pondered the Mary Ann situation all morning. She still hadn't come up with any logical answer when James arrived at noon. But her first concern was telling her manager about Vinnie's impromptu visit the night before, and warning of his planned return that afternoon.

"I think it highly sensible that Detective Reese be on the

premises when our friend BookBuyer75 returns," he said with a grimace as she finished. "Something about that man does not sit right with me."

"He's kind of messed up, but I'm not sure he's a bad guy, overall. I just wonder how things would have worked out for him if he'd gotten his bequest when he was supposed to. We're talking a pretty nice chunk of change," she added, telling him the revised figure that she had calculated upon rereading the document.

James raised a brow in surprise.

"That is, indeed, quite a bit more than we thought. If the money is still invested somewhere, after twenty years the gentleman could find himself sitting on a considerable fortune."

Darla let herself imagine for a fraction of an instant what that would be like. Of course, she'd been incredibly blessed herself, in being her great-aunt's sole beneficiary. But the truth of her situation was that most of the estate had been tied up in property. And while she wasn't exactly land-poor, as the expression went, she hadn't yet traded in the ten-year-old Mercedes for a Lamborghini.

"Or, on the other hand," she pointed out, "Vinnie's father might have blown the money years ago, and there's nothing left now for him to claim. And all giving him the trust document will do is make him even more miserable and bitter than he already is."

"Hmm. That is a valid point, but I do believe that ethically we are bound to give the paperwork to him; besides, he might ultimately have discovered the document himself, without our interference. As to what happens afterward, it is none of our affair. Devotee as I am of Hawthorne, I still will be happy to see that volume out of all our lives later today."

Darla nodded.

"Agreed. But I'm still kind of curious to know how the story of Miriam and Donatello ends," she replied, referring to the book's main characters. "Remind me to buy a paperback copy for myself the next time I place a stock order."

While they were speaking, Robert had come down the stairs from the coffee lounge. "The regular coffeepots are set," he told them as he pulled on his coat and reached beneath the counter for his backpack. "Anyone want me to pick up lunch when I go to the deli?"

"If you don't mind," Darla said with a smile as she reached for her own bag to find some cash. "I'll take my usual."

"Turkey Reuben, vinegar-style potato salad, pickle instead of chips," he recited with a grin, having been through the drill a few times before.

But as she handed over the money, she recalled that she hadn't yet run over to check on Mary Ann.

"Robert, when you take Roma for her walk on the way to lunch, can you see how Mary Ann is doing? And if she needs lunch, too, you've got enough with what I gave you to cover it." At his nod, she added, "And if anything seems wrong, come back here first before you go to the deli."

As Robert started for the door, James said, "I fear I was remiss, as well. I did not look to see whether her store was open when I arrived at work."

"Actually, I'm sure she'd prefer we didn't hover over her. But until Reese solves her brother's murder, I'm not comfortable knowing she's there alone. At least Robert will be with her at the estate sale the next couple of days. But I can't help wonder where she really was the morning Mr. Plinski was murdered." She proceeded to tell him what little Reese had related to her.

"I fear we simply will have to trust Detective Reese in this matter," James told her when she'd finished. "Knowing

Mary Ann, I am confident that her silence was not a capricious decision on her part. In time, she will let us know the full story, assuming it is any of our concern."

It was a good forty-five minutes later when Robert returned bearing a large and slightly greasy bag. "How was Mary Ann?" she asked as she helped him unload the food onto the counter.

He shrugged. "She's good. She's all ready for the estate sale tomorrow. We have to be there before nine, so we have to leave around eight." He paused for a bite of his pickle and added, "Mr. Hodge was there, too. He's got a car, so he's going to drive us."

Hodge would be with her? Darla took a considering bite of her own pickle, absently savoring the crunch and blast of garlic. On the one hand, she was glad Mary Ann wasn't alone while dealing with her grief. On the other, she was spending an awful lot a time with a man who, given their sixty-year separation, was pretty much a stranger.

While James handled things downstairs, Darla and Robert went upstairs to finish their lunch. Hamlet tagged along, a single insistent *meow* reminding Darla that she had to save a bit of turkey for him. While she disassembled her sandwich to accommodate His Royal Fuzziness, Robert pulled out a tea tray from beneath the coffee bar's main counter and carried it over to their table.

"Your turn," he reminded her as he set down the tray with its crossword puzzle–style board and arrangement of wooden tiles.

Darla smiled. She'd recently introduced her young barista to the word game, having found an old but unused set tucked on a shelf high in the storeroom. He'd been amazed to learn that the similar game app he'd played with his friends had actually been based on it. They managed to each play a turn or two during lunch, and Darla had been amused with how quickly the youth had taken to the low-tech version.

"Just one turn today," she told him, peering over the loft's half wall for a look at the shop floor below. "Looks like James is going to need a hand in a minute."

She made quick work of her turn—best she could manage was adding an "A-R-E" to an available "C"—and ate half her sandwich, and then disappointed Hamlet by rewrapping the rest for lunch the next day. Leaving Robert to his turn—he triumphantly slapped down an "X" on a double-point square that could be scored from two directions—and to finish his meal, she hurried back downstairs to assist James.

By the time they had handled the small afternoon rush of customers, a glance at the wall clock showed it was quarter to three. James had gone on his own lunch break, though he'd volunteered to forgo it. Knowing Reese would be there, she'd insisted her manager get his late lunch, though now she was wondering if she should have taken him up on his offer.

Where are you, Reese? she wondered, checking the clock again. Last thing she wanted was to drop her bombshell on Vinnie without backup. And then, only a couple of minutes behind schedule, the detective walked through the door. He gave her the slightest nod of acknowledgment, his mirrored gaze sweeping the room.

"Don't worry, we're all clear," she hurriedly told him. "There aren't any other customers for the moment, and Vinnie isn't here yet."

He nodded again and took off his sunglasses.

"Let me scope out the best view of the counter where I've got a bit of cover. Say, I smell garlic," he commented as he headed for the shelves. "Did someone make a deli run? I'm starving."

She watched as, after a couple of false starts, he settled on a spot in the biography section. There, the shelving was slightly angled to accommodate the children's section behind it. He pulled a book from the shelf and opened it while assuming a casual pose that gave him an unobstructed view of the front. Satisfied that nothing was going to happen without Reese to see it go down, Darla pulled the copy of *The Marble Faun* from beneath the counter and settled in to wait.

At three o'clock, she stared nervously at the front door, not wanting to be taken by surprise when he walked in. But ten minutes later, Vinnie still had not shown up. At quarter after, she wandered over to where Reese waited, still pretending to read his book.

"I don't know why he's late," she grumbled. "We said three o'clock."

"Maybe he had a problem with a customer over at the bridal shop," was the detective's reply. "Give him a few more minutes."

The front bells jangled just then, and Darla started. But when she poked her head around the shelving unit expecting to see Vinnie, she instead saw James returning from his lunch break, followed by a new customer.

Spying her standing in the shelves with Reese, her manager headed in their direction. "Has Mr. Modello already come and gone?" he softly asked as he joined them.

Darla shook her head. "He hasn't shown up yet. Maybe I should give him a call and see if he's still coming."

"Give it another five," Reese instructed, "then make the call. And what was the verdict on the deli? Any chances there's any leftovers you don't want?"

Rolling her eyes, Darla went upstairs to the lounge while James shrugged off his coat and went to help the middle-aged man who'd followed him in. She returned a few moments later trailed by Hamlet and carrying the other half of her turkey Reuben sandwich.

"Here," she said as she shoved it into the detective's hands. "Don't get any of the Thousand Island dressing on the stock."

While Reese made quick work of the sandwich—much to the dismay of Hamlet, whose emerald eyes shot green daggers in his direction—Darla returned to the counter. At twenty after three, she reached into the drawer under the counter for the business card that Vinnie had given her. "Which should I call, cell or business number?"

Book now tucked under his arm, Reese wiped a bit of dressing from his chin and tossed the crumpled napkin and wrapper into her trash can. "Try the mobile number first. Go ahead and use your landline, so he can see it's the bookstore calling. If he answers, just find out if he's on the way. If he's not, see if you can get him to reschedule for later today. If you don't get him, don't bother with a message."

Nodding, Darla punched in the numbers for the man's mobile line. She held her breath while it rang five times and then switched over to voice mail.

"No answer," she told Reese as she ended the call. "I'll try the shop next."

"Use your cell to call the bridal shop. If someone else besides him answers, I don't want them seeing your store name popping up on any caller ID."

Darla frowned, not quite certain why that was important, but she complied, reaching under the counter for her phone. "If it's not Vinnie who answers, should I talk to Daniel or just say I'll call back?"

"If Mr. Modello isn't there, keep it short and sweet. Don't explain, give your name, or leave a message. Just find out if he's expected back anytime soon. Oh, and try not to sound too Texan."

She shot him a look at that last, even as she conceded he had a point. Slipping into a few "y'all's" or a "how're yew's" during the conversation likely would cause whoever answered to remember the call.

Taking a deep breath, Darla dialed the other number. This time the phone was answered on the second ring.

"Davina's Bridal, where every bride is special," she heard Daniel say in a credible imitation of a radio announcer's full-bodied voice. "How may I help you?"

Daniel, she mouthed to Reese, pointing at the phone. Aloud, she clipped out, "Vincent Modello, please."

"I'm afraid he's not in. This is Daniel. May I help you instead?"

"I do need to speak with him personally. Do you happen to know when he'll be back?"

"Unfortunately, Mr. Modello has taken a few days off, but if you would care to leave a message . . ."

"Thanks, I'll check back later," she said, and hung up.

Turning to Reese, she said, "That's odd. Daniel just told me that Vinnie is on vacation. Vinnie didn't mention that when we set up our appointment."

"Why would he need to? You weren't meeting him at the bridal shop," Reese suggested. "Try his cell number one more time, and if there's still no answer, leave a message."

Switching out phones again, Darla redialed Vinnie on the landline. As before, the call went to voice mail.

"Hello, Mr. Modello," she said after the beep. "This is Darla from Pettistone's Fine Books. I'd expected you at three today to pick up that copy of *The Marble Faun*, and it's now three thirty. Please call me to reschedule."

She gave both of her phone numbers and then hung up. "What next?" she asked Reese.

The detective shrugged. "For you, nothing unless Modello calls you back . . . then you call me. I'm going to see if I can find an address on him. The way you said he was acting over that book, it's pretty odd he suddenly can't make time to pick it up, even if he is on vacation."

With a final "Thanks for the sandwich," he left the book on the counter and headed for the door. She watched him go, then happened to glance at the book's title. She gave an amused snort.

"*The History of the Pinkerton Detective Agency*," she read aloud to Hamlet, who still looked peeved over the loss of the sandwich. "So, you think Reese grabbed the first book he could put his hands on, or you think he picked this one deliberately?

"Oh, never mind," she grumbled right back at him as the cat flopped onto his haunches and tossed a furry leg over one shoulder. "And I'm the one who should be complaining. That sandwich was going to be my lunch tomorrow. Now, go help James with the customers."

Tossing the Pinkerton book back onto the counter, she reached for her copy of *The Marble Faun*.

"It should be titled *The Bad Luck Faun*," she muttered with a snort, "because that's all it's been so far. James is right. I need to get this book to Vinnie before it causes any more trouble."

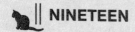 || **NINETEEN**

BY SIX O'CLOCK, DARLA STILL HAD NOT HEARD FROM VINNIE. She'd gone from being more than a bit irritated at his inconsideration to growing worried about his welfare. Maybe the man had decided to forget the Hawthorne novel and had gone off on some other wild-goose book hunt. Or maybe he'd up and quit his job at the bridal shop, and Daniel was covering for him. But no matter the explanation, she was pretty well out of patience with fauns and brides and secrets in general.

"Now, Pinky does know that you were referring to a.m. and not p.m. when you told him to be here at nine tomorrow?" James asked as he gathered his overcoat and coffee thermos in preparation to leave for the evening.

Darla smiled. "He knows. And before Robert left, he promised he'd call Pinky at least twice to make sure he was awake and on the way. So don't worry, we'll be fine until you come in at noon. And like I told you, this will be a perfect dry run for when Robert is on vacation."

"Agreed . . . but that does not mean I will breathe easily again until we lock the doors Saturday night. Speaking of which, are you certain that I cannot help pay the tab for Detective Reese and his fiancée's engagement party?"

"This one's on me," Darla assured him. "Just be there with bells on, or whatever the Professor James T. James equivalent is."

"I can assure you, it is *not* bells."

Darla's smile broadened. "I didn't think so. And tell Martha I'm looking forward to seeing her there. I didn't get a chance to chat with her much the last time the book club met."

Promising her that he would, James headed into the night, Darla close on his heels to lock the door after him.

"Don't worry, no one is going to pull another Vinnie on me," she told Hamlet, who was watching to make certain she followed through.

A few minutes later, the pair were upstairs in the apartment again. After feeding Hamlet, who still seemed a bit miffed over the sandwich issue, she grabbed a chunk of cheese to hold her over until she'd made her own supper and went to her desk to check her personal email. As she opened the program, the first thing she spied was a message from a familiar and unwelcome name. Scrolling past it, she went through the rest of her messages first. Then, with no other unread messages remaining, she gritted her teeth and opened his.

The message was briefer this time, but still pushing the same agenda.

Hey, Darla, haven't heard back from you yet. I know you're busy, but I'd really like to see you when I'm in town. Mom still asks about you, and she never misses an opportunity to tell me what an idiot I was

to let you go. So shoot me a message back and let
me know if supper is on. Remember, I'm picking up
the tab.

This time, it was signed

Your favorite (well, maybe not so favorite)
ex-husband.

"Argh!" she groaned aloud, drawing a questioning look
from Hamlet, who was now sprawled along the back of the
horsehair sofa.

"It's him again. Why doesn't he go bother whatever-the-
heck-her-name-was who he cheated on me with, instead?"
she muttered, not caring that James would be struck to the
heart had he heard that last twisted bit of syntax.

But when Hamlet made no reply, she shrugged. "Yeah,
I don't know, either. But what do you think? Should I write
back and tell him to get lost? Or just block his email address?"

"Or, I know," she said with a small, evil grin. "I *could*
be nice and say yes, and then make him take me to the most
expensive place I can find and stuff myself to the gills. You
know—appetizers, soup, salad, entrée, dessert—the whole
enchilada. Except not nearly as cheap. And then bring home
most of it in a giant doggie bag so you and I can enjoy our
own little feast together the next night. What do you think?"

The cat blinked and gave a small *mrumph* that she took
to mean *Go for it*. Evil smile still in place, she started to hit
"Reply" . . . and then paused.

"Wait. I know what he's up to, Hammy. He's just doing
this to make himself look like Mr. Magnanimous. I go to
supper with him, he pays the big tab, and he's done. He
thinks he's made up for all the crap he put me through. Well,

no way am I going to help him ease his conscience. He *should* feel guilty."

With that, she hit the "Delete" key, sending his message to the trash file.

"Settled," she muttered in satisfaction as she got up from the computer again.

Strangely in the mood for enchiladas now, she reached into her freezer and pulled out a handmade version of the filled corn tortilla staple that she'd previously bought from a local Mexican restaurant. Once she'd eaten, she turned on a bit of mindless television and played the role of couch potato until it was time for bed.

Just around midnight, she awoke from dreams of a mis-tuned strings section playing a concert in her bookstore to realize the sound she heard was Hamlet.

Rowwwwww. ROOwwwww. ROOOWWWWW!

"What's wrong?" she sleepily managed as she sat up.

He leaped from the bed and trotted to the closed door. *ROOOWWWWW!*

Fully awake now and on alert, Darla threw back the covers. "What is it, Hammy?" she whispered as he pawed at the doorknob. Then a shiver ran through her. "Is someone out there?"

Of course, no one could be, since she had an alarm both downstairs and up, which would have gone off if someone tried to get past it. But something obviously was very wrong.

Flipping on her bedside lamp, she grabbed a pair of jeans and a sweatshirt tossed over the chair in the corner and hur-riedly dressed. Then, grabbing up the baseball-bat-like Chil-ean rain stick beside her dresser that was the closest thing she had to a weapon, she eased open the bedroom door.

Hamlet went flying out.

"Hammy," she softly called as she hurried after him, rain

stick tightly clutched in hand. She should have been surprised but was not when she saw where he'd gone . . . straight to her front window. She could see him silhouetted in the faint silver glow from outside, stretched to full length with his paws on the sill and black nose pressed to the glass.

"Is he back?" she whispered as she joined him there. "Is it the skulker?"

Sure enough, she saw a dark, manlike shadow detach itself from the rest of the darkness. A faint red glow abruptly brightened—the ember of his cigarette—and then faded and spiraled downward. Darla gave her head a disgusted shake. A skulker and a litterbug, both.

"What do you think, Hamlet? Should we take a little midnight walk of our own and see who's down there?"

At the word "walk," the cat abruptly abandoned his post for the front door. It had been cold enough out that they'd not taken their usual walks of late, so Hamlet appeared more than ready for a little midnight excursion.

Setting down the rain stick, she pulled Hamlet's harness and lead from the hook near the door and buckled him in. She pulled on her navy blue down jacket, which would be dark enough not to advertise her presence on the street, and then tugged on her leather walking boots. Checking for gloves and scarf, she took her phone and keys from her purse, grabbed hold of Hamlet's leash, and started out the door.

She deliberately didn't turn on the stairwell light as she felt her way down the steps, since its glow would show through the front door window and announce her presence. By the time she reached the entry landing, her heart was pounding in fearful anticipation. Did she really dare go out into the night to confront whoever was lurking there?

"Wait, Hammy," she hissed as she sidled up to the door's curtained window. "Let's see where he is first."

She eased the curtain aside just a fraction and cautiously peered out. Then she frowned. "He's gone," she told the cat. "Are you sure that wasn't just some random guy headed home after a night out?"

By way of answer, Hamlet reared up and pawed at the doorknob.

"Okay, okay, we'll go check it out." Because, of course, the skulker might still be there and simply now out of view.

Darla's heart pounded faster still as she deactivated the alarm and, quietly as she could, unlocked all her front door's knobs and latches. Hamlet's leash was securely looped around her wrist as she slipped out onto the stoop and locked the deadbolt behind her. Stuffing the keys back into her pocket, she gripped her cell phone with her free hand, tempted to call Robert or Jake to meet her outside. But the youth had an early morning and needed his sleep, while Jake would only lecture her for wandering out into the dark on her own with some unknown person there on the street.

"We can do it, Hammy," she whispered to the cat as she steeled herself and walked down the concrete steps with him into the cold night.

She realized as they reached the sidewalk that she'd left the rain stick back in the apartment. She could go back for it . . . but by the time she got back downstairs again, the skulker might be gone. And given the recent tragedy next door and the drama with Vinnie and his book, no way was she going to pass on a chance to finally determine her midnight visitor's identity.

As they started down the sidewalk, the first thing that hit her was the acrid smell of secondhand cigarette smoke. The discarded butt still smoldered where the figure had dropped it. Buoyed by a flash of righteous indignation that was tempered by a sudden urge to cough, she paused and ground the butt with her boot heel until the red tip flickered out. Then, waving away the remaining cigarette stench, she glanced around her again.

The sidewalk on either side of the street appeared clear of pedestrians, for the moment. But, of course, most of the brownstones featured garden apartments, meaning there were plenty of walls and railings and stoops and stairs behind which anyone might hide. And the midnight shadows would only further cloak them.

The shiver that swept her was not entirely because of the cold. *You're being ridiculous*, she scolded herself. *Even if there is someone out here, how does he know you're not just a regular Jane taking her cat on its usual midnight walk?*

Hamlet, however, already had a plan and a destination in mind. He gave the leash a tug and started toward Bygone Days.

Darla followed after, keeping a close eye on her surroundings. The back of her neck tingled like Hamlet's whiskers as she anticipated an attack with every shadow she crossed, and she hunched deeper into her coat for what little protection it offered. Of course, it could simply be her imagination creating danger where none lurked, she tried to tell herself.

The smoke smell had dissipated. Either the skulker had gone inside somewhere, or else he hadn't lit a replacement cigarette. But at least that did eliminate one possible person who could be that shadowy figure, she told herself . . . namely, Vinnie. For hadn't the man talked about his childhood asthma and how his father's smoking had made his illness worse? No way would he, as an adult, become a smoker.

That still left infinite other possibilities as to who the skulker could be.

By now, they had reached Mary Ann's stoop. Hamlet halted there, then lightly bounded up the first step before glancing over his shoulder at Darla.

"You want to go inside?" she whispered as she took another step up. "But, why—oh!"

For as she peered inside the window, a single small light suddenly flared somewhere deep within. She'd barely had time to wonder why Mary Ann had turned on a lamp, when a shadow momentarily blocked it from view. Someone had walked past the window . . . and from the shadow's shape she was sure it wasn't Mary Ann.

Hodge, perhaps? Maybe he was there with Mary Ann again. And maybe, like Hamlet, he had heard a sound outside and crept downstairs in the darkness to check on it. Maybe he'd found nothing, and then Mary Ann had flipped on a light so he could see his way back upstairs.

It was a perfectly reasonable scenario, Darla tried to tell herself. Yet there'd been something oddly furtive about that shadow's movement, as if making its way in an unfamiliar place while trying to remain unnoticed.

She slipped her cell phone from her pocket and crouched on the topmost step of the cold stoop, hunching her body around the phone as she opened it so that its glare wouldn't be noticeable inside the shop. *Don't assume*, she told herself. *Give Mary Ann a call and see if everything is all right.*

She could hear the phone ringing in her ear, and also faintly through the store's window glass, the twin rings forming a stereo effect. The shadow flashed past the window again, causing Darla to gasp. But after another couple of rings, the call went to the store's recorded message, carefully spoken by Mary Ann.

Thank you for calling Bygone Days Antiques and Col-

lectibles. We are assisting a valued customer at the moment, so kindly leave a message and we will be happy to phone you back momentarily.

Darla ended the call before the beep sounded. Mary Ann was in there, she was certain . . . and if Darla could hear her phone ringing from outside, then surely the old woman had heard it, too. But why didn't she answer?

Her uneasiness returning, she shot Hamlet a look. The cat was seated with his nose almost touching the door, obviously waiting for a human to let him in. She hesitated, recalling that the last time she and Jake had essentially broken into the store out of concern for Mary Ann's safety, their sudden appearance had come at a highly inopportune moment. But she trusted Hamlet's instincts, and he obviously thought something was amiss with the old woman.

Swiftly, she raised the phone again and hit a button. She'd call Jake and get her take on the situation before trying anything drastic.

It took a few rings before the PI answered, her voice thick with sleep as she said, "Hello." And then, sounding confused, she added, "Darla?"

"Sorry to wake you," Darla whispered into the cell, "but I'm sitting on Mary Ann's stoop. Hamlet thinks something's wrong. I tried calling her, but she didn't answer, even though I saw a light go on inside the store. Plus I know I saw someone moving around in there."

"Hamlet thinks something's—oh, never mind," Jake cut herself off. "Look, kid, if you really think Mary Ann's in trouble, call 9-1-1."

"But remember last time?" she softly urged. "I hate to ask, but can you come out and take a quick look?"

"Sorry, no can do."

"I know it's late, but if you could just throw on your coat and run over here—"

"I can't." Jake cut her short. "I'm not there."

"But where—?"

"I'm on a date," she replied in a soft if very precise tone. "You know. A date."

"Oh. Sorry."

Darla felt herself blush as she took Jake's meaning, even though no one was there to see her embarrassment. But Jake was continuing, "Look, give Mary Ann one more call. If she doesn't answer, call me back and I'll throw on my, uh, coat and hurry back over there."

"I'm calling her now." Darla hung up, then gave Hamlet a determined nod. "One more time, Hammy."

Swiftly, she went back to her "recently called" screen and pressed Mary Ann's number again and silently counted the rings as she waited for it to connect. She'd begun to fear the call would again go to voice mail, when at the last minute she heard Mary Ann's quavering voice answer, "Hello?"

"Mary Ann," she replied in relief. "It's Darla. I was afraid something had happened to you, and—"

"Why, Jake." The old woman cut her short. "Whatever are you doing calling me at this time of the night?"

"Mary Ann, it's Darla. I'm out here on your stoop. I saw a light on inside your shop, and I thought I saw someone moving around. Are you all right?"

"Now, Jake," she replied. "I don't know why you and Fiorello worry so much about me. You know that I haven't slept well at all ever since that surgery last year. It's really not necessary for you to keep checking up on me."

Jake? Fiorello? Surgery?

Darla felt her stomach clench as a very terrible suspicion gripped her. Lowering her voice, she said very slowly,

"Mary Ann, is someone there with you keeping you from talking?"

"Of course, my dear. Of course. And now, I really must try to go back to sleep. Give Fiorello my love," she said, and hung up the phone.

Hands shaking, Darla hurriedly dialed Jake again.

"Someone's in there with her," she softly cried as soon as her friend answered. "She was saying all sorts of strange things, and when I asked her if someone was keeping her from talking, she said, *of course*. I've got to do something."

"Don't do a thing except call 9-1-1," Jake shot back in a low voice. "If someone *is* holding her, last thing we need is for you to be taken hostage, too. I'm heading there now, and I'll call Reese, too. You stay put and just keep your eyes open until a patrol car shows up."

"But I can't just—oh, no!"

For even as she started to argue with Jake, Darla heard from within the antiques store a faint, high sound, like a scream being cut off. At the soft keen, Hamlet leaped at the door and pawed at the knob.

"It's Mary Ann," Darla choked out in a rush. "I just heard—it sounded like she screamed. Jake, I don't have time to call 9-1-1. I've got her spare keys, so I'm going inside."

"Don't you dare, Darla Pettistone!" Jake yelled back at her . . . or, rather, yelled as loud as she could while still whispering. "I'll make the call for you, but don't go inside under any circumstances."

"You'd go in," Darla pointed out, then hung up the phone before Jake could reply.

Turning her phone ringer off, she stuffed the cell into one coat pocket and then pulled her key ring from the other. Fingers shaking, she quickly located the old woman's door keys. Carefully, she inserted the key into the deadbolt and turned it as quietly as she could. Then, shoving the keys back into her pocket, she tightened her grip on Hamlet's leash and slowly opened the door.

Immediately, she could hear the soft sounds of two people arguing: a woman's determined if shaking voice that was Mary Ann's, and a second, angry male voice that sounded familiar, although she couldn't identify it. Slipping past the door, she hurriedly punched in the alarm code and eased the door shut behind her and Hamlet, praying that the intruder had been so intent on his dispute that he hadn't heard the hinges creak or noticed the momentary change of light as the door opened and closed.

Just to be certain, she stood half crouched with Hamlet a moment, listening. But even when it was apparent her entry hadn't been noticed, she continued to hesitate, uncertain what to do next. The voices seemed to be coming from the second-floor landing. If Mary Ann was still talking, that had to mean she was relatively unharmed, though that situation could change at any moment. Darla shook her head. She had to find a way to distract the intruder long enough for the old woman to break free. If she could lure the intruder downstairs . . .

A plan abruptly occurred to her, though it would require Hamlet's assistance, as well as getting to the stairway quickly, and unnoticed. A look at Hamlet showed him primed for action, all but marching in place on his leash. Shedding her bulky coat there in the aisle, she gave the cat's lead a gentle tug. Doing her best to imitate his cat walk, she moved softly but swiftly toward the back of the store.

Once at the register, she could hear the voices above more clearly.

"I don't know anything about that book," Mary Ann was

insisting. "I told you we don't inventory anything but the most valuable volumes when we set up an estate sale. The rest are priced in tiers, and we only list how many, not the titles."

As Darla scooted behind the counter, she could hear the man shouting, "The book was there at the end of the sale. I saw it, and then some idiot packed it away with a bunch of others before I could get to it again. I need to know the names of everyone who bought books at that sale. I want that book!"

She shuddered at the venom she heard in the intruder's voice. They had to be talking about her copy of *The Marble Faun*. But who besides Vinnie would have reason to want it? Who could know that a copy of the secret trust had been hidden within its cover? Obviously, the same person who'd attacked Mr. Plinski with the pillow.

The pillow.

Abruptly, something about the pillow rang an alarm bell in her head, but she didn't have time to worry about that now. Instead, she began feeling about in the darkness there behind the counter.

She heard Mary Ann give a sharp cry of pain just as Darla found what she'd been searching for . . . the long length of silver chain that Mary Ann had used to tie herself up in protest. Spurred on by the sound of her elderly friend's fear, Darla swiftly carried the chain to the staircase. Moving carefully lest the chain slip and jingle, she looped one end on the open newel post and then laid out the rest so that it ran parallel to the bottom step, ending at the wall. That accomplished, she picked up Hamlet.

"You're on, boy," she whispered in his ear. "Just stay where I put you."

Removing his leash, she hefted him onto the seat of the

gliding stair lift. She waited a couple of heartbeats to make sure he was settled and pressed the "On" button for the lift. Then she swiftly concealed herself around the corner of the wall.

Unleash the felines! she wildly thought as, with a soft clink and hum, the chair began moving up its guide rail toward the second-floor landing above.

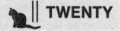 **TWENTY**

"WHAT IN THE—?"

A flashlight beam abruptly shined upon the lift chair as it made its inexorable way up to the second floor, Hamlet seated upon it.

"What did you do, lady? If you think you can trick me—"

"It's just the neighbor's cat," Darla heard Mary Ann say with lofty dignity while the gliding chair continued its upward journey. "He comes over to visit sometimes. He's very clever. He's even learned to press the buttons on the stair lift chair so he doesn't have to walk up."

"Yeah, well, let's see just how clever that cat is."

Something large and rectangular came flying down the stairwell, hitting the wall just above the stair railing. The resulting loud splat caused Darla to jump. And, not surprisingly, it made Hamlet spring up from the seat with a yowl and go flying back down the steps toward Darla.

Don't hurt my cat, you jerk!

It took everything Darla had not to shout the words, but she had no choice. For in the moment that the book had gone sailing down the steps, the intruder had taken a few steps down toward her. The flashlight he carried had briefly illuminated the long and wicked-looking knife he held in his other hand.

Armed. She didn't dare try to provoke the man, not with Mary Ann still within his reach. She needed to get him down the stairs, and quickly.

With that, she hit the "Stop" button on the lift chair, waited a few breaths, and then punched the "Down" button.

"What the—someone's doing that," he yelled as the chair began moving back toward the lower level now. "I know someone's in here. Whoever you are, you better show your face, or I'll cut the old lady."

She hit the "Stop" button again.

"Come on out," he called, shining the flashlight down the stairs. For the moment, she was concealed behind the wall and safely out of sight. But she had to get him down those steps before it occurred to him to flip on all the lights.

Slipping off one of her boots, Darla took a steadying breath and then tossed that shoe away from her toward the aisle, where it landed with a clatter.

"All right, wise guy, one last chance, and then I'm coming down there."

Just what I want you to do.

Carefully, she pulled off the second boot and tossed it in the same direction, wincing when the resulting clatter was followed by a small crash.

"That does it!"

The intruder came down the stairs . . . but not at the breakneck pace she'd counted on. Instead, he was moving with caution, one step at a time. Darla could see that he wore a full ski mask to cover his features, not that it mattered at the moment.

She bit back a groan. If he didn't put on a bit of speed, she wasn't going to be able to follow through with her plan. And once he was past the bottom step, she'd be no better off than Mary Ann and at the mercy of his knife.

Frantic, she flailed in the dark, trying to lay hands on something else she could toss.

And then, with a guttural yowl, Hamlet came flying up the stairs in the man's direction, taking him by surprise and sending him off balance.

The flashlight swung wildly about, its beam bright enough that Darla could see the man stumble as the cat twisted through his legs. An instant later, he'd lost his knife as well as his footing, with the weapon cartwheeling down the stairs and clattering to the ground not far from where Darla stood.

The intruder regained his equilibrium almost immediately; then, with a guttural sound, he was rushing down the steps like a greased pig toward her, just as she'd planned.

Almost there. Almost there. Almost there.

Heart slamming in her chest, Darla bit her lip and held her ground. She'd have one chance to make her plan work . . . and if it failed, she and Mary Ann would both be at the man's mercy. She waited until the intruder reached the final step. And then, with a mighty effort, she yanked the chain she'd tied around the newel post upward. The long series of metal links tangled between his legs and sent the man crashing facedown to the floor, almost at her feet.

Darla didn't check to see if he was injured or simply stunned. Instead, she rushed to unfasten the chain's end from around the newel post. Channeling her inner cowgirl, she whipped the chain around the man's feet, then pulled his arms behind and wrapped his wrists together, virtually hog-tying him.

Mary Ann, meanwhile, came scurrying down the steps, long flannel nightgown flying behind her. At the bottom of the stairs, she paused to flip on the overhead lights.

"Darla," she cried, voice quivering, while Darla squinted against the sudden illumination. "Thank goodness you and Hamlet came. This terrible man was the one who murdered Brother, and he was back again trying to find this silly book he said we sold at the estate sale. He threatened to kill me, too, if I didn't tell him where it was."

"He's not going to kill anyone," Darla replied in an out-raged voice. "Jake is on the way, and she should have already called 9-1-1. We just need to wait a few minutes, and the police will be here. But in the meantime, I want to know who this guy is!"

With that, Darla managed to drag the prone figure over so that he was now on his back. He groaned and blinked. A faint smell of cigarette smoke emanated from him, along with what smelled like cologne or aftershave. Resisting the impulse to give him a good kick or three, she instead knelt beside him and pulled off the ski mask.

The first things she noticed were his heavy black eyebrows and a shock of bleached blond hair. She assumed that once it had been gelled and spiked, though now it lay plastered to his skull. Perhaps it was the late hour, or the sudden adrenaline crash, but it took a moment for her to realize who it was.

"Daniel!"

And then another realization struck—the explanation for the alarm bells in her head a few minutes earlier—and she gasped.

I suppose I always thought of guns and knives as the

*weapons of choice in a random murder, not silly embroi-
dered pillows.*

"You knew," she choked out as the remembered comment
from the man returned to her. "You knew exactly how Mr.
Plinski was murdered, when the police were keeping that
fact confidential. You were the one who killed him."

"Yeah, you figured it out," he said with a sneer, all trace
of affectation gone from his voice, so that Darla realized
why she hadn't recognized him as he'd spoken before. "I
guess you think you're pretty clever, don't you?"

"I guess I am," she replied, "because I have the copy of
The Marble Faun you're looking for."

Then, as his muddy brown eyes widened at that, she
added, "Oh, and I also found the copy of the secret trust that
your grandfather hid inside it. I know that Vinnie was supposed to get a giant bequest from his dead grandfather. But
your father was the trustee, and instead of giving the money
to your brother, he kept it for himself. And he planned that
when he died, it was all going to you. The only thing he—
and you—had to make sure of was that Vinnie never found
out about the secret trust."

"And he's not going to find out about it," Daniel clipped
out, abruptly struggling against his bonds. And then, with
a sudden clanking of chain, he shook himself free.

The magician's chain, she thought in dismay. *It isn't just
the locks. Some of the links must also have a quick-release
trick to them.*

Looking just as surprised as Darla felt at his unexpected
escape, Daniel momentarily froze. But before Darla could
scramble out of reach, he recovered himself and shot a quick
hand out to grab her upper arm.

She gave a little shriek of shock and pain as his fingers
clamped tightly into her flesh.

"All right," he snapped out as he scrambled to his feet and dragged her up after him, then bent and retrieved his knife. "You and me and the old lady are going to go get that book, and then we're all going to take a ride."

"No, we're not," came a quavering voice behind them followed by the unmistakable sound of a rifle being cocked.

She and Daniel glanced behind them to see Mary Ann aiming her brother's lever-action 1894 Winchester—the one Jake had said was hidden under the counter—directly at Daniel.

"Now, young man," she commanded, rifle butt firmly pressed into her flannel-covered shoulder and barrel steady, "you're going to let Darla go and sit down on those stairs until the police come. Do you understand?"

Daniel responded with something unsettlingly like a growl but released his grip on Darla and took a seat, as ordered. And then they all heard the sudden pounding on the store's front door, followed by the welcome call of "NYPD, open up!"

JAKE ARRIVED JUST AS TWO OF THE RESPONDING POLICE OFFICERS WERE walking a handcuffed Daniel out to one of the two patrol cars parked outside the antiques store. Of the two young cops who remained in the store, one was questioning Mary Ann. The other—having politely relieved the old woman of her rifle—was busy ascertaining that the weapon was indeed an antique and, thus, not subject to the local gun laws. Peering out the front window, Darla saw a long and somewhat familiar-looking dark sedan pull up at the curb. Jake hopped out of the backseat and came rushing up the steps.

Darla noted in private amusement that her friend's curly

hair looked wilder than usual. Obviously, she'd not had a chance to comb it back into submission following her "date."

Jake rushed up the steps and identified herself to the second cop, who seemed more interested in posing as Lucas McCain than he did in securing the scene. Her first stern words to Darla were, "All I'm going to tell you is, don't you ever pull a boneheaded stunt like that again. I'll leave the rest of the lecture to Reese when he comes to get your statement tomorrow."

"I'm sure he'll have plenty to say," Darla agreed, finding herself shaking a little in delayed reaction to everything that had just gone down.

Because, of course, Jake was right that she'd taken a foolhardy risk in confronting an armed intruder. Her adrenaline was still racing, even though the danger was long past, for she knew full well that her impromptu plan could have gone terribly wrong. But no way could she have waited outside the building while Mary Ann was inside being threatened.

Working to keep her voice steady, she continued, "All that really matters is that we finally know who killed Mr. Plinski, and why. But I wasn't alone. Hamlet was my backup—or maybe I was his. Speaking of which . . ."

Having done his part to distract Daniel, Hamlet had vanished into the far corners of the darkened store while Darla—and then Mary Ann—finished the job. Darla hadn't worried about him, for while they waited for the police, she had spied the wily feline perched on the shoulder of the poodle-skirt-wearing mannequin, his green gaze watchful.

Now she called in his direction, "Hamlet, you can come out now."

To her relief, the big black cat promptly materialized

right behind her. Darla had already retrieved her boots and his leash while the officers were taking care of Daniel. Now, she snapped the leash onto Hamlet's harness. "I'm going to ask the officer if I can walk Hamlet back to the apartment so he'll be safe, and then come back."

"I'll go with you, and you can give me the CliffsNotes version of what went down."

But as they walked out of the brownstone, Darla saw that the long, dark sedan that had dropped Jake off was still parked at the curb not far from the remaining patrol car.

"What about your date?" she asked the PI.

Jake shrugged. "Eh, I'd say it's pretty well over for tonight."

But by then the vehicle's rear door had opened, and as she and Jake approached the car, a short, darkly handsome man dressed in a custom wool overcoat climbed out. Leaning against the vehicle's open door, he asked Jake in an accented voice, "Stay, or go?"

"I'll stay, you go," she told him as she paused at the car.

He nodded. "And tomorrow night?"

Jake gave him a hint of a sly smile and simply said, "Yes."

At that, he climbed back inside, and a moment later the sedan slipped away from the curb and purred off into the night.

Darla stared after the car, wide-eyed, before turning back to Jake. "Don't tell me—it can't be—wasn't that Alex Putin?"

Her friend gave a careless shrug, and Darla decided it was her turn to lecture.

"I can't believe you're actually dating the czar-father of the local construction industry. I know you went with him to the martial arts tournament last year, but I figured that was a one-off kind of thing. But to actually have a relationship with the guy! I mean, he's . . . that is, isn't he . . . ?"

"He's an upstanding businessman who happens to be a former client. And he and I just happened to hit it off. And, not that it's any of your business, but we've been hitting it off pretty regularly the past couple of months."

She paused and added with another sly smile, "You know what they say about men and shoe sizes? Let me put it this way. Alex may be short, but he definitely wears size twelves."

"Ugh. TMI," Darla muttered as they reached her stoop and headed up the steps. *So much for lecturing*, she told herself. She'd just learned more than she ever needed to know about her friend's love life.

"Come on in out of the cold while I run upstairs with Hamlet," she said, quickly changing the subject as she unlocked the front door. "I'll tell you everything I know on the way back, and maybe we'll figure out the last piece of the puzzle—whatever happened to Vinnie."

"AND WHAT IS THIS LIST?" JAMES ASKED THE NEXT MORNING ONCE DARLA had gotten him up-to-date on the previous night's events. Indicating the paper she'd been jotting notes on, he read aloud, "*The Fool's Guide to Wills and Estates*. N. C. Wyeth website: Round Table legend pictures. Arthur Miller's *The Crucible*. *The Brothers Karamazov*."

"That's my official Hamlet book-snagging list," she said with a smile and a fond look at the sleuthing feline in question, who was lounging nearby on the counter. "You know how he always seems to know what's going on when something bad happens? I've been thinking back over the clues he tried to give me, but I have to say he was a bit more subtle than usual. That, or I was dumber."

"Well, the first one is self-explanatory, since a secret trust was at stake here," James replied. "As for the Wyeth paintings, they were used to illustrate a volume titled *The Boy's King Arthur*, which story is filled with brotherly conflict, betrayal, and abandonment between fathers and sons."

"I've got *The Crucible* covered," Darla interrupted. "It was Miller's way to illuminate the evil and absurdity of the McCarthy Communist witch hunts of the 1950s. And I'll admit that I haven't read *The Brothers Karamazov*, but I do know it's about Russian brothers."

"More specifically, Dostoyevsky wrote about an unpleasant father and brothers born of two different mothers," James clarified. "So it appears that Hamlet was once again at the top of his game. And it would seem that even Mr. Modello himself was fooled by his brother. Have they located him yet?"

"Actually, I was starting to worry last night that Daniel had done something to Vinnie, too," Darla replied, her words turning grim again. "After all, he'd already killed Mr. Plinski trying to get him to tell where that blasted book had gone to, and he probably would have done the same to Mary Ann if Hamlet hadn't raised a ruckus."

"Anyhow," she went on, "the whole disappearing-Vinnie thing is probably the wildest part of the story. Reese told me this morning that he'd gotten hold of Vinnie last night. He really had taken a few days off unexpectedly. Would you like to guess why?"

When James shook his grizzled head, Darla smiled a little. "It turns out he didn't need any of our help . . . not ours or Hamlet's or even Reese's attorney friend's. Vinnie received a registered letter from the attorney's office that had written the original secret trust twenty-five years ago. Apparently, an intern had run across the document in an old file, did the math on the likely age of Vinnie's grandfather, and figured out that trust should have been settled. So he's been busy with the lawyer putting documentation together to bolster his case against Daniel. Reese says there's a good chance Vinnie will get a pretty good portion of his bequest after all these years."

"That is excellent news for Mr. Modello," James concurred. "And now you do not have to concern yourself with the ethics of revealing what you found in the book. Though perhaps you will still want to drop off that copy of *The Marble Faun* to him at the bridal shop."

Darla smiled. "That's my plan for lunch today, finally unloading that bad-luck book. The rest of the time, I'll be keeping an eye on Pinky. He's doing pretty well with the coffee drinks, but he's still having problems with the early hours."

Though with all the previous night's activity, she'd barely dragged her own self out of bed at eight, just enough time to get showered and dressed and breakfasted and let a yawning Pinky in at nine. Robert and Mary Ann had left on schedule, as well. The youth had sent Darla a text thirty minutes earlier letting her know that the estate sale was off to a good start.

"I am sure Pinky will settle in by tomorrow," James assured her. "And I have to say I am looking forward to the engagement party. It will be nice seeing matters return to some semblance of normality again."

"Hey, when we're talking about a party, who wants normality?" Darla gave her manager a smug nod. "I'm predicting on a scale of one to ten that this party's going to be a solid eleven. Just you wait and see."

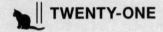 **TWENTY-ONE**

THE *TING-TING-TING* OF A KNIFE TAPPING A WATER GLASS signaled that the postsupper speeches were about to begin. The tapper was the groom-to-be, and as the din of conversation in the private banquet room of Thai Me Up settled, Reese stood.

Darla privately thought that, dressed as austerely as he was in a white dress shirt with black tie and trousers, the detective looked more like he was observing a wake than celebrating his upcoming nuptials. The future Mrs. Fiorello Reese, however, was festive enough for them both. Her sparkly sweater dress of blue and red swirls caught the light with her every move, while her sky-high do had been sprayed into submission with a freeze-spray that contained a liberal sprinkling of glitter.

"Everyone, I have a few announcements to make, if that's okay with our hostess," he said with a look in Darla's direction. At her smile and nod, he continued, "First off, I have to say, it's been a great party so far. Having all of you here to celebrate me and Connie like this . . . well, it means a lot."

He paused while everyone applauded this, and Darla spared a fond look around the room. It was a small but friendly gathering. Seated at the head of the table were Reese and Connie, with James and Martha to their right, and then Robert and Sylvie. Jake and Alex Putin—Darla couldn't yet look at the man without thinking about size twelve shoes!— sat to the left of the happy couple, followed by Mary Ann and Hodge. The other seats were filled by Hank and Hal Tomlinson and their dates, while Doug Bates had brought along one of the co-owners of the children's specialty toy store a couple of doors down from his doughnut shop. Darla had asked Steve Mookjai to sit in as a guest, and so he had a chair there as well.

When the applause died down, Reese said, "I want to start by remembering someone who should have been with us tonight. Rest in peace, Bernard. You're missed, and you won't be forgotten."

He raised his champagne glass, and a somber murmuring of "Bernard" filled the room before everyone joined him in drinking to Mr. Plinski.

Then he set down his glass and smiled. "I've got another toast to make, too, and this one's a happy one. And you don't know how hard it's been to keep it a secret these past few days. I'd like everyone to raise a glass to our newlyweds, Hodge and Mary Ann Camden, who made it official down at City Hall a few days ago."

Delighted gasps filled the room, and calls of *congratulations!* followed as the second toast was made. Catching Reese's gaze, Darla gave him a questioning look, and he nodded. *So that was where Mary Ann was the morning of her brother's death*, she thought with a small pang on her elderly friend's behalf, remembering the old woman's white brocade suit, and her big smile that day.

A jovial Hodge stood, while Mary Ann modestly studied her plate. "Thank you, Detective Reese. Mary Ann and I didn't mean to keep all of you in the dark like this. You understand that, given the circumstances, we didn't want to make a production of our nuptials. But she and I have discussed it, and we intend to have a religious service the first of the year just to really make things official. And all of you will be invited."

More applause followed this, and Darla smiled, happy that the elderly pair would have a second date to celebrate that wasn't the same sad anniversary as Mr. Plinski's death.

Then Reese raised his glass a third time. "Finally, I would like to toast our hostess, Darla Pettistone, who put together this bash tonight. You're a good friend, Red. Connie and I appreciate everything you've done for us."

This time it was Darla modestly staring at her plate as the group applauded her. When the clapping died down, she rose.

"Thanks, Reese, and everyone else," she slowly began. "I have to tell you, excited as I was to start a new life with the bookstore, it was pretty hard moving away from Dallas. A few times in the first month, I really thought I'd made a terrible mistake. But now, after almost two years, I'm not sure I'd ever be able to go back home to Dallas again. Because Brooklyn . . . my store . . . my friends . . . that's all home now."

Smiling, she said, "And since I'm probably going to get weepy if I say anything more, why don't we all stretch our legs for a minute, and then we'll have the beautiful engagement cake that Doug made, and we can keep making toasts until Steve throws us out."

Laughter and applause followed this, and then everyone rose and began milling around while Steve went to see if the cake was ready to be brought in. Darla was chatting with Martha when she felt a tap on her shoulder and turned to see Hodge.

"Excuse me, ladies," he said. "May I borrow Darla for just a moment?"

"Sure," Martha agreed with a smile. "We'll finish catching up later on."

As Martha strolled off, Darla gave the man an expectant smile. "Congratulations, Hodge. That's wonderful news about the wedding. Now, what can I do for you?"

Hodge nodded toward the room's far corner. There, a shrinelike table was presided over by a small statue of Kwan Yin, which Darla had learned from Steve was the goddess of compassion. The fragile white flowers that surrounded her had already begun to droop, and a scattering of petals lay like snowflakes at her feet.

"Can we talk in private for a minute?" the old man asked.

She followed him over there, assuming he wanted advice on his and Mary Ann's upcoming wedding. Instead, after glancing about to make sure no one else was within earshot, he said, "I need to tell you something, but I need to ask first that you promise not to repeat what I'm about to say to anyone else . . . especially not Mary Ann.

"Don't worry," he added, obviously reading on her face the sudden concern that had swept her at his words. "It's nothing terrible, but I want someone to know for the record."

She considered that a moment and then nodded. "All right, I promise. Go ahead and tell me."

The words came out quickly, as if he'd rehearsed them.

"It has to do with Mary Ann's parents, and the fact they were arrested by the government back in the fifties for being

Communists. She's trying to spare my feelings, but I know that Bernard finally told her that I was the one responsible for turning them in."

"That's what she told me," Darla confirmed. "She forgave you, though. She realized you were still a teenager and overly idealistic when you did it, and that you truly thought you were doing the right thing."

Hodge nodded and gave her a sad smile. "Mary Ann has a good heart. She tries to see the best in everyone. And that's why I lied to her, though it was more a sin of omission than anything else. I let her think I turned them in, but I didn't. It was Bernard."

"Mr. Plinski?" She stared at him, dumbfounded. "Are you saying that he actually turned in his own mother and father to the feds?"

"He did. It was just like Mary Ann said. He was young and overly idealistic, and he thought his parents were on the wrong path. He never thought they'd go to jail; he just figured some government official would put a big scare into them, and they'd cut out all that crazy stuff."

He paused and sighed. "But then Mr. and Mrs. Plinski got tossed into prison, and Bernard realized he'd made a terrible mistake. He was afraid for Mary Ann to find out what he'd done, so he asked me if I'd take the blame. I didn't want to, but I couldn't have her hating her own brother. So I agreed. And now that he's dead, I really can't tell her. But I needed to set the record straight with someone."

"Hodge, you're a true hero," Darla said, giving his arm a pat. "I'll keep your secret, until you tell me not to."

Then she gave him a quizzical look. "You probably already hashed this out with Reese, but I know that you went to Bygone Days the morning you and Mary Ann were married, but it was after she'd already left. Why were you there?"

The old man hesitated, glancing in his bride's direction to make sure her attention was turned elsewhere. Then he said, "I went to see Bernard. I was hoping I could settle things between us—all of us—and convince him to attend our little ceremony. I wanted to surprise Mary Ann. Nothing would have made her happier than seeing her brother there."

"And he refused, of course."

"He did . . . but he also gave us his blessing. And he did agree to meet us for a celebratory dinner that night. But then . . . well, you know what happened."

"But does Mary Ann know all this?" Darla asked in surprise.

Hodge shook his head. "I thought it best to wait until things settled down a bit. But we'll be having a small memorial for Bernard sometime after Thanksgiving, and I'll tell her then."

Before she could reply to that, however, a flurry of movement near the door caught her attention. *The cake!*

"Time for dessert," Darla told the old man with a smile. "Come on, let's take a look. I know Doug did a fantastic job."

But "fantastic" was faint praise for the large two-layer cake iced in white rolled fondant with gilt flowered stenciling all around the sides. Where the layers met, what looked like strands of gold beads wrapped around it, like pearls encircling a beautiful woman's neck. The topper was a veritable bouquet of white fondant roses with gilded edges. The overall effect was one of classy beauty without crossing over into being girly or fussy.

And, as to be expected, a chorus of oohs and aahs accompanied the cake's appearance, along with the requisite cell phone photos to be posted on social media. Doug took the accolades in stride, though Darla could see he was pleased with everyone's reaction. But she noticed a strained expression on Connie's face that surprised her. Surely the cake wasn't too plain for her?

Another round of toasts followed, and everyone returned to their seats while Steve presided over the cake cutting. After one taste of the gloriously light dessert, Darla swiftly changed her mental vote from *Don't dare cut that gorgeous cake* to *Would it be rude to take a second piece home?*

But Steve had barely served the last piece and resumed his own seat when a cell phone whose ring Darla recognized as Reese's went off.

"Darn it, Fi," Connie burst out, slamming down her fork and bringing all conversation to a halt. "Can't we have one night out that's not spoiled by your job?"

He glanced at his caller ID and shook his head. "Hang on, I'll handle this," he told her as he quickly left the table to take the call. He was back a moment later, and from his expression Darla could tell he wasn't happy. Resuming his seat, he turned to his fiancée and said, "Sorry, Conn, we've got a slight change of plans. I hate to tell you, but—"

"No!"

This time, the fork went flying, narrowly missing Hank and landing somewhere beneath the table where the engagement presents were lined up. She shoved back her chair and stood.

"I can't take it anymore, Fi," she cried, lower lip trembling. "It's always running late and leaving early, and dead people lying around, and calls in the middle of the night. I know it's your job and all, but . . ."

She trailed off. Then, with a determined expression, she yanked off the diamond engagement ring and slammed it on the table.

"I love you, Fi, but I can't do this. I can't marry you!"

Not waiting for a response, she snatched her purse off the back of her chair and made a beeline for the door.

The room was stunned into momentary silence so profound that Darla was certain she could hear the dying flower petals dropping around the Kwan Yin statue. Then Reese, whose expression was that of a man who'd been smacked over the head with a baseball bat, abruptly shoved back his chair and stood.

"Connie!" he shouted after her, though she was long since out the door. "Wait, you don't understand."

Steve and Hodge, meanwhile, leaped from their chairs as well, and quickly put restraining hands on him.

"Talking now is no good," Steve warned him. "You must leave her be. Let her be mad for a while, then talk."

"Steve's right. Let her cool off and think about it," Hodge urged. "I was married for forty years the first time. I know."

"But how's she going to get home?" Reese demanded, now looking like that baseball bat had hit him in the solar plexus.

"I've got a car," Hodge told him. "Let me see if I can catch her—she'll talk to an old man like me—and then Mary Ann and I will take her home."

At Reese's nod, he hurried off in the direction Connie had gone, then returned a few moments later. "She's still here, waiting on a car. She agreed to let us give her a ride instead. Mary Ann?"

His wife rose to join him. She paused as she reached Reese, who'd sunk back down into his chair.

"Don't worry, my dear," she told him, patting his bulging biceps with a fragile hand. "Things always work out for the best."

Once the Camdens left, the rest of the party began making their excuses as well, murmuring words of sympathy or encouragement as they walked by Reese. Jake and Alex were the last to go, and the former shot Darla a questioning look. Darla lightly shook her head in return, and Jake nodded her understanding.

And then, as the banquet room door closed behind the pair, it was just her and Reese alone in the silent room. Darla got up from her chair at the foot of the table and took the seat next to him.

"So what was the call?"

He'd been silently studying the ring that Connie had flung aside. At her question, he looked up and gave her a faint smile.

"Remember your suggestion about the special surprise? Well, that was Pinky calling to tell me that his friend who was supposed to give him a ride bailed, so he was going to walk, but that meant he was going to be even later than he already was. So I was gonna ask Connie if her special surprise could happen another time, and then my whole life just blew up in my face."

"Reese, I'm so sorry," she told him, sympathetic tears brimming in her eyes. "Maybe if she sleeps on it, she'll realize she didn't mean it."

Reese shook his head. "Nah, Red, she meant it. I guess I shoulda known, a broad like her needs a guy who'll pay attention to her every waking minute. And I just can't make that happen."

He twirled the ring between his fingers and then nodded toward the table with all its gifts. "What should I do about those?"

"If you're talking etiquette, the presents go back to the givers. If you mean logistics-wise, I'm going to settle up with Steve now, and I'll ask if he can hold them for a couple of days until everyone can pick up their gifts in person."

She returned a few minutes later and told him, "Everything's taken care of, so I'm going to head home now. Will you be all right?"

He nodded and stuck the engagement ring in his shirt pocket. "I'll get over it," he said, though Darla suspected the casual response covered a truly trampled heart. "I guess seeing the dress before the wedding turned out to be bad luck, after all."

Then, with a shrug, he added, "Can I give you a lift back?"

"If you're sure you don't mind, that would be great. Let me get my stuff."

She retrieved her gift from the table and then, feeling only slightly guilty, grabbed a couple of slices of engagement cake that Steve's staff had individually boxed.

The short ride back to her brownstone was a silent one, though Reese made sure to jump out and hold open the car door for her once they'd arrived. "You need help carrying any of that up?" he asked, his smile wry as he watched her juggle the cake boxes.

"I'm good," she assured him. "Give me a call tomorrow if you feel like talking."

"Yeah, sure. Thanks."

But he waited until she'd reached the top of the stoop to call to her, "Hey, Red. Up until the last few minutes it was a really great bash. Thanks."

Once inside her foyer, she glanced back through the window to see that he was still parked along the curb, no doubt waiting to make sure she got inside okay. When she made it up to her apartment a few moments later, Hamlet was waiting at the door with a score of noisy demands.

Giving him a quick, "Hang on, Hammy," she flipped on the lights and set down her things on the dining table, and then headed to the window. She was just in time to see Reese's battered sedan pulling away from the curb two stories below. *What a gentleman*, she told herself, her attitude only partially facetious. He'd waited to see her lights come on in the apartment before he left.

That, or he'd decided to try calling Connie before he drove off.

"Tough night, Hammy," she told the cat as she went into the kitchen to check his food and water. Reaching into the drawer for a fork, she went back to the dining table. There, she retrieved the white-and-gold gift-wrapped box, along with one neatly boxed slice of cake, and went to her computer.

While she waited for her programs to boot up, she unwrapped the gift box and pulled out the vintage cake topper she'd bought for the couple. Studying the slightly battered figures, she couldn't help but compare them to Reese and Connie's crumbling relationship. Then, fork in hand, she opened the cake box and took a bite.

"I'd share," she told Hamlet, who'd padded in to join her, "but you're not supposed to eat processed sugar."

She opened her email and then, on impulse, checked her trash file. The email from her ex was still there. Not certain why she did it, she dragged the message into her inbox and then hit "Reply."

Dear Troy,

she wrote between bites of cake,

Sorry for the delay in writing back. It's been a pretty hectic week. But, sure, we can get together when you're in town. Call me at the bookstore when you get settled, and we'll pick a time and place. My cell number is in my signature file. Remember, you're paying.

She hit "Send" before she could change her mind, and closed the laptop case before she could recall the message. Then, forking up another bite of cake, she joined Hamlet on the sofa.

"Yeah, I know, I should have told him never to write me again, but what can I say? I'm a soft touch. Everyone deserves a second chance and, who knows, maybe he's really sorry. Maybe he's really changed."

Or, maybe not.

But even if he turned out to be the same old Troy, she was a brand-new Darla, she reminded herself in satisfaction. She'd left Dallas an angry and somewhat frightened divorcée, not quite sure what her great-aunt's bequest to her really meant for her future. Now she was an independent businesswoman running a successful store and surrounded by good friends, while living quite contentedly alone in the heart of what had once been a strange city. Being able to get through a civil evening with her ex-husband would prove to her, if not him, that he really *had* been an idiot to let her go.

"You know how people are always talking about closure," she told Hamlet. "Well, that's what seeing Troy again will be. Then it's onward and upward, as C. S. Lewis put it."

She waited for a hiss, or a leg fling. But for once, Hamlet refrained from a snarky reply. Instead, quite politely, he reached a paw toward what was left of her engagement cake.

"Oh, why not?" she said with a chuckle as she dabbed a bit of fondant on his paw. She smiled fondly at him as he took an experimental lick, and then quickly finished off the icing. Giving him another tiny taste, she added, "Besides, there's nothing better than sharing dessert with your best friend. And when it comes to best friends . . . well, Hammy, you're most definitely the cat's meow!"

Connect with Berkley Publishing Online!

For sneak peeks into the newest releases, news on all your favorite authors, book giveaways, and a central place to connect with fellow fans—

"Like" and follow Berkley Publishing!

facebook.com/BerkleyPub
twitter.com/BerkleyPub
instagram.com/BerkleyPub

Penguin
Random
House